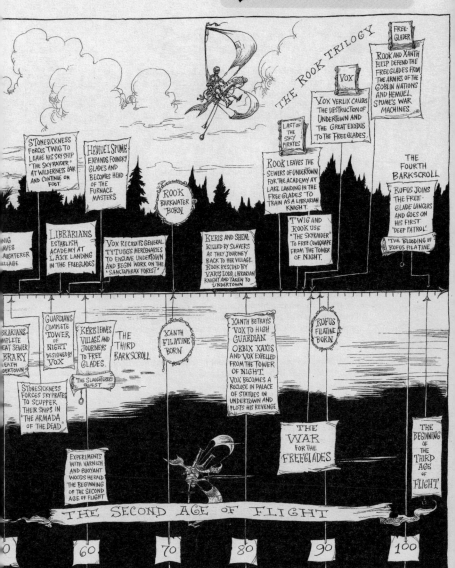

KU-645-868

THE ROOK TRILOGY

FREE-GLADER
ROOK AND XANTH HELP DEFEND THE FREEGLADES FROM THE ARMIES OF THE GOBLIN NATIONS AND HEMUEL SPUME'S WAR MACHINES

VOX
VOX VERLIX CAUSES THE DESTRUCTION OF UNDERTOWN AND THE GREAT EXODUS TO THE FREEGLADES

LAST OF THE SKY PIRATES

ROOK LEAVES THE SEWERS OF UNDERTOWN FOR THE ACADEMY AT LAKE LANDING IN THE FREE GLADES TO TRAIN AS A LIBRARIAN KNIGHT

THE FOURTH BARKSCROLL
RUFUS JOINS THE FREE-GLADE LANCERS AND GOES ON HIS FIRST 'DEEP PATROL'

STONESICKNESS FORCES TWIG TO LEAVE HIS SKY SHIP "THE SKY RAIDER" AT WILDERNESS LAIR AND CONTINUE ON FOOT

HEMUEL SPUME EXPANDS FOUNDRY GLADES AND BECOMES HEAD OF THE FURNACE MASTERS

ROOK BARKWATER BORN

LIBRARIANS ESTABLISH ACADEMY AT LAKE LANDING IN THE FREEGLADES

VOX RECRUITS GENERAL TYTUGG'S MERCENARIES TO ENSLAVE UNDERTOWN AND BEGIN WORK ON THE "SANCTAPHRAX FOREST"

KERIS AND SHEM KILLED BY SLAVERS AS THEY JOURNEY BACK TO HER VILLAGE. ROOK RESCUED BY VARIS LODD, LIBRARIAN KNIGHT AND TAKEN TO UNDERTOWN

TWIG AND ROOK USE "THE SKYRAIDER" TO FREE COWLQUAPE FROM THE TOWER OF NIGHT.

'THE BLOODING OF RUFUS FILATINE'

TWIG LEAVES SLAUGHTERER VILLAGE

GUARDIANS COMPLETE TOWER OF NIGHT DESIGNED BY VOX

KERIS LEAVES VILLAGE AND JOURNEYS TO FREE GLADES

THE THIRD BARKSCROLL

XANTH FILATINE BORN

XANTH BETRAYS VOX TO HIGH GUARDIAN ORBIX XAXIS AND VOX EXPELLED FROM THE TOWER OF NIGHT. VOX BECOMES A RECLUSE IN PALACE OF STATUES IN UNDERTOWN AND PLOTS HIS REVENGE.

RUFUS FILATINE BORN

LIBRARIANS COMPLETE GREAT SEWER LIBRARY BENEATH UNDERTOWN

THE SLAUGHTERER'S QUEST

STONESICKNESS FORCES SKY PIRATES TO SCUPPER THEIR SHIPS IN "THE ARMADA OF THE DEAD"

EXPERIMENTS WITH VARNISH AND BUOYANT WOODS HERALD THE BEGINNING OF THE SECOND AGE OF FLIGHT

THE WAR FOR THE FREEGLADES

THE BEGINNING OF THE THIRD AGE OF FLIGHT

THE SECOND AGE OF FLIGHT

0   60   70   80   90   100

THE LOST BARKSCROLLS
A CORGI BOOK 978 0 552 55599 9

First published in Great Britain by Doubleday,
an imprint of Random House Children's Books
A Random House Group Company

Doubleday edition published 2007
Corgi edition published 2008

1 3 5 7 9 10 8 6 4 2

The Random House Group Limited supports the Forest Stewardship
Council (FSC), the leading international forest certification organization.
All our titles that are printed on Greenpeace-approved FSC-certified
paper carry the FSC logo. Our paper procurement policy can be
found at www.rbooks.co.uk/environment

Corgi Books are published by Random House Children's Books,
61–63 Uxbridge Road, London W5 5SA

www.kidsatrandomhouse.co.uk
www.rbooks.co.uk

Addresses for companies within The Random House Group Limited
can be found at: www.randomhouse.co.uk/offices.htm

THE RANDOM HOUSE GROUP Limited Reg. No. 954009

A CIP catalogue record for this book is available
from the British Library.

Printed and bound in Great Britain by
CPI Bookmarque, Croydon, CR0 4TD

THE EDGE CHRONICLES

THE LOST BARKSCROLLS

PAUL STEWART & CHRIS RIDDELL

CORGI BOOKS

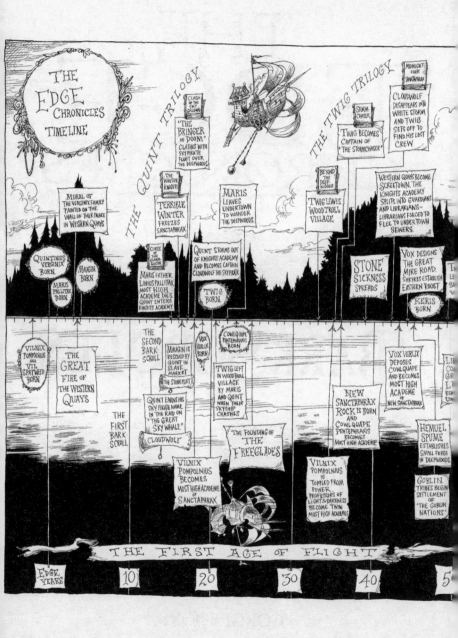

THE EDGE CHRONICLES TIME LINE

THE QUINT TRILOGY

THE TWIG TRILOGY

CLASH OF THE SKY GALLEONS
"THE BRINGER OF DOOM" CLASHES WITH SKY PIRATE FLEET OVER THE DEEPWOODS

STORMCHASER
TWIG BECOMES CAPTAIN OF 'THE STORMCHASER'

MIDNIGHT OVER SANCTAPHRAX
CLOUDWOLF DISAPPEARS INTO WHITE STORM AND TWIG SETS OFF TO FIND HIS LOST CREW

MURAL OF THE VERGINIX FAMILY PAINTED ON THE WALL OF THEIR PALACE IN WESTERN QUAYS

THE WINTER KNIGHTS
TERRIBLE WINTER FREEZES SANCTAPHRAX

MARIS LEAVES UNDERTOWN TO WANDER THE DEEPWOODS

BEYOND THE DEEP WOODS
TWIG LEAVES WOODTROLL VILLAGE

WESTERN QUAYS BECOME SCREETOWN. THE KNIGHTS ACADEMY SPLITS INTO GUARDIANS AND LIBRARIANS - LIBRARIANS FORCED TO FLEE TO UNDERTOWN SEWERS

QUINTINIUS VERGINIX BORN

MAUGIN BORN

MARIS PALLITAY BORN

CURSE OF THE GLOAMGLOZER
MARIS' FATHER, LINIUS PALLITAY, MOST HIGH ACADEME DIES. QUINT ENTERS KNIGHTS ACADEMY

QUINT STORMS OUT OF KNIGHTS ACADEMY AND BECOMES CAPTAIN CLOUDWOLF THE SKYPIRATE

TWIG BORN

STONE SICKNESS SPREADS

VOX DESIGNS THE GREAT MIRE ROAD. SHRYKES ESTABLISH EASTERN ROOST

KERIS BORN

VILNIX POMPOLNIUS AND VEL SPATHWEID BORN

THE GREAT FIRE OF THE WESTERN QUAYS

THE SECOND BARK-SCROLL
MAUGIN IS RESCUED BY SLAVE MARKET
THE STONE PILOT

VOX VERLIX BORN

COWLQUAPE PENTEPHRAXIS BORN

TWIG LEFT IN WOODTROLL VILLAGE BY MARIS AND QUINT WHEN THEIR SKYSHIP CRASHES

VOX VERLIX DEPOSES COWLQUAPE AND BECOMES MOST HIGH ACADEME OF NEW SANCTAPHRAX

LI CO GR BE UN

THE FIRST BARK-SCROLL

QUINT EARNS HIS SKY PIRATE NAME IN THE RAID ON 'THE GREAT SKY WHALE'
CLOUDWOLF

'THE FOUNDING OF THE FREEGLADES

NEW SANCTAPHRAX ROCK IS BORN AND COWLQUAPE PENTEPHRAXIS BECOMES MOST HIGH ACADEME

HEMUEL SPUME ESTABLISHES SMALL FORGE IN DEEPWOODS

VILNIX POMPOLNIUS BECOMES MOST HIGH ACADEME OF SANCTAPHRAX

VILNIX POMPOLNIUS IS TOPPLED FROM POWER. PROFESSORS OF LIGHT & DARKNESS BECOME TWIN MOST HIGH ACADEMES

GOBLIN TRIBES BEGIN SETTLEMENT OF 'THE GOBLIN NATIONS'

THE FIRST AGE OF FLIGHT

EDGE YEARS   10   20   30   40   5

THE FIRST
BARKSCROLL

CONTENTS

INTRODUCTION

The young apprentice librarian hurried up the steps of the Great Library, his brown homespun robes flapping. He crossed the threshold beneath the imposing statue of the first High Librarian, Fenbrus Lodd, and entered the vast circular building. He picked his way between the forest of tall pillars, each one studded with climbing-pegs, pausing only to breathe in the familiar smell of woodcamphor and bark-mildew. All round him, motes of glittering dust danced in the shafts of golden light that streamed in through the windows.

Looking up, he saw the barkscrolls hanging in great clusters from the shadowy vaulted rafters. Countless precious manuscripts, meticulously transcribed in woodink onto bark parchment and carefully stored by generations of librarians stretching back to the time of Kobold the Wise, stored in the Great Library of the Free Glades.

Learned treatises on Deepwoods creatures hung

beside works on medicine and woodlore. First-hand accounts of sky battles from the First Age of Flight hung next to cloudwatching manuals and sagas from the Goblin Nations. Works on every aspect of the Edgelands and its history – from the destruction of Old Undertown to the War for the Free Glades – could be found high in the rafters of the Great Library, their dusty pages full of sky pirates, leaguesmasters, knights academic and strange goblin tribes.

The librarian stopped before one of the great pillars and read the copperwood plaque at its base. Then, tucking the hem of his robe into his belt, he began to climb the great column, taking the jutting rungs two at a time. He was eager to find the treatise on sweetwood timber which he needed to complete the study on buoyant wood he was working on. High up in the rafters, he eased himself down into one of the hanging-baskets and, seizing a rope, pulled himself through the air . . .

'Sapwood, shankwood, stinkwood . . .' He read off the plaques on the roof-timbers overhead. 'Sweetwood.'

Taking care not to up-end the precariously swinging basket, he reached across and pulled towards him the dusty scroll-holder that hung from a hook beneath the plaque. Peering inside the carved wooden tube, the librarian frowned. Instead of Arboris Helquix's recent study of sweetwood he'd been expecting, there were four dusty, long-forgotten barkscrolls inside.

Despite the best efforts of the librarians, sometimes those less skilful in the baskets would knock the scroll-holders and dislodge their contents, sending them tumbling to the floor far below, like falling leaves. Apprentices were supposed to sweep them up and return them to the correct rafters, but mistakes did happen.

Who knows from what shadowy corner of the library these ancient scrolls had come? thought the librarian, as he pulled them out of the holder and held them up.

They certainly looked a good deal more interesting than old Helquix's interminable account of leaf shapes and woodgrain. The outside margins of the scrolls were covered in intricate illuminations of ancient sky ships, hooded stone pilots, strange goblins with curling tendrils, and great battles.

The librarian sat down and settled himself in the hanging-basket, his heart pounding and his mouth suddenly dry. Slowly, with trembling fingers, he unfurled the first of the yellowing scrolls and began to read . . .

THE DEEP WOODS

THE TWILIGHT WOODS

THE EDGELANDS

The Edge.

For Jack, Katy, Anna, Joseph and William

CLOUD WOLF

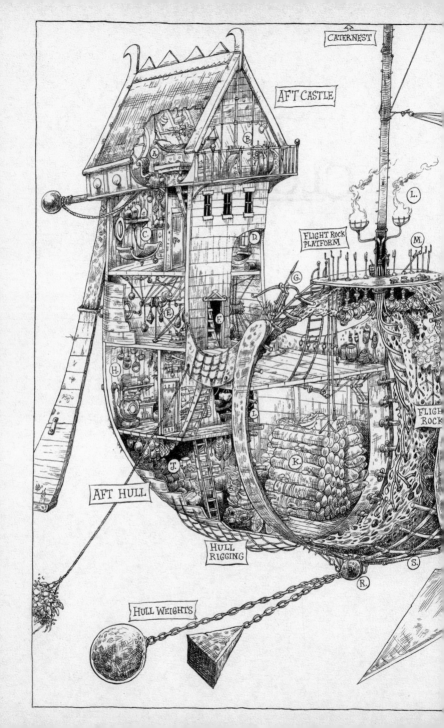

CATERNEST

AFT CASTLE

FLIGHT ROCK
PLATFORM

L.

M.

A.

B.

O.

C.

D.

G.

S.

E.

F.

H.

I.

FLIGHT
ROCK

J.

K.

AFT HULL

HULL
RIGGING

S.

R.

HULL WEIGHTS

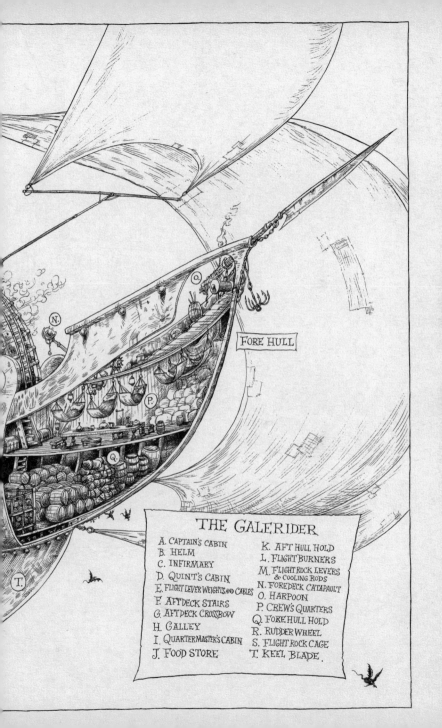

FORE HULL

THE GALERIDER

A. CAPTAIN'S CABIN
B. HELM
C. INFIRMARY
D. QUINT'S CABIN
E. FLIGHT LEVER WEIGHTS AND CABLES
F. AFTDECK STAIRS
G. AFTDECK CROSSBOW
H. GALLEY
I. QUARTERMASTER'S CABIN
J. FOOD STORE

K. AFT HULL HOLD
L. FLIGHT BURNERS
M. FLIGHT ROCK LEVERS & COOLING RODS
N. FOREDECK CATAPAULT
O. HARPOON
P. CREW'S QUARTERS
Q. FORE HULL HOLD
R. RUDDER WHEEL
S. FLIGHT ROCK CAGE
T. KEEL BLADE

. CHAPTER ONE .

WILDERNESS LAIR

'Prepare for descent, Ramrock,' Wind Jackal called to his stone pilot. His hands ran expertly over the bone-handled levers, tweaking the sails and adjusting the hull-weights. 'We're going down.'

'Aye-aye, captain,' Ramrock shouted back. Clad in the characteristic stone-pilot garb – a thick hooded coat and heavy boots – he worked calmly to raise the temperature of the rock. The torches flared as he pulled the heating lever, the bellows blew the scorched air into the stone cage and, as the rock within began to glow, so the *Galerider* began to descend.

Quint looked over the balustrade of the sky pirate ship and shuddered. Was his father mad? the youth wondered. Going down *there*, into the Edgelands!

Situated between the Deepwoods and the yawning abyss beyond the Edge, the Edgelands was an inhospitable rocky wasteland, swirling with thick, treacherous mists, where spirits and nightmares shrieked and howled, and the gloamglozer – the wickedest creature in all the Edge – was said to dwell.

Quint crossed to the helm. 'Is this wise, Father?' he said.

'Steady on the boom, Master Queep!' Wind Jackal bellowed back along the sky ship to his quarter-master. 'Grappling-hooks at the ready!' He glanced round at his son. 'Wise?' he said.

'I thought we were heading for Sanctaphrax,' said Quint. 'You told me the Most High Academe had requested an audience.'

'He has,' said Wind Jackal. 'But something else has come up. Something far too big to be ignored.'

'Father?' said Quint.

'A carrier-ratbird arrived last night bearing a message from Ice Fox . . .' The storm winds buffeted the side of the sky ship with ferocious force. Wind Jackal lowered the neben-hull-weights to compensate. 'A sky-pirate assembly has been called for this evening,' he continued, 'away from prying eyes, here at Wilderness Lair. And I don't have to tell you how unusual that is, Quint. The old skycur must be on to something big.'

'But what about the Most High Academe?' Quint asked.

'Sky willing we'll complete our business and be back in Sanctaphrax in time to keep our

appointment,' said Wind Jackal. 'And if we are not; well, Linius Pallitax and I go back a long way, and what is half a day between old friends?' He peered down. 'Lower the mainsail!' he boomed. 'Furl the jib!'

Quint shrugged and returned to the balustrade.

As the *Galerider* descended through the clouds, Quint caught flashing glimpses of the rocky land-scape below; vast glistening grey slabs with jagged fissures between them. And there, where the sul-phurous mist thinned for a moment, was the tall mast of another great sky pirate ship slicing through the gloom.

'We're not the first,' Quint shouted to his father.

'Nor shall we be the last,' Wind Jackal replied. 'A great pirate armada is gathering. It can mean only one thing.'

'What?' Quint asked.

'A sky battle,' his father replied simply.

*

Wilderness Lair was not so much situated *in* the Edgelands as *beneath* it. Through the gaps in the mist, Quint could see other sky pirate ships coming in from all directions and sailing over the jutting lip of rock. As Wind Jackal followed them, Quint gasped as the *Galerider* was suddenly battered by the full strength of the incoming storms.

Slowly, carefully, his father brought the sky ship round and headed back towards the cliff-face. Beneath the overhang, Quint saw a dozen or more sky pirate ships clinging to the sheer rock. He held his breath as the sky ship dipped sharply in the sky and threatened to roll. The wind howled. The mist swirled. The rockface came closer.

'Fire the fasting-spikes!' Wind Jackal bellowed. 'Launch the grappling-hooks!'

A volley of metal shot through the air and landed with muffled thuds and clangs. Some fell away, but others held firm. The sky pirates tugged at the ropes and secured them tightly. The *Galerider* came to rest alongside the other sky ships. Together, they clung to the vertical cliff-face like a cluster of rock-limpets.

Quint sighed with relief and glanced round. 'Look!' he shouted and pointed to his left. 'It's the *Fogscythe*! And the *Mistmarcher*.' He turned the other way. 'And there's the *Windspinner*.'

His heart swelled with pride to see how many had come from all corners of the Edge in answer to Ice Fox's call. Sky pirates might be loners, but when the need arose, they would band together like no-one else.

Each sky ship was distinct from its neighbour, depending on the fighting techniques favoured by the individual captains. The *Fogscythe* was fitted with curved fore-blades which could slice through the sails and rigging of enemy ships; while the elegant *Windspinner* had, fixed to its aftcastle, an intricate catapult that hurled molten pitch onto an opponent's flight-rock to send the ship into a spiralling descent.

'And look,' said Wind Jackal, nodding towards a two-mast vessel with a great brass harpoon at its prow. 'It's the *Cloudbreaker*. Ice Fox himself must already be here.'

The moment the *Galerider* moored, sky pirates from the adjacent ships lowered gangplanks and rope-bridges both to connect the fleet and to allow access, one with the other – for those daring enough to brave the flimsy walkways in such weather. Soon the *Galerider*, like all the other sky pirate ships in the growing fleet, was bustling with activity.

Old friends greeted one another warmly. Acquaintances were rekindled. Stories were swapped. And as more and more sky pirate ships

broke through the cloud cover and attached themselves to the cliff-face, so the party-like atmosphere
grew increasingly rowdy. Queep discovered that a
long-lost cousin had become the *Mistmarcher*'s head
cook, while Steg Jambles – a bluff, bearded
character – went off in search of his old flat-head
sparring partner, Hogmutt, who had been crewing
on board the *Fogscythe* the last time he'd heard from
him.

Quint, too, would have liked to explore the other
ships. He wanted to meet Grist Greystone, the
grizzled quartermaster of the *Fogscythe*, and talk to
him about his role in the infamous ironwood
blockade. He wanted to examine the catapult
mechanism of the *Windspinner*. But Wind Jackal was
adamant.

'You're to remain here where I can keep an eye on
you,' he said.

'Oh, but Father,' Quint protested, 'I'm not a child
any more. I can look after myself.'

'Quint, Quint,' chided Wind Jackal. 'Don't always
be in such a hurry to grow up. Whatever you may
think, there's still much you have to learn. Believe
me.'

Quint nodded. 'Yes, Father,' he said irritably.

With the approaching darkness came the night-
chorus of the Edgelands. Deep rumbling groans
and low chattering drowned out the constant roar

of the wind; shrill, blood-curdling cries set Quint's heart racing. Suddenly, staying on board the *Galerider* didn't seem such a bad idea after all, and he followed his father around as he lit the oil lamps and tallow lanterns.

All at once, a loud, almost mechanical, voice filled the air. It was Ice Fox. Everyone turned in the direction of the noise to see the sky pirate captain himself standing in the caternest of the *Cloudbreaker*, a megaphone raised to his lips. A second individual was standing beside him, head held high.

'My friends,' Ice Fox bellowed above the noise of the battering storm. 'Eighteen of you I summoned to Wilderness Lair. Eighteen sky pirate ships are here.' He paused. 'I have important news.'

The pirates stopped talking and listened closely.

'Undertown is a free city with free citizens,' said Ice Fox. 'It is written in the constitution that no-one is permitted to enslave another. Yet the leaguesmen flout this law. They press-gang any they find to crew their ships – and kill those who refuse!'

There was a rumble of indignant murmuring.

'Who among us has not heard of the *Great Sky Whale*?'

The muttering grew louder. The *Great Sky Whale*, a vast four-mast league ship, was notorious throughout the Edge for the riches it transported – and the barbaric treatment of its crew.

'This youth,' Ice Fox continued, nodding to the gangly figure beside him, 'who, three days since, managed to escape from the *Great Sky Whale*, can bear witness to the terrible conditions on board. The ceaseless labour. The pitiful rations of food. The incessant beatings . . .' He looked around. 'An unimaginable existence for a sky pirate.'

'You can say that again!' someone shouted.

'Bloodsucking leaguesmen!' another cursed. 'Something should be done to teach them a lesson!'

'Something *will* be done,' Ice Fox broke in. 'For the news I bring is that the *Great Sky Whale* is currently travelling from the Deepwoods to Undertown, laden with jewels . . .'

'But the ship travels with the entire Hammerhead Goblin Guard on board,' a voice pointed out. 'And you know what they say about those hammerheads. Cruel, pitiless . . .'

'Fight to the death as soon as look at you!' added another.

'And what about the armed escort fleet?' asked a

third. 'Thirty league ships there were at the last count, all bristling with weapons . . .'

Ice Fox raised his hands for quiet. 'I have inform-ation that for this trip the *Great Sky Whale* is travelling without an escort fleet and with only a single hammerhead guard company on board.' A hush descended. 'Apparently, the Leaguesmaster, Marl Mankroyd, has commissioned the boat . . .'

A ripple of anger went round. The Leagues-master's reputation went before him.

'. . . unbeknown to the other leaguesmen,' he went on. 'You know how treacherous they can be, even among themselves. He has just completed an illicit jewel deal with the glintergoblins of the Northern Mines and the *Great Sky Whale* is carrying a small, but priceless, cargo of black diamonds. Mankroyd was hoping to feather his own nest without any other leaguesmen finding out. But with no escort fleet, and but a single company of the hammerhead guard,' he said, spelling it out, 'we shall pluck the treasure out from under his nose!'

A roar of approval went up.

'And we will free the captive crew.'

The roar grew louder.

'We will destroy the evil slave vessel once and for all!'

Ice Fox's words were drowned out completely by the shouting of the sky pirates. Quint turned – a broad grin plastered across his face – to see his father looking oddly sombre.

'Who is this youth that brings such unexpected tidings?' Wind Jackal called across to Ice Fox.

'This is Pen,' Ice Fox replied, and raised his arm high in the air. 'Former bootspit to the Leaguesmaster himself. Now, a freeman once more.'

'Pen . . . Pen . . .' Wind Jackal murmured thoughtfully. The name was unfamiliar – yet the face of the gangly youth with the huge hands and feet was not. Where had he seen him before? He shook his head.

'We shall depart for the Deepwoods at daybreak,' Ice Fox continued. 'We shall use ratbirds to track the *Great Sky Whale* in the vastness of the Deepwoods. When they find it, we must strike as one, for even without its escort ships, the *Great Sky Whale* is still the most formidable of all league ships. But we shall overpower it by force of numbers.' He paused and looked around. 'And when we do, the treasure of the *Great Sky Whale* will be ours!'

A tumultuous cheer – the loudest so far – went up. They could do it. They *would* do it!

. CHAPTER TWO .

RATBIRDS AND TURBULENT-FOG

Quint barely slept a wink that night. He lay in his hammock, tossing and turning with excitement. He would be first on board the *Sky Whale*. He would be brave and resourceful. He would make his father proud.

With such thoughts he drifted off to sleep, only to be woken a moment later by the sounds of the Edgelands themselves – for this was a forsaken place. The vast cliff-face fell away into blackness, with cloud banks breaking against it like raging waves. The mists and clinging fog swirled cease-lessly, conjuring up strange apparitions and ghoulish faces, while the winds howled and whistled through the cracks and crevices of the rock; a ghastly chorus of wailing shrieks and anguished cries.

With a shudder, Quint pulled the covers up over his head, and turned his mind away from the unseen horrors out there, and back to the coming battle. His eyelids grew heavy . . .

'*Waaaa-iiiee!*' came a blood-curdling screech, and Quint was wide awake once again.

'What *is* that?' he wondered nervously.

And so it went on. All night. By sunrise Quint had already abandoned any attempt to sleep, and was dressed and ready. As the first patches of pink light dusted the sky, he went up on deck.

It was a chilly morning. The mist clung to him like wet clothes.

'Quint!' came Wind Jackal's surprised voice. 'You're up early.'

Quint turned to see his father in the misty shadows at the rear of the ship. Steg Jambles was with him. They were standing either side of a large cage, each holding a ratbird in his hands.

'I couldn't sleep,' he said.

'Too excited, eh, Master Quint?' said Steg. 'I know the feeling.'

Quint nodded. He didn't mention the grinding fear which had gripped him every time one of the spirits or ghouls – or whatever they were – had cried out.

'Odd-looking little things, ratbirds, aren't they?' he said to change the subject. He tickled one under the chin. 'How will they find their way?'

'I've taught them to seek and home,' Steg Jambles explained. 'They use sun-angle and wind-direction,

35

plus they have an acute sense of smell. The scarf of that youth, Pen, has been cut up and distributed amongst all of us,' he said, removing a fragment of spotted cloth from his top pocket and rubbing it round the ratbird's snout. 'Its scent will guide the ratbirds to the great league ship. While this,' he said, passing a smooth musk-rock pebble back and forth across the cage door, 'will help them to return.' He threw the creature into the air. 'Now fly, ratbird. Fly!'

The ratbird switched its tail, flapped its furry wings and, with a squeaky screech, was gone. Wind Jackal's ratbird flew after it, followed – in quick succession – by the half dozen others which had been waiting in the cage. The same procedure was being repeated on all the other sky pirate ships. And as the curious flying creatures were swallowed up by the dense, swirling mist, the sky pirates fingered the lucky charms around their necks and prayed for a swift and successful return.

36

'Now the ratbirds have gone, it is time for us also to set forth,' said Wind Jackal. 'Raise the gang-planks!' he bellowed. 'Unhitch the walkways. Prepare the flight-rock, Ramrock.' He took his place at the helm. 'Detach the fasting-spikes!'

The next moment, the *Galerider* and the rest of the sky pirate fleet soared into the sky like a great flock of winged raptors. Quint raised his head and shuddered with pleasure as the wind blew into his face. Skysailing! There was nothing in the world that came even close to the wonderful sensation of soaring across the sky.

'Quint!' Wind Jackal called out. 'Come and take the helm.'

Quint jumped to it eagerly. And while his father operated the bone-handled levers behind him, adjusting the sails, fine-tuning the hull-weights, Quint turned the great wheel this way, that way, feeling the sky ship responding to his touch like a wild and wilful creature. Far, far ahead – where the rocky Edgelands met the forest – he caught the first glimpse of the tallest treetops, tipped with silver and gold from the rising sun.

'The Deepwoods!' he exclaimed.

'Aye, lad, there they are,' said Wind Jackal. 'And somewhere above their sprawling vastness, the *Great Sky Whale* awaits.'

*

Several hours were to pass before the *Galerider* reached the Deepwoods, by which time the weather had deteriorated.

'Where are those ratbirds?' Wind Jackal muttered, as he scanned the horizon with his telescope.

Quint removed his own telescope and joined in the search. Apart from several of the other sky pirate ships – now widely spread out across the sky – the only airborne creature to be seen was a lone rotsucker, flapping across the sky with a sealed caterbird cocoon dangling from its taloned feet. The Deepwoods looked vast enough to conceal a hundred mighty league ships.

'What do we do?' Quint asked.

'We keep looking,' said Wind Jackal. 'And we remain patient.'

Midday came and went. Late afternoon turned to early evening. Quint scoured the horizon until his eyes hurt. Would they ever see the ratbirds again?

'Ratbirds on the starboard bow at two hundred strides,' shouted Spillins, the ageing oakelf lookout. 'Two of them . . . No, three.'

Wind Jackal bellowed for Steg Jambles. It was important that, as ratbird keeper, he be there on deck to see the aerial display put on by the birds when they reached the sky ship. For like woodbees, whose curious wiggle-dance informed the rest of the hive about a source of nectar, so the dips and dives of the ratbirds' flight would reveal the direction and distance of the object they had been sent out to seek.

'Ratbirds at fifty strides,' cried Spillins.

'Steg!' roared Wind Jackal for a second time. 'Where are you?'

'Here, captain,' came a breathless voice.

'The ratbirds are over there,' said Wind Jackal urgently.

'I see them,' said Steg. The ratbirds were getting closer. If they simply returned to their cages, then hunger had been their motive for returning. But if they performed their dance . . .

The three creatures flew once, twice, three times round the mast and suddenly soared back into the sky. 'Thank Sky for that,' Steg muttered. A moment later, and just as suddenly, they tumbled back down, turning somersaults as they dropped. With less than a stride to go before smashing into the deck, they pulled out of the dive and landed on top of the cage. Wind Jackal turned to Steg.

'How many somersaults did you count?' he asked.

'Twelve,' said Steg. He frowned thoughtfully and Quint watched his lips move as he made calculations. 'The *Great Sky Whale*,' he announced at last, 'is positioned at three degrees west of north-north-west.' He paused. 'At about twenty thousand strides off.'

Wind Jackal nodded. 'Which, with these winds, is a good night's travel away.' He turned to his son. 'You're looking exhausted, Quint,' he said. 'Go and get some sleep.'

'But, Father . . .' Quint protested.

'You won't miss any of the excitement,' his father said. 'I'll wake you the moment we catch sight of the *Sky Whale*. Now go.' He looked round. 'Steg,' he said. 'Take the helm.'

'Aye-aye, cap'n,' Steg replied.

Quint stood aside. He was far too tired to put up any resistance. His father was right. The previous night had left him fit for nothing. He really did need to get some sleep.

Down below deck, Quint climbed into his hammock. The cabin was quiet and dark, his covers were warm, and the gentle sway of flight was soothing. With the howls and shrieks of the Edgelands no more than a distant memory, Quint was asleep within seconds.

In the early dawn light, Wind Jackal paced the upper-deck thoughtfully. Steg was standing at the helm.

'That lanky youth with the big hands and feet,' Wind Jackal said. 'The one with Ice Fox – did you recognize him?'

Steg shook his head. 'Can't say as I did, captain. Why?'

'I'm not sure,' said Wind Jackal. 'There was something familiar about him.' He shuddered. 'Something I didn't like . . .' he said, and added, 'It's a good job Quint isn't around to hear his father prattling on like some superstitious old gabtroll.'

Steg looked at Wind Jackal evenly. 'Where I come from, we take such things seriously,' he said. 'My old grandma – Sky rest her spirit – reckoned that premonitions, intuition and the like, were all part of the

"silent language". *Turn away, and rue the day*, that's what she used to say.'

'Turbulent-fog at four thousand strides, and rising,' Spillins' strident voice announced from the caternest.

Turbulent-fog rising! Both Wind Jackal and Steg looked round and recoiled in horror.

Normally, turbulent-fog was a low-sky phenomenon, seldom rising up much higher than the tops of the Deepwoods' trees, and therefore easy to fly over. But not this time. This time, the vast wall of fog which extended from horizon to horizon also towered far, far above the tree-line. Wind Jackal had to think quickly. In less than five minutes, the sky ship would be swallowed up.

Thick and viscous, yet as full of air-pockets as hammelhorn cheese, turbulent-fog was notorious. The sticky air played havoc with flight-rocks, blocking their porous surface, reducing buoyancy and causing them to sink. This would have been manageable if it hadn't been for the pockets of icy, crystal clear air trapped inside the fog, for each time a sky ship penetrated one of these, its flight-rock would 'breathe' again, and soar upwards. Many was the Undertown tug, barge and even unwary league ship that had been shaken to pieces in its violent down-pull and up-draft.

'Turbulent-fog at a thousand strides!' shrieked the oakelf.

'Sky protect us all,' Wind Jackal murmured as he

pressed the amulets round his neck to his lips.

'Captain!' Steg Jambles cried out in alarm. 'What are we going to do?'

Wind Jackal reached out, gripped the bone-handled levers and breathed in deeply. 'We'll try to fly above it. Hang on tight, Steg. If we can't, it'll have to be a vertical rise!'

Steg gasped.

Wind Jackal lowered the stern-weights. He lifted the prow-weights and raised the sails. With a lurch and a sigh, the *Galerider* soared upwards. The wall of fog came closer. It was like scaling a mighty waterfall.

'Get ready to douse the flight-rock on my order, Ramrock!' he shouted to his stone pilot.

'Turbulent-fog at five hundred strides!'

'Come on, my lovely,' Wind Jackal urged the sky ship as, creaking and cracking, it rose higher and higher. 'You can do it!'

The bank of fog came closer. If they could just rise that little bit faster, they would avoid being swallowed up . . .

'Impact in five seconds!' the oakelf called.

Wind Jackal's expert fingers raced over the rows of levers – raising here, lowering there. The sky ship rose more quickly.

'Four!'

'We're not going to make it,' shouted Steg.

'Three . . .'

'Douse the flight-rock!' Wind Jackal bellowed.

Ramrock pulled a lever. The flight-rock was instantly smothered with chilled earth. It groaned and creaked as it cooled. Immediately, the sky ship soared skywards, almost vertically and at breakneck speed. Despite their best efforts, however, there was nothing that either the captain or his stone pilot could do to evade the oncoming fog.

'Impact!' Spillins bellowed.

The instant it entered the sticky purple-grey fog, the *Galerider* stopped rising. The fog choked the porous flight-rock and the sky ship began a slow, shuddering descent. Neither Ramrock nor Wind Jackal could steady it.

The *Galerider* dropped through the dense stickiness, gathering speed as it went. All of a sudden the fog disappeared and the sky ship hit its first big air-pocket. The air was cold and crystal clear all around them.

'Rope yourselves down!' Wind Jackal bellowed to the crew-members up on deck, as he seized a tolley-rope of his own and tied it round his waist.

The pores in the surface of the rock expelled the claggy fog and sucked in the pure, clean air, causing the flight-rock itself to become abruptly super-buoyant. With a judder and a lurch, the sky ship rocketed up into the air as if fired from a mighty

catapult. Terrified, the crew cried out and fell to the deck, clutching hold of anything they could find. Higher and higher the *Galerider* flew, right up to the top of the air-pocket – and back into the fog itself.

Immediately, the sky ship slowed down, and then began to sink once more. Steg Jambles and Ramrock both climbed to their feet. Wind Jackal lowered the sails. Down in his cabin below deck, Quint picked himself off the floor and looked round with surprise. One moment he'd been in his hammock dreaming of how proud he'd just made his father, the next he was flying across the room.

He rubbed his eyes and tried to gather his thoughts. Had they found the *Great Sky Whale*? Were they about to attack? He frowned. 'Why didn't Father wake me? He promised he would!'

Quint slipped on his longcoat and parawings, checked that his knife was on his belt and left the room. As he hurried up the stairs the sky ship juddered violently. Below him, he heard the frantic screeching and squawking of the ratbirds which lived in the bowels of the ship. The next moment . . . *FWOOOPFF!* The *Galerider* was rocketing upwards for a second time.

Quint fell to his knees and gripped the rope-banister with both hands. His stomach heaved. His head spun. 'What's happening?' he groaned. 'I've never known it so rough before.'

. CHAPTER THREE .

ATTACK!

'The ship won't take much more of this, captain,' Steg Jambles moaned as the *Galerider* came out of an ascent, travelling so fast and reaching so high that old Spillins up in the caternest had actually blacked out.

'Steady, old friend,' Wind Jackal replied, as he realigned the port hull-weights. 'The fog's thinning.'

The rest of the fleet was nowhere to be seen. Had they escaped the terrible fog? Wind Jackal could only pray that they had. Steg Jambles squinted ahead. 'We do seem to be dropping less quickly,' he said.

'Father, what in Sky's name is going on?' came a voice.

Wind Jackal turned. 'Quint!' he said. 'I thought you were safely tucked up in your hammock.'

'What, with all this upping and downing?' said Quint.

'Hold on tight,' said Wind Jackal through clenched teeth. 'It's not over yet.'

They hit another air-pocket. The *Galerider* listed sharply to one side and surged upwards. Quint fell to the floor, skidded across the deck and slammed into the fore-balustrade.

'Quint!' Wind Jackal bellowed.

'Grab this rope, Master Quint,' Steg Jambles shouted as he tossed the end in his direction.

Quint, who was clutching hold of the spindles of the balustrade, released one hand and seized the rope. He wound it round and round his arm and held on grimly. The upward force drained the blood from his head, making him giddy. He let go of the wooden spindle and slithered back down the sloping deck.

'Quint!' Wind Jackal cried out a second time. With the tolley-rope still tied around his own waist, he dived after his son. His hands grasped at a bony

ankle and held on tight. The rope went taut. Wind Jackal tightened his grip.

At that moment, the sky ship left the vast pocket of air and abruptly slowed down once more. The descent through the sticky fog began again. This time, however, something was different. Instead of gathering speed, the *Galerider* slowed until it was hovering at one height. Then it righted itself.

Wind Jackal lifted his head and looked round. The fog was thin and wispy; neither dense enough to make the flight-rock plummet, nor so crystal clear that it would exaggerate the stone's natural buoyancy.

'We made it,' he breathed. 'But at what cost?' He noticed the rigging, torn away from the masts and hanging limp; and the sails, some slightly torn, some completely shredded. 'Sky alone knows how many of the others have made it.' He shook his head. 'I fear you'll have to wait to experience your first sky battle, Quint.'

The great sky pirate fleet shattered? Quint could hardly believe it. He walked over to the side of the sky ship. Behind them the great wall of fog was receding. In front, the sky was becoming clearer with every passing second. He narrowed his eyes and squinted into the distance.

'Look!' he shouted excitedly. 'Over there.'

Wind Jackal raised his telescope and focused on the dark spot where Quint was pointing. 'It's probably just another rotsucker,' he said. 'Or a caterbird. Or . . .' He paused. 'It's the *Fogscythe*!' he exclaimed.

'It is!' Quint cried triumphantly. 'And over there!' he said, swinging his outstretched arm around to the left. 'Is that the *Mistmarcher*? And beyond that a ways, that must be the *Windspinner*. Look, you can see the great catapult fixed to its aftcastle.'

Wind Jackal nodded. 'And not looking *too* much the worse for wear,' he said thoughtfully.

'Better still is what's above us,' said Steg Jambles.

'Above us?' said Quint.

Steg nodded up into the sky, high above their heads, where a sturdy craft in pristine condition was sailing across the sky with a further half dozen sky ships following behind in a V-shaped form-ation. They looked like a migrating skein of gullet-geese.

'That's the *Cloudbreaker* up in front!' Quint announced excitedly.

'So I see,' said Wind Jackal. 'Why, that wily old skycur, Ice Fox. He only managed to get above the turbulent-fog, didn't he?' He chuckled. 'He must have been up there the whole time, waiting to see how many of us got through.'

'They're signalling us,' said Steg, as a flashing light glinted from the *Cloudbreaker*.

Although loners, the sky pirates had several ways

of communicating with each other. And while ratbirds were used for long distances, reflective slivers
of silver marble were the chosen means of convey-
ing information over shorter stretches of sky.

'League . . . ship . . . at . . . north . . . west . . . four . . .
thousand . . . strides . . .' Wind Jackal said, as the
message built up, letter by letter. 'Follow . . . us . . .'
He turned to Quint. 'Looks like it's on again,' he
said.

Quint grinned. 'My first sky battle!'

By three thousand strides away from the league
ship, most of the sky pirate ships which had set off
from Wilderness Lair had formed themselves into a
fleet, headed by the *Cloudbreaker*.

The crew of the *Galerider* was getting ready. Up on
deck, Steg and Quint carried out makeshift repairs
to the rigging and sails. Spillins was hammering the
broken side-panels of his caternest back into place.
Grim and Grem, cloddertrog twins, were using
their enormous bulk to shift the great sky-harpoon
back into position; while Ratbit – a wiry, swivel-
eyed mobgnome – was down beneath the ship,
checking the rudder-wheel and hull-weights.

Below deck, Queep the quartermaster hurried
from stockroom to store, returning the spilled
supplies to their rightful places and tying everything down in preparation for the oncoming battle.

Ramrock was, as always, with his beloved flight-rock, venting and re-boring it as best he could.

'You need a full steam-irrigation,' he was muttering, 'and as soon as we return to Undertown, that's the first thing you'll get. But for the time being, this will have to do . . .'

At two thousand strides away from their destination, everyone on board the *Galerider* was ready. Wind Jackal locked the bone-handled flight levers in place and took Quint aside.

'There's something I must tell you,' he said.

Quint frowned. 'Father?' he said.

'I know you're excited,' he said. 'I remember how *I* felt when your grandfather took me on my first sky pirate raid – and that was a small affair compared with this . . .'

'I . . . I won't let you down,' said Quint. 'I'm going to make you proud of me . . .'

'I know you are, son,' said Wind Jackal warmly. 'Steg says you've volunteered for the advance boarding party. Is that true?'

'Yes, Father,' said Quint. 'I want to be there right from the start. I want to be first on board and . . .'

'No,' said Wind Jackal firmly. 'It's out of the question. The advance boarding party is made up of the toughest and most experienced pirates in the fleet. Grim and Grem from our sky ship; Hogmutt from the *Fogscythe* . . . It's no place for a first-timer.'

'But Father . . .'

'Sky above, Quint, don't you think *I'd* like to go in the first wave? But my place is here, with the *Galerider*. And your place is here next to me. Besides, have you any idea how brutal those hammerheads can be?' Then, seeing the look of disappointment on his son's face, his voice softened. 'You can go in with the second wave,' he said. 'With Steg and the others, when the hammerhead guards have been knocked out and it's safe. But only then. And only with my say-so. Is that understood?'

'But . . .'

'That's enough!' he snapped. 'You will do as I tell you!'

And Quint fell silent, knowing his father well enough to realize that if he uttered another word, he would not be allowed on the league ship at all. All the same, the decision hurt.

At a thousand strides, the look-out on board the *Cloudbreaker* spotted the *Great Sky Whale* for the first time. Word instantly went round the rest of the fleet. Quint raised his telescope to his eye.

'There it is!' he cried out excitedly.

'No mistaking it,' said Wind Jackal. 'It's the largest sky ship that's ever sailed. It must be at least ten times the size of the *Galerider*.'

Quint stared in awe. 'Four masts, four flight-rocks, eight sky rafts. And a solid-gold figurehead . . .'

'Yes, and a company of fearsome hammerhead guards, don't forget,' Wind Jackal interrupted. 'So you mind what I told you.'

Quint nodded sullenly.

Despite its size and formidable array of weaponry, the *Great Sky Whale* was a cumbersome vessel; a ridiculous triumph of design over function. It was slow and notoriously awkward to sail – yet as a symbol of brute force it was awe-inspiring. That, presumably, was why Marl Mankroyd had decided to use the ship in his gem dealings. Now, with the fleet of swift, manoeuvrable sky pirate ships bearing heavily down on him, Wind Jackal, Ice Fox and the other sky pirate captains were all

hoping that it was a decision he would live to regret.

As they approached the great looming league ship, the sky pirate ships fanned out. Then, at a given signal and using cloud-cover to conceal them whenever they could, they swooped in on gusting cross-winds. One by one, they surrounded the huge vessel – like woodwasps circling a hammelhorn – taking up pre-arranged positions and holding them.

Ice Fox surveyed the scene below him, a smile playing on his lips. There were no guards on the deck of the *Great Sky Whale*. Three of the four caternests were empty, while the look-out in the fourth seemed to be asleep. The captain was nowhere to be seen. He was about to be punished for his complacency. Ice Fox nodded to his quartermaster, who in turn signalled to all of the watching, waiting sky pirates. The mirror flashed out a single word.

Attack.

With deft fingers, Wind Jackal lowered the prow-weights and raised the stern-weights. The sky ship tipped obligingly forwards. The stud-sail was raised, the jib was tilted. They were off.

Down through the sky they sliced. The *Great Sky Whale* loomed up before them. At the last possible moment, Wind Jackal lowered the mainsail completely and came in parallel to the great carved balustrade near the stern on the starboard side. This was exactly the point where it had been agreed the *Galerider* would make its attack.

Quint gasped with delight. He'd never witnessed his father sailing with greater precision. The *Galerider* closed in on the *Great Sky Whale*. Wind Jackal marshalled his crew.

'Stave-hooks and tolley-ropes,' he bellowed. 'Advance party, prepare to board.'

All round the gargantuan league ship the scene was repeated as the grappling-hooks of the sky pirate ships flew across the divide, found their target and held fast – to the bows, the aftcastle, the hull-rigging, the masts. And at the individual captains' command the first wave of sky pirates scrambled aboard.

They found the deck deserted. Could the league ship be completely unguarded?

All at once a horn sounded and the doors at the top of the deck-stairs burst open with a resounding crash. A phalanx of hammerhead goblins strode out on deck. The swoosh and jangle of swords, scythes and daggers being drawn filled the air. For a moment there was an eerie silence as the disbelieving sky pirates stood rooted to the spot. Suddenly, the hammerheads threw back their heads and, with one voice, gave a high-pitched scream of rage and hurled themselves at the invaders.

The next moment, all was sound and fury. Clashing

metal and splintering wood. Blade-thrust and
hammer-blow. Banging, thudding, screaming.

Quint strained at the balustrade, his heart thumping, as the ghastly scene unfolded before his eyes.
On the poop-deck, Grim and Grem – the great
cloddertrog twins – were fighting back to back,
surrounded by a dozen screaming hammerhead
guards swinging their evil daggers and serrated-
edged swords. There was a deafening clang of metal
on metal as the cloddertrogs' studded clubs struck
the crescent-shaped shields of the goblins.

Above them, at the helm, a desperate battle was
developing between the boarding party from the
Windspinner and a group of hammerheads led by a
huge battle-scarred veteran in a plumed helmet.
Two, three, four sky pirates fell to his fearsome
sword. The others dropped back in disarray.

Elsewhere on the sky ship, Quint could see the

battle was going equally badly for the pirates. If a single company of hammerhead goblins could wreak such havoc, he thought, then with a full guard on board, the league ship would be impregnable.

Then, just as it looked as if the sky pirates were staring defeat in the face, the hammerheads seemed to lose heart. Was it the casualties they'd sustained? Or was it that they could see the second wave of sky pirates preparing to board?

As the battle on board hung in the balance, several of the sky pirate ships detached themselves to attack the league ship at other points. The *Fogscythe* flew up above the level of the deck and, with the great curved blades at its prow, began severing the ropes that held the sails in place. The *Thundercrusher* hovered above the aftcastle, swinging its great pendulous wrecking-ball into the wooden structure with loud, splintering crashes. While the *Windspinner* – its braziers bubbling with boiling woodtar – catapulted the scalding black pitch down onto the first of the league ship's flight-rocks.

From the *Galerider*, Quint watched it all; white-knuckled, unblinking. The second wave of sky pirates who were now boarding had definitely tipped the balance. Wherever he looked, the hammerhead guards were in retreat, disappearing down into the depths of the sky ship.

With cries of victory, the sky pirates pursued them.

'Come on,' Steg Jambles said to Quint. 'Let's join them!'

Quint hesitated; his father's words rang in his ears. *Maybe with the second wave.* This *was* the second wave, after all. And there was Pen, the gangly youth, crossing onto the league ship from the *Cloudbreaker*. If *he* was allowed to board . . .

Steg climbed up onto the balustrade and jumped across the gap to the league ship. 'Well?' he called back. 'Are you coming?'

Quint glanced

around the deck of the *Galerider*. Wind Jackal was nowhere to be seen. 'Yes,' he said. 'Yes, I am!' He seized a rope hanging down from the sail cross-beam above his head – still loose after the turbulent–fog – and swung across to the deck of the *Great Sky Whale*.

'Good lad,' said Steg. 'We'll make a sky pirate out of you yet.'

'This way!' bellowed a voice.

Quint turned to see a flat-head sky pirate rallying half a dozen others round him, and setting off down below deck.

'That's my old mucker, Hogmutt,' said Steg. 'Let's follow him.'

Without giving it a second thought, the pair of them set off. Through the narrow doorway they went and down the stairs. One flight. Two flights. . . Quint looked round. There wasn't a hammerhead goblin in sight.

As they reached the second quarter-landing, he heard a low hum of muffled voices; pitiful groans, sighs, wails. He turned, and there through the narrow opening before him was a terrible scene. Two hundred, maybe more, skeletal figures – mobgnomes, gnokgoblins, woodtrolls and cloddertrogs – sat chained to a central iron bolt-shaft, each one gripping a rope attached to the upper spar of a giant set of bellows. Down they pulled it, and the furnace-heated air whistled along the giant pipes that led to the flight-rocks. With a creak, the bellows sprang back. The slaves grunted with effort as they pulled the ropes back down again. Up. Down. Up. Down. Relentlessly . . .

'What is this?' gasped Quint.

'These are the underdeckers,' said Steg. 'Slaves, every one of them, condemned to warming the huge flight-rocks which keep this accursed vessel afloat. If the bellows were to stop, the rocks would cool and the *Great Sky Whale* would hurtle.'

'Hurtle!' exclaimed Quint.

It was the term every sky sailor dreaded. As they all knew, since cold rock rises and hot rock sinks, skysailing depended on controlling the temperature of the flight-rock. Untended, a cooling flight-rock became increasingly buoyant and – out of control – hurtled upwards into open sky, taking its sky ship with it.

'Over here,' yelled Hogmutt, dashing off down a broad wood-panelled corridor.

They turned from the toiling slaves. 'Quick,' said Steg, seizing Quint by the arm. 'He must have discovered the treasure.'

They found him in front of a low arched door. ''Cording to that Pen character,' he was saying, 'this should be the treasury-room.'

'Then what are we waiting for?' shouted Steg

Jambles. 'Smash the door down.'

Hogmutt stepped back, lowered his shoulder and rammed the door. There was a loud thud – but the door didn't budge. A swarthy brogtroll from the *Windspinner* stepped forward.

'Let me try,' he said.

There was a second, louder, thud. Still the door did not move. The sky pirates drew their clubs and cudgels and were about to batter it down when Quint spoke up.

'Are you sure it's locked?' he said.

Steg Jambles strode up to the door and tried the handle. It opened with a creak.

'I don't believe it,' Hogmutt groaned.

'Forget it,' said Steg Jambles. 'Let's see what's inside.'

One by one the group of sky pirates went in. They found themselves in a large dark room shot with beams of light from the high portholes and containing a collection of caskets and chests. Quint stared at them, his heart thumping.

'Do you think this is the treasure?' he said.

'Only one way to find out,' said Steg.

They crossed the room. Quint pulled the lid of a chest open, and gasped. It was half-full with gold and silver, and jewels that sparkled like multi-coloured fire. And, from the yelps of surprise and delight from the rest of the room, it was clear that the

other chests the sky pirates had examined were the same.

'Wealth beyond our wildest dreams,' Hogmutt bellowed, and a cheer went round.

'So, the rats have nibbled at the bait,' roared a voice.

The sky pirates spun round to see Marl Mankroyd, the Leaguesmaster himself, standing in the doorway.

'It's a trap!' Steg hissed in Quint's ear. 'Quick, lad!' He held open the treasure chest. Quint jumped inside and closed the lid.

'Pi-rats!' Marl Mankroyd sneered. And as he chuckled at his own joke, two dozen armed hammerhead goblins appeared behind him. 'Guards, seize them! Disarm them and tie them up – but do not kill them.' He smiled unpleasantly. 'You are to be executed back in Undertown as an example to others, to put an end to this accursed sky piracy once and for all.'

The room filled with hammerhead goblin guards armed to the teeth. The pirates were trapped like piebald rats in an Undertown sewer. They dropped their weapons and were immediately seized and roughly bound and gagged.

Curled up on the bed of jewels, Quint listened to the Leaguesmaster barking orders. 'Tighten those ropes! Gather up their weapons! And when you've finished, I want you back up on deck!'

Soon, it fell silent. And in the darkness of his confined hiding-place, Quint trembled with fear, waiting to make his move – wondering what that move should be.

You've been stupid and careless, he told himself. You've walked straight into an ambush. You should have guessed. You should have known . . .

On the upper-deck of the *Galerider* Wind Jackal was muttering the self-same words to himself. All around the horizon – and closing in fast – were league ships. Thirty of them at least.

Wind Jackal chewed his lower lip, shuddered, and cursed. It had all been too easy. He should have known. He should have stopped the second wave from boarding the *Great Sky Whale*, cut his losses and made a dash for it. But now it was too late. He looked across at the helm where his son had last stood, taking the wheel.

'Quint,' he whispered, 'where *are* you?'

. CHAPTER FOUR .

THE SKY BATTLE

There was turmoil and confusion in the sky pirate fleet as the league patrol ships drew nearer. One after the other, individual sky pirate captains decided to abort the attack and flee, even if it meant abandoning some of their finest fighters. Within minutes, the fragile union of the pirate fleet had collapsed and Ice Fox had bellowed his final order down his megaphone – 'Everyone for himself!'

Wind Jackal was desperate. He sent Ramrock to scour every inch of the *Galerider* for his son. The last of the other sky pirate ships were departing as the first patrol ships came close enough to fire sky-harpoons and cannon-rocks. Wind Jackal raised his telescope to his eye to get a closer look at the attackers.

'Ruptus Pentephraxis,' he growled a moment later, as he focused in on the figure at the helm of the lead ship. 'I might have known!' And he slapped his forehead angrily as he finally remembered where he'd seen 'Pen', the gangly youth, before.

Once, when he and Ruptus Pentephraxis had fought a duel on a sky raft high over the Mire, he'd been lurking in the shadows behind the leaguesman and, when Wind Jackal had begun to get the upper hand, had fled to get help. But his name was not Pen. It was Ulbus. Ulbus Pentephraxis, for he was Ruptus's son – a vicious individual with a growing reputation for murder and assassination. At the time, Wind Jackal had left Ruptus with a small scar – and both he and his son with a huge grudge.

Ramrock came dashing up the stairs to the helm. 'Quint is nowhere to be found,' he panted.

'Oh, Quint!' Wind Jackal bellowed with rage and fear.

'I saw him, captain,' Spillins called down from the caternest. 'Aboard the *Sky Whale*. He and Steg Jambles took the aftcastle stairs down below deck.'

Wind Jackal glanced across at the league ship to see that there were guards there now, minding the stairway. He saw something else too. Grim and Grem were sprawled out across the rear of the deck. They looked as identical in death as they had in life. Wind Jackal groaned. His two best fighters had been killed. There was nothing for it. He couldn't leave. He would have to board the *Great Sky Whale* himself to rescue his son.

'Ramrock!' he called to the stone pilot. 'Take the helm. And be prepared for a quick getaway when I return.'

He looked down over the balustrade at the mid-section of the aftcastle. It was here that the officers' quarters were usually situated – luxurious chambers with carved beds, thick carpets and heavy curtains at their large, oval portholes. As the battle raged on, and the patrol fleet closed in, Wind Jackal launched himself off the side of the *Galerider*.

His parawings clicked open and he leaned for-wards, tipping the wings to one side and gliding down through the air in a wide spiral. A porthole came closer. He tugged the wings down and swung round until his feet were out in front.

'Down a tad more,' he muttered, 'and . . .'

Smash!

Wind Jackal hurtled through the glass, landed heavily on the floor and rolled over. He picked himself up and looked round.

'Bullseye!' he exclaimed.

In his hiding-place inside the treasure chest, Quint pushed the lid up and peeked out through the crack. Apart from the low murmur of conversation, it was quiet down in the hold. Six sky pirates were lying in a row, bound and gagged behind the treasure chests. Two hammerhead guards, dressed up in their armour of heavy breastplates and helmets, had been left inside the chamber to watch over the prisoners, while a third – Quint had overheard – had been put on the locked door outside.

The two hammerheads inside were sitting on caskets by the door. 'All this treasure just lying here,' one of them was saying. 'I'm sure they wouldn't miss a few gold pieces. Or a couple of gems . . .'

'No point,' said the second guard. 'They're all fake.'

'Fake?' the first said, shocked. He stood up from the casket and lifted the lid. At the same time, Quint slipped out of his chest, dropped to the floor and lowered the lid silently. 'Are you sure it's fake?' the guard was saying.

'Glass and ironwood, the lot of it,' the second guard confirmed. 'Specially made for the ambush.'

The first guard bent over, retrieved a golden coin and bit it. '*Puh . . . puh . . .*' he spluttered, and spat the splinters from his mouth.

'Told you!' said the second guard triumphantly.

Quint slithered across the floor – keeping behind the barrels and boxes – and on towards the shadows in the corner where Steg Jambles, Hogmutt and the others lay.

'The only real treasure on board is up in the Leaguesmaster's chamber,' the guard continued.

Silently, Quint reached the bound sky pirates. He slipped his knife from the sheath on his belt and sliced through the ropes at Steg's wrists and ankles. Steg wriggled free, tore off his gag and began undoing his neighbour's knots. Within seconds, all six of the sky pirates were free.

As the ropes round Hogmutt's legs came loose, his boot knocked against one of the treasure chests.

'What was that?' the two hammerheads asked one another.

'It was *this*!' roared Steg Jambles as he leaped from the shadows and hurled a casket at the startled guards. As it struck the heavy-set goblins full in the face, it exploded into shards of splintered wood and a shower of fake jewels and coins. The guards crashed to the floor.

'See to them,' said Steg. 'I . . .' There was a grating noise as the key slid into the lock. Steg raised his hand for hush. Hogmutt picked up one of the guards' discarded swords, moved behind the door and lifted his arm, ready.

The handle slowly turned. The hinges creaked, then – *BANG* – the door suddenly flew back – missing Hogmutt by a hair's breadth. Quint stared. There in the doorway was a figure with his foot raised and his sword drawn, a hammerhead guard unconscious at his feet.

'Father!' he exclaimed, then, remembering what he'd done, he dropped his head. 'I . . . I'm sorry.'

'Never mind that now,' said Wind Jackal, stepping into the room. 'We've got to get out of here, and fast. The patrol ships are closing in all round.' He hesitated. 'And this whole sky ship's crawling with hammerhead guards.'

He looked round, rapidly assessing the situation. Three unconscious guards, eight sky pirates . . .

'Tie them up,' he ordered. 'Quint, Jambles, put on the hammerheads' breastshields and helmets.'

'But why . . . ?' Quint began.

'Just do as I say!' Wind Jackal growled.

The sky pirates made their way back up the staircases in a long line. Quint, Steg Jambles and Wind Jackal himself were dressed up as guards, the rest of the sky pirates were their prisoners.

As they passed the third landing, Wind Jackal glanced at his son. 'That's where I got in,' he said, nodding towards an opened door. Quint looked into the room. There was broken glass all over the carpet. 'Marl Mankroyd's personal chamber,' Wind Jackal added.

Quint hesitated. 'Is it?' he said. There was a small, ornate chest at the end of the four-poster bed, and the guard's words came back to him – *the only real treasure on board is up in the Leaguesmaster's chamber*. 'Wait, Father,' said Quint. 'There's something you should know . . .'

Five minutes later, as they continued up the stairs, all the sky pirates' pockets were stuffed full of precious black diamonds – the contents of the now empty chest.

At the second quarter-landing, Wind Jackal motioned them to be still for a moment. 'Turn right at the top of the stairs,' he instructed them in a gruff whisper. 'Do not stop until we reach the *Galerider*. Ramrock should have lowered it down beneath the bulge of the *Sky Whale*'s hull and run up the white flag. They'll think she's surrendered.' He looked round. 'And if anyone challenges us, I'll do the talking. All right?'

A chorus of grunted assent went round.

'Let's go,' he said.

'Father,' Quint said urgently. 'The slaves! We must free them!'

Wind Jackal turned and saw the great bellows with the wretched underdeckers chained into position below them – even now continuing to tend to the flight-rocks. A mixture of emotions crossed his face: pity, anger, disgust. 'You're right, Quint,' he said. 'We must free them. But be warned, all of you. Once the flight-rocks are untended, this ship will begin to hurtle. We will have five minutes at most to escape.'

'And the slaves?' said Quint.

'I'll take care of that,' said Wind Jackal.

He strode over to the massed rows of toiling slaves, chained as they were to the central bolt-shaft. He struck the main bolt a mighty blow with his sword. The metal buckled, the wood splintered and the chains jangled down through the stifling air.

'Friends!' Wind Jackal announced. 'You are free. Make for the sky rafts and save yourselves. We'll buy you time to escape.' He turned back to the sky pirates. 'Come!' he bellowed. 'We must hurry.'

Shouting out their heartfelt thanks, the slaves rushed down to the lower decks where the sky rafts were secured. Wind Jackal and the others made their way to the upper decks, picking their way through the debris and the dead. All around them – both on deck and up in the sky – the fighting had subsided, and the decks were crowded with the many hammerhead goblins who had been waiting to ambush the sky pirates.

It was a well-sprung trap, thought Wind Jackal bitterly. Thank Sky, most of the pirates had already escaped. Now it was their turn.

Wind Jackal caught sight of the top of the *Galerider*'s caternest poking up above the balustrade, and they were just heading towards it when, all at once, a furious voice ripped through the air.

'Where are you taking those prisoners?'

Wind Jackal looked up. Two heavy-set guard captains were standing on the deck above them, hands on hips.

'They're to be sky-fired,' Wind Jackal replied.

'By whose orders?' one of the guards demanded.

'By the orders of the Leaguesmaster himself,' Wind Jackal stated boldly.

Marl Mankroyd appeared from behind the guards, the treacherous 'Pen' by his side. 'I've ordered no sky-firing,' he hissed. 'Come here, the three of you. Explain yourselves.'

'What do we do now?' Quint asked his father under his breath.

Suddenly the *Galerider*, with Ramrock at the helm, reared up behind them, and came in level with the deck of the *Great Sky Whale*.

'Run!' bellowed Wind Jackal.

The first of the sky pirates vaulted over the balustrade and on to the *Galerider*. The hammerhead guards drew their scythe-like swords with an evil hiss, and bore down on the rest of the sky pirates. Wind Jackal and Steg Jambles fell back to meet them.

Quint leaped on board the *Galerider* and, landing with a heavy thud, had the wind knocked out of him. He looked back. Steg and his father were battling valiantly with four guards. With a start, he saw, coming in from the east, the lead league ship with the fearsome Ruptus Pentephraxis at its helm. A great spike protruded from its prow. Any second now it would spear the *Galerider* and fix it to the *Great Sky Whale* like a butterfly pinned to a board.

'Come on!' Quint bellowed to his father. 'Now! Or you'll get cut off!'

'Let's go!' Wind Jackal shouted to Steg Jambles and the pair of them spun round, made a dash for the edge of the deck and leaped across to the *Galerider*.

The moment they landed, it soared upwards into the sky under Ramrock's expert touch. Just in time, for beneath them there was a tremendous *CRASH!* as Ruptus Pentephraxis's league ship – unable either to slow down or change course – rammed the *Great Sky Whale*, its great spike shattering the rear of the starboard hull and sending vast chunks of splintered wood from both sky ships tumbling down through the air.

From the swiftly retreating *Galerider* came the sound of cheering and jeering. They'd escaped. They'd stolen the Leaguesmaster's treasure. As for the slaves, even now, the sky rafts were flying free from the juddering *Sky Whale* – its cooling flight-rocks already straining in their cages, pulling the great vessel upwards.

Then all at once, with a creaking groan, the huge ship suddenly hurtled upwards, taking the hammerhead guards and its captain with it and disappearing beyond the clouds into open sky.

Quint cried out for joy. The enemy leaguesmen had been defeated; the wicked *Great Sky Whale*, destroyed. They had won the battle! A sky pirate's life didn't get much better than this!

. CHAPTER FIVE .

NAMED

It was late afternoon. The sky pirates had been celebrating since daybreak. Far in the distance, the glittering towers and spires of Sanctaphrax had finally come into view. Quint was standing at the helm with his father, Wind Jackal. Despite the upbeat rowdiness of the rest of the crew, he was in a reflective mood.

'The whole incident shows just how quickly and unpredictably grave situations can arise,' he was saying to Quint. 'Grim and Grem both dead . . .'

'Sky take their spirits,' Quint murmured.

Wind Jackal turned to him. 'Yet you did well, my son,' he said. 'Very well – despite your disobedience!'

'I said I was sorry,' said Quint quietly. 'And it wasn't all my fault anyway. If Ice Fox hadn't been deceived and . . .'

'I know, I know,' said Wind Jackal, resting his hand on his son's shoulder. 'Yet it was a close shave

80

for all that. I was lucky this time. One day I might not be so lucky . . .'

'But Father . . .' Quint protested.

'Let me finish, Quint,' Wind Jackal told him. 'If anything should happen to me, you will become master of the *Galerider* and then you will need a sky pirate name.' He paused. 'I will give it to you now,' he said and squeezed Quint's shoulder. 'You've earned it.'

'A sky pirate name?' said Quint. 'But don't sky pirates choose their own names when they become captains?'

'Some of the newer upstarts do,' said Wind Jackal scornfully. 'But traditional pirate families do things differently. We always have. For us, sky piracy is in the blood, and our names are handed down through the generations. My father gave me my name. Now it is time for me to give you yours. But remember, until you become the master of your own ship, it is a secret name – a name it would be unfitting for you to reveal to anyone.'

'I shan't,' Quint promised. 'But what is the name you have chosen?'

Wind Jackal came closer. He looked round, then spoke two words loud and clear into his son's ear. 'Cloud Wolf.'

'Cloud Wolf,' Quint whispered reverently.

'That's right,' said Wind Jackal. 'And that is the

last time you must utter the name before it is time for you to use it.'

Quint nodded.

'And now,' said Wind Jackal, returning to the flight-levers, 'we must hurry if we are not to be late for our appointment with my old friend, Linius Pallitax, back in Sanctaphrax.' He raised the sails and re-aligned the hull-weights for maximum speed.

'I wonder what he wants of us?' said Quint.

'I don't know,' said Wind Jackal, 'but when the Most High Academe of Sanctaphrax summons you to his palace, it must be a matter of the greatest importance.'

'A new adventure!' whispered Quint.

'Yes,' said Wind Jackal, looking out across the broad sky. 'Perhaps the greatest adventure yet.'

THE END

THE SECOND BARKSCROLL

THE
STONE PILOT

THE TERMAGANT TROG COLONY

. CHAPTER ONE .

THE PROWLGRIN PUP

I Maugin, was once a stone pilot. I have flown through the heart of ice-storms, battled albino rotsuckers over the Mire, fought against sky galleons amidst blazing ironwood pines, the air black with choking smoke . . . And throughout it all, I kept my sky ship afloat. I must use my skills now, on this sadness that threatens to destroy me. Tend it carefully, bring it back under control and use my memories like the pulleys and levers on a flight-rock platform, just like the stone pilot I once was . . .

I close my eyes, breathe deeply and go back, back to the very beginning, where it all started in the Great Trog Cavern far beneath the Deepwoods. It was there that I, Maugin, daughter of Loess, granddaughter of Loam, great-great-great-granddaughter of Argil, the first Cavern Mother, was born. Today, I am eighty-eight seasons of the bloodoak old, which is, even for termagant trogs, a great age – and yet I look barely twelve.

And that is my great sadness; a sadness I keep wrapped up inside me like a carefully tended flight-rock in a sky-ship cage – sometimes sinking, sometimes rising, but with me always.

Now, as I stand here by the lake of lonely Riverrise and stare out across the endless Deepwoods, my heart grows heavy, like a hot rock heated by the burning flames of memory. And, like a sinking flight-rock, the sadness – that terrible weight at the very centre of my being – is threatening to drag me over the edge and into the black void below, from which there can be no escape . . .

But I must go back to my earliest memories, memories of the wondrous cavern, place of my birth. Tears come to my eyes when I think of it . . .

It was beautiful, so beautiful. Stout, pillar-like roots from the trees growing in the forest up-top spanned the air, from the vaulted ceilings above, down to the soft earth of the cavern floor below – roots that provided for our every need.

As well as the roots of the sacred bloodoak, there were many, many others. Some, like the sweet-lullabee and the yellow-sapwood, provided nourishment; some – ironwood, leadwood and copperwood pines – yielded the raw materials for our dwellings; while others, such as the beautiful wintertree and delicate dew-willow, glowed softly, bathing the cavern in a soothing pastel light.

And then there was the underground lake of crystal-clear dew-water. Beside it, where the tangle of roots fanned out, we trogs built our cabins of paper, piled one upon another to form a trogcomb of dwellings. They were round and snug, separated one from the other by communal walkways, and whenever anyone was home – day or night – each one was lit up from within by flickering root candles.

Oh, how I loved to stand by the dew lake. I would gaze at the shimmering lights of the trogcomb reflected in its still waters, waiting for my beloved mother, Loess, to return from the root harvest.

I can recall her so clearly, even after all these seasons, standing tall in her paper robes, magnificent tattoos covering her strong arms and gleaming bald head. Thin, weedy trog males would trot along beside her, carrying her huge scythe and root-tap, while she carried a trug laden with lullabee shoots and sapwood nectar for our supper. When I saw her, I would let out a cry of delight and rush back to our cabin to light the root candle and spread the paper supper-cloth before she arrived home.

Then, after our meal in that small, glowing dwelling-place, my mother – her papery clothes rustling – would sit me on the floor and comb and plait and bead and braid my hair, all the while telling me stories. Wonderful tales, they were, of the termagant trog sisterhood, and of Argil, the first Cavern Mother, and how she had founded our colony beneath the roots of a sacred bloodoak tree, digging out the first small cavern with her daughters, and creating a tiny dew pond. Safe from the terrors and dangers of the world up-top, the colony prospered, and the cavern grew into the mighty trog cavern I knew so well.

Down there, amidst the glowing roots and glistening lake, there was no snow, no rain, no hurricanes or storms. The cavern sheltered us. It kept us cool when the woods up-top shimmered in the heat, and kept us warm when the ironwood pines groaned beneath layers of snow and ice. And not only did the cavern shelter us, but it protected us as well.

Up-top, as every trog knew, the countless Deepwoods tribes were forever fighting, with pitched battles constantly breaking out as marauding hordes pillaged and ransacked each other's settlements and villages. Fearsome shryke battle-flocks, savage hammerhead goblin war parties and roving bands of slavers preyed on the weak and unwary. And as if that wasn't enough, the terrifying creatures of the forest – from halitoads and hover-worms to wig-wigs and snickets – lay in wait behind every tree and in every shadowy glade.

Hidden away down in our cavern, we trogs remained safe while tribes fought and creatures devoured each other in the world up-top. And if any unwanted visitor got too close to our cavern entrance, then the sacred blookoak – together with its deadly sidekick, the tarry vine – soon took care of them. Most of those up there knew from bitter experience to avoid any glade where a bloodoak had taken root, and we termagant trogs were left in peace to enjoy life in our beautiful caverns far below the hustle and bustle of the world above us.

And so it was that we became the most secretive of all the tribes in the vast Deepwoods. Few up-top had ever seen a termagant trog for themselves. In fact, as I was to discover, there were many who believed that we didn't actually exist at all, but were simply the stuff of old gabtroll tales.

All this I learned as a young trog at my mother's knee, as she combed and braided my beautiful flowing orange hair – hair that we both knew I would lose when I reached my twelfth season of the bloodoak and turned termagant at the Blooding Ceremony. Ah, the Blooding Ceremony! That extraordinary transforming event, which can happen only once in a trog's lifetime . . .

There it is again; the sadness, heavy in my heart – unbearably heavy. I must be careful or it'll sink me. I must try to lighten it; to cool the sadness, like an over-heated flight-rock cooled by the cold earth released bit by bit with the drenching-lever . . .

I know, I'll think of Blink . . .

Yes, that's it. Blink. My darling little prowlgrin pup. He could only have been a few hours old when I first laid eyes on him, nestling in my mother's huge, outstretched hands.

'*There* you are, Maugin, my little dew-blossom,' she said brightly, her bloodshot eyes twinkling as she handed me the little creature. 'I've brought you something.'

I smiled. Although huge and fearsome, termagant trog mothers are exceptionally tender and nurturing to their young. By encouraging their daughters to keep pets they believe that they, in their turn, will become good mothers. Loess was no exception.

'What is it?' I asked.

Gazing up at me through large trusting eyes was a furry orange creature with strong back legs and a huge mouth.

'Up-top they're known as prowlgrins,' Loess smiled. 'This one's a pup. A clutch hatched out in a copperwood pine just above the tunnel mouth, and it fell into one of our nets ... They make good pets – they're affection-ate, easily trained, and we don't have to worry, because they're not talkers.'

We trogs never allowed any creature into our cavern that might give away the secret of our existence.

97

'It's only a pity that it's a male,' she said, and chuckled. 'What are you going to call him?'

I looked down at the tiny creature, and as I did so, his mouth parted, almost like a smile, and his two great big yellow eyes closed momentarily.

'Blink,' I said. 'I'm going to call him Blink.'

From that day on, Blink and I were inseparable. I fed him on fat pink grubs from the gnarled roots of dew-willows, which he'd only eat after I'd squished them and their wriggling had stopped. Then he'd bark excitedly and wag his thin, whiplash tail while I dropped the slimy things into his gaping mouth.

As Blink quickly grew on his diet of root grubs, we explored every part of the cavern. We would paddle in the dew lake, chase each other through the root clusters and play hide-and-seek amongst the paper cabins of the trogcomb. There was only one place Blink would not go near, and that was the great cluster belonging to the blood-oak, which lay at the very centre of the cavern.

When these roots glowed red, he would yelp with

fear and back away, as if sensing that up-top, the sacred bloodoak was gorging on some unfortunate prey. It was just as well, for pets weren't allowed inside the dome of the root cluster where the tap-root grew and the Blooding Ceremony took place . . .

But I must try not to think of that.

Blink's favourite place was below the mouth of the entrance tunnel. Whenever we went there, he'd get excited and skittish and begin to leap high on his powerful legs, his tongue lolling out of his wide mouth and a wild look in his yellow eyes as he sniffed at the air coming in from outside. Sometimes, it was all I could do to drag him away from the entrance tunnel on the end of the sumproot rope I had, by then, taken to attaching to his collar. He was getting stronger by the day.

When I told Loess of his behaviour, she smiled and gently ruffled my hair.

'What you have to remember, my little bloodoak-acorn,' she said, 'is that Blink's natural home is up-top, in the highest of the high treetops. He can sense it calling to him . . .'

'But his home is here with me!' I protested. 'He's *my* Blink, and I love him!'

'Your Blooding Ceremony is soon,' Loess said kindly. 'After that, your feelings will change. You'll have no more time for pets, and you'll be ready to raise a daughter of your own.'

'I'll always love Blink!' I cried, hugging the pup fiercely.

'You've raised him well, but if you want to really prove your love, you'll let him go before you turn termagant,' Loess replied.

I can feel the tears returning to my eyes as I remember my beloved mother's words. She was right, of course. I knew it, even back then, as a young trog of twelve seasons. What I didn't know – couldn't have known – was how this act of love was going to change my life for ever.

I remember it as if it were yesterday. Loess and the trog sisters had examined me, noting that my hair had a deep orange lustre, my white skin a pearly bloom, and that my eyes were glistening brighter and bluer than ever before. I was ready to turn termagant, they declared, and hurried away to prepare the tap-root. My Blooding Ceremony would take place the next day. There remained one last thing to do.

With a heavy heart and trembling fingers, I awoke, took hold of Blink's leash and set off for the cavern's entrance tunnel.

I was taking my darling prowlgrin pup up-top to set him free.

I remember the feel of the sumproot rope in my hands as I gripped it tightly and an increasingly skittish Blink dragged me up the tunnel towards the world above. We brushed past the nets that kept creatures out of the cavern, slipped round a sharp corner and up a gentle slope . . .

And there we were, in a small hollow beneath a curved root of a copper-wood pine, looking out across a sunlit glade. All around were mighty trees and lush Deepwoods veg-etation – sallowdrops, dellberry bushes and saw-fronds. But what I remember most – more than the sun's dappled light or the swaying of the trees; more than the hum of woodbees or the dis-tant whooping of a far-off fromp – was the shock of feeling the wind on my face.

Down in the protecting

cavern, the air was warm and still. The only breeze was the gentle waft of a paper screen falling across a cabin door. But here, the feeling of wind on my face was shocking, as if I had suddenly shrunk to the size of a seed-head and was about to be blown away into the Deepwoods and lost for ever.

My heart started pounding, I struggled for breath and my knees felt weak. I dropped the sumproot rope – and with a yelp of delight, Blink leaped out into the glade and off through the trees.

'Goodbye, Blink!' I called after him, my head spinning as the pup disappeared from view. 'Goodbye, boy!'

I turned, and was about to stumble back down the tunnel, still shocked by the feel of the wind ruffling my hair and rustling the paper cloak I was wearing, when a sound rang out.

'Yeeaaoowaargh!'

It was a howl of pain. It chilled my heart and drove all other thoughts from my head. Blink was in trouble! I had to do something.

I had to help him.

I flung myself from the hollow and ran through the glade and into the trees. The next moment I burst through the undergrowth into a small, shadowy clearing. And there, lying on his side, a thick barbed arrow sticking out of his chest, was Blink.

'No!' I cried out. I ran forward and sank down

beside him, cupping his head in my hands.

The wounded pup looked up at me, his great yellow eyes seeming to appeal to me for help. Then he blinked – once, twice . . . The eyes misted over and the third time they closed, they remained shut.

'Oh, Blink!' I sobbed, scalding tears welling up in my eyes and streaming down my cheeks. 'Blink. Bl—'

Crack!

From behind me came the sound of a breaking twig, followed by a low, rumbling growl. . .

. CHAPTER TWO .

WOODWOLVES

I turned round slowly, hardly daring to breathe, to find myself staring into two glowing yellow eyes. A huge grey creature with tufted ears and glistening fangs was standing at the far edge of the clearing. The great white mane of fur round its throat stood on end as it tensed its powerful legs in readiness to pounce. Unable to tear my eyes from the cruel stare of the great whitecollar woodwolf, I backed slowly away on trembling knees.

From the forest behind the snarling beast came the bloodcurdling howls of the rest of the pack as they picked up the scent of blood. Suddenly, the woodwolf sprang – followed by two, three, four others that burst into the gloomy clearing in a cloud of dust and a swirl of leaves. I let out a high-pitched scream and curled up in a tight ball, expecting at any moment to feel the pain of those terrible fangs tearing into me.

Instead, the clearing filled with the hideous

sounds of snarling and snapping as the savage wolves fell upon the body of Blink, my darling pet. I couldn't bear to look, and instead scrambled to my feet and ran full-pelt from that terrible place, back into the undergrowth.

I kept on running – running till my head pounded, my lungs burned and I feared my heart would burst. I jumped over streams, I leaped fallen logs; I dodged thornbushes and boulders. And as I ran, a terrible panic rose in my chest.

I was lost and alone in this vast, terrible place full of long thorns which scraped and tore at my shoulders and back, and strange plants and berries which released pungent, heady odours as my feet trampled them. And worst of all was the terrifying feel of the wind on my face, making me gasp and sob, and struggle for breath.

At last, exhausted, I could bear it no longer. I collapsed on the forest floor and lay there, tattered and torn and half out of my mind. I wanted to hide, to disappear into the ground and escape from the vast terrifying openness of the world up-top. My fingers clawed at the earth. And as they did so, they released a sickly, rancid odour which made me gag . . .

Behind me, coming closer through the trees, I could hear the snarling growls and excited yelps of the woodwolves. They were following my scent. It wouldn't be long now, I thought to myself, scalding tears running down my cheeks, before I too was torn apart, just like Blink.

Crack! Crack! Crack!

Suddenly there were twigs snapping behind me. I glanced round over my shoulder, and there – coming through the dense undergrowth towards me, moving like water sluicing through sand – were four of the woodwolves.

Their red eyes blazed, their blood-stained nostrils snorted, their tongues – dripping with saliva – lolled over their sabre-like teeth. I could hear them, panting and slavering, their paws pounding, their bodies swooshing through the undergrowth and, as they approached, I could *smell* them, too. The stale odour of their fur. The gagging tang of their rotten-meat breath . . .

I buried my face in my hands, my eyes shut tight, and gasped. The earth beneath me smelled worse than the woodwolves.

'Yarrghaaoow!'

The howling screech slashed through the air like a blunt knife, sending jarring shudders down my neck and spine. I looked up, but didn't understand at first what was happening.

The woodwolf seemed to be *flying*!

The next moment, there was a whistling *swoosh*, and out of the corner of my eye I caught a flash of green. Heart racing, I turned to see a long green tendril wrap itself round the belly of a second woodwolf once, twice, three times, and wrench it from the ground. It followed its hapless companion through the air, yelping and whimpering as it disappeared into the shadows of the forest.

I lay there for a moment, watching the space in the air where the two creatures had been hovering a moment earlier. The other two wolves let out piercing squeals, turned on their heels and fled. Slowly, I got to my feet and looked up.

I was in a glade of dark red earth, flecked with jagged white shards of what I took to be rocks, but which on closer inspection turned out to be bones. At the centre of the clearing stood a colossal tree, its roots sinking down into a great mound of skulls, ribcages and leg bones. Its mighty trunk pulsated with glistening lumps and grotesque nodules, and from the top, where its great branches sprouted, the sound of a thousand mandible-like teeth gnashing filled the air.

'M . . . Mother Bloodoak,' I whispered in awe, sinking to my knees before the sacred tree.

What I witnessed next still fills me with horror and revulsion when I recall it. The two woodwolves were clasped in the deadly embrace of the tarry vine, its thick roots anchored deep in the pulsating trunk of its host, the bloodoak. The whiplash tendrils of the vine raised the unfortunate creatures high in the air and dangled them over the great gaping mouth of the flesh-eating tree. For an instant they hung there, wriggling and writhing and letting out bloodcurdling screaming howls. Then, with a spasm, the vines released the wolves into the tree's gaping maw.

A horrible crunching sound was followed a few moments later by a thick column of blood and bones which exploded from the bloodoak's jaws. The lumps and nodules on the trunk greedily

sucked the blood in as it streamed down, the entire tree shuddering and pulsating in sickening convulsions.

Down below, in the Great Cavern, I knew that the domed cluster of the bloodoak would be glowing red as the roots filled with blood, and the sacred tap-root would be bulging. When I was down there, in the beautiful, glowing cavern, I'd never thought of the nightmarish scene unfolding up-top every time the bloodoak fed – the feeding which enabled each Blooding Ceremony to take place. And for the first time, I felt a terrible sadness well up within me – sadness I have lived with now for so long.

As I stood before the sacred bloodoak, I wanted to forget everything, to return to the beautiful cavern of my birth and to my beloved mother, and to wipe all thoughts of the terrible world up-top from my mind. My mother had told me that I'd change when I turned termagant and, standing there in that terrible glade, frightened and alone, that was what I wanted to do more than anything in the world.

I glanced about me, trying to get my bearings. Below my feet, I knew, was the Great Cavern, which meant that the entrance tunnel couldn't be far away. I looked around the glade, searching for the copperwood pine. And there in the distance it stood, its reddish gold branches standing out from the sallowdrop trees all round it.

I raced towards it, running as I'd never run before, panting loudly, my hair streaming out behind me. And as I reached the edge of the glade, I saw a smaller sunlit clearing further on, and the copperwood pine with the shadowy hollow beneath its curving roots.

'The tunnel,' I breathed.

Leaping over a jutting boulder and negotiating the ridges of tree roots poking up through the surface of the earth, I hurried on. Past a lullabee I went, past a bank of jangling flowers. All at once the clearing was before me, drenched in late afternoon sunlight. I rushed into it, happiness welling up inside me. For there,

on the far side, in the hollow beneath the roots of the copperwood pine, was the entrance.

'Mother,' I gasped, stumbling those last few strides. 'I'm coming. . .'

But then, just as I was crossing the clearing, there was a flurry of movement in front of me and two of the woodwolves stepped out from the shadows. They barred my path, their fangs bared and the white hair around their necks standing on end.

I skidded to a halt, terror screaming in every pore of my body. Desperately, I looked around.

Four more woodwolves appeared at the edges of the clearing, one to my left, one to my right and the other two behind me. I was surrounded by the pack. Once again I found myself staring into the cruel yellow eyes as the creatures advanced towards me, the circle growing smaller, like the tightening of a noose.

Then, above the low rumble of the woodwolves' throaty growls, I heard another sound. Higher-pitched. Metallic . . .

Clink! Clink! Clink!

. CHAPTER THREE .

ZELT PINK-EYE

'Well, well, well,' came a rough, brutish voice. 'What have my clever boys caught for me *this* time?'

At the sound of the voice, the woodwolves pricked their ears and whimpered eagerly. I looked up and saw, towering over me, the strangest figure I'd ever seen. He was tall and stooped, with incredibly long, spindly legs and arms, and huge hands with thin spidery fingers. His body was completely round, and he had almost no neck. Beneath the layers of grime, his face was as white as snow, except for one brown blotch that extended from above his left eye to halfway down his cheek. The eye set within this brown patch was milky – like a pebble in a stream. The other was pink.

He was wearing a long jacket made up of hundreds of different patches, each the skin of a Deepwoods creature – some mottled, some spotted, others soft and furry, or striped and feathery – all patched together in a sort of quilt. From the heavy leather belt around his circular belly hung dozens of traps, snares, collars and chains which clinked gently when he moved.

'Easy, boys,' he growled. 'Don't damage the merchandise.'

Five of the six woodwolves took a step back. The sixth, a hungry glint in its eye, took a step towards me, its teeth bared.

'Tozer!' grunted the strange figure angrily, one of his huge hands straying to his belt. 'Easy, I say!'

Suddenly, his hand snapped forward. It was gripping a coiled whip which swished through the air and landed with a loud *crack* on the woodwolf's snout. The creature yelped and fell back with the others, eyeing me resentfully as it did so.

'That's more like it,' he said. His eyes narrowed. 'Now, let's have a look at you.'

Leering unpleasantly, he swaggered forwards and broke through the circle of woodwolves – tickling the one he'd just punished behind the ear as he did so. It nuzzled against him and licked his palm.

'So, little one,' he said, turning his attention to me, 'what in the name of Earth and Sky is a tiny little slip of a thing like you doing out here in the middle of the Deepwoods? Why, there isn't a village or settled glade for miles.'

Reaching out, he took me gently by the arm and helped me to my feet. I shuddered as a gust of wind blew through the glade, rustling my paper cape and ruffling my hair.

'My, my, but you're a delicate little thing,' he crooned, tilting his great mottled head to one side and eyeing me up and down with his one good eye. 'Old Zelt will have to treat you gentle like.' He gave a wheezing laugh and snapped a delicate pair of manacles around my wrists.

I tried to cry out, to beg him to let me go – but I could not. It was as if the wind had blown my voice away, and however hard I tried, up here in the great vastness of the world up-top, I was unable to make a sound.

He looked around, his good eye narrowing suspiciously. 'I can't see no sign of clan or kin, can you, boys?'

The woodwolves yelped and nuzzled round Zelt's spindly legs.

'So, finders keepers, I reckon!' With that, he picked me up and slipped me neatly into a great sack that hung from one side of his belt, and I found myself plunged into darkness.

What followed was the first real journey of my life. And although I didn't know it then, it was to be the start of many journeys. In fact, one journey has led into another and another and even now – so many long seasons of the bloodoak later, as I stand here at Riverrise – I know my journeying is not yet over.

But all that lay in front of me as I curled up in the comforting blackness of Zelt Pink-Eye's sack, the hateful wind no longer on my face. The steady swaying and the heavy tramp told me I was being carried ever further from my beautiful cavern home.

As he walked, Zelt hummed tunelessly and whistled to his wolves, and the traps and snares on his belt clinked. In the depths of the sack, I felt great waves of sorrow break over me.

I thought of my beloved mother, Loess, in our glowing cabin in the trogcomb, and how she would be preparing my paper robes ready for the Blooding Ceremony. I pictured the sisterhood gathering in the dome of the Bloodoak Root Cluster and making ready the tap-root.

And as I imagined their faces – the pain and worry and distress etched into their features as they searched in vain for me in the cavern – tears welled up in the corners of my eyes and trickled down over my cheeks, and silent sobs racked my body. They would be calling for me to come quickly, their cries ever more desperate, for they knew as well as I that a trog who misses her Blooding Ceremony will never get another chance to turn termagant. I was sobbing freely now, and the trickle of tears had turned to a flood.

Suddenly, I was absurdly grateful to the slaver's sack which, for now at least, shielded me from the terrible world up-top.

'Here, Tozer! Filzer! Ribb!' the slaver's muffled voice sounded, calling to the wolves.

And from outside, I heard the woodwolves whimper and snarl with agitation as the slaver used his whip to bring them to heel.

I don't know how long we travelled. One hour? Three hours? Six ... ? Locked up inside the darkness of the sack, it was impossible to tell. But although I couldn't see, I could sense the changing ground over which Zelt tramped, by listening to the sound of his great heavy feet – now slapping down on rock, now scrunching over sand, now soft and padded on thick grass growing in soft, loamy-smelling soil. Every footstep he took was transformed into a visual image of our surroundings as the dense forest gave way to glades and clearings, which turned to marshland, pasture, scree, and back again.

Moreover, despite the thickness of the coarse sack, I could sense smells – and even colours. The earthy dampness and the lush greenness of crushed meadow grass; the dusty smell of gravel, acrid, dry and grey; the peaty, rich brown odour of muddy marshland. And as I lay in that swaying sack, I realized that I possessed talents of perception that I hadn't noticed before in my comfortable cavern home.

Despite all this, here in the darkness, it was of course my ears that gave me the most information on the world we travelled through. I could hear a rising wind in the trees, the coming and going of babbling streams, the low moans and muffled sighs of the woodwolves which trotted after us . . . And, above it all, soft yet insistent, the *clink, clink, clink* of the collection of traps and snares hooked to the slaver's belt.

I had no idea of our destination, yet the further we went, the more I dreaded ever reaching it.

It was later – much later – when I heard voices in the distance. I'd grown used to the solitary nature of our march, and the sound made me instantly uneasy. One was shouting; giving orders and barking commands. Others sounded lost and frightened. There were plaintive denials and tearful pleas . . .

As we got closer, I picked up the smell of blazing torches dipped in pine-resin and wax, and braziers stuffed full of oily timber that gave off thick, pungent smoke. The voices grew louder and Zelt's gruff voice rang out in greeting.

'What's all this? Leaving without me, Griddle?'

A thin wheedling voice sounded in reply. 'Of course not, Zelt, me old mate. Just harnessing the hammelhorns to save time. We'll set off at daybreak.'

Zelt gave a throaty laugh, and there was the sound of one of his great hands slapping a back.

'So, what took you so long, Zelt?' Griddle asked. 'Can't be much merchandise out there, so far from

the settled glades.'

'You never can tell, Griddle,' came the reply, and I felt the sack lurch as Zelt unhooked it from his clinking belt. 'What do you make of this, eh?'

The sack gave another lurch and I tumbled out onto the soft, dusty earth of a forest clearing. It was dark and, all around, burning torches cast nightmarish shadows over the great wooden wagon and squat, hairy beasts in harness before me. A small goblin with a pointy, twitching nose thrust his face into mine and narrowed his small, cruel-looking eyes.

'Darned if I know, Zelt,' he hissed. 'Still, let's get it loaded. Everything's got to be ready. If we don't leave at daybreak, the merchandise is going to start dying on us before we reach market.'

With that, he grabbed me roughly by the arm and dragged me towards the great gaping door of the wagon.

'Careful, Griddle!' Zelt protested, hurrying behind. 'Don't damage it. It's a delicate little thing . . .'

'*Pah!*' snapped Griddle, flinging me roughly through the door, into the fetid, inky blackness. 'Perhaps *too* delicate, Zelt, me old mate,' he hissed, slamming the heavy wooden door shut, 'for the bidding hook!'

. CHAPTER FOUR .

THE SLAVE WAGON

That night and the following day were among the strangest of my long life. It was there, in the darkness of that foul-smelling slave wagon, that I learned much of the evils of the world up-top, and shed bitter tears for the cavern life I now knew I was leaving behind for ever. For even if I was to escape and find my way back to the cavern, I had now missed my Blooding Ceremony and would never turn termagant. I was an outcast.

The wagon was full of the 'merchandise' I'd heard Zelt Pink-Eye and his partner, Griddle, talk of. They settled themselves outside, at the front of the covered wagon, on comfortable seats from which they whipped the hammelhorns into motion as the first light of dawn broke. From the dark, stuffy interior, we could hear them laughing and joking and passing a bottle of woodgrog back and forth between them as they boasted of what fine specimens they'd secured for the bidding hook.

At each mention of that dreaded contraption, I felt my heart flutter, and even now – all these seasons later – the sound of those two little words still fills me with dread. And I clearly wasn't the only one. As my eyes became accustomed to the gloom, I began to make out the features of the merchandise around me, and catch snatches of their whispered conversation.

It seemed that every Deepwoods tribe and creature was represented in that wagon – and many I have since become familiar with. But back then, when I was a mere slip of a trog of twelve seasons, they were all so strange and wonderfully exotic. There were ghostwaifs, even smaller than me, with huge fluttering ears and big sad eyes. Crimson-haired slaughterers huddled next to tousle-haired woodtrolls; gnokgoblins and tree goblins cowered beside sad, weeping mobgnomes . . .

'I was out fishing when it happened,' someone close by was saying. 'Terrible bad luck.' The voice sounded friendly, I thought, soft and with a lilting burr. 'Course I'm not blaming her, but if my Rilpa hadn't said how much she fancied a little bit of sweetwater chubbock for her supper, I wouldn't have been there, rod, hook, net and a pot full of woodbottle grubs in hand.'

The axles squeaked and the timbers creaked as the lumbering wagon continued across the bumpy forest floor, jolting and jarring us as the ironwood wheels seemed to find every tree-root and boulder in the pitted track.

'Went down to a place we mobgnomes know as Mogred's Elbow, I did,' the voice went on. 'A great deep pool at a bend in the Edgewater River. Sat me down 'neath a spreading sallowdrop tree. It was warm, peaceful, my eyelids grew heavy ... Next thing I know, I've been caught, and in me own net. Me *own net*! Can you believe it?'

Whoever it was that he was telling his story to must have muttered something sympathetic in response, but I didn't catch what it was.

'That weaselly little goblin caught me. All bones and sinews – and he had a vicious whip,' he added, and I could hear the pain in his voice. 'Clapped me in irons and dragged me away.' He paused for a moment. 'What on Earth are Rilpa and the young'uns gonna do without me?'

To my left, other voices – three of them – were arguing.

'This is what comes from seeking new pastures.' The voice sounded tetchy.

'But the tilder-grazing there was perfect – sweet young meadowgrass.'

'It might have been sweet, but it was too far from the village hammocks. I warned you, Glottis, but you wouldn't listen. You never do . . .'

'Come on, now,' broke in a third voice, older and wearier than the others. 'He didn't do it on purpose.'

'I never said he did. All I know is that if we hadn't taken the herd so far away, this would never have happened.'

'Well, it's no good crying over spilt tildermilk, Spleen,' said the older slaughterer. I could just see his sad, red face in the gloom as he turned to his companions. 'And at least we led the slavers away from the village . . .'

As the wagon rumbled on, I found myself listening to someone else – a young woodtroll who was seated some way to my right. He looked about my age, and was being comforted by the strangest individual in the whole wagon – a creature with large flapping ears and eyes on the ends of stalks, which she kept moist with her long, slurping tongue as she talked. It was my first sight of a gabtroll, and I'll never forget her.

'In your own ... *slurp* ... time, m'dear,' she whispered. 'And don't fret yourself.'

'It's like I said,' the frightened woodtroll's voice whispered back. 'I did what I shouldn't do – what *no* woodtroll should do, let alone a young'un. I strayed from the path.'

The gabtroll patted his shoulder gently.

'We were out mushroom-gathering. Me, my big sister Briary and cousin Towselbark, each of us with a plaited trug that we were racing to fill first. Course, we were sticking to the path, only venturing off a few steps after mushrooms if we could actually *see* a clump growing.'

129

'I understand . . . *slurp* . . .'

'Anyway, Briary and I started arguing. She reckoned half of the stuff I'd picked was inedible. Toadstools, she said they were. Poisonous toadstools. And she started tossing them away. I got so upset, that . . . that . . .'

'There, there, now . . . *slurp* . . . It's all right.'

'But it's *not* all right, is it?' the young'un sobbed. 'I ran off; I strayed from the path . . . That'll show her, I thought. Now she'll be sorry. But the only one I showed was me!' As the hushed whispers continued, I could tell that the woodtroll's tears were flowing freely now, and I felt tears spring into my own eyes. 'I was running across this stretch of ground when – *whumpf!* – this net I'd stepped onto was triggered. It hurtled up into the air with me inside it. The drawstring pulled shut and I was left, dangling from a branch, high up in the air, wrapped up so tightly inside the net I could barely breathe, let alone cry out for help . . .' He sniffed. 'Two days I hung there. No one found me – until the slaver came. Cut me down, he did. Tossed me into a sack and slung me from his belt . . .'

Suddenly, it all became too much for me and I burst into tears. The gabtroll shuffled over and ran a stubby hand over my head.

'Oh, my dear,' she soothed. 'Don't take on so . . .

My, but you're a delicate little one ... *slurp!* Well I never!' Her stalk-like eyes came towards me and looked me up and down. 'Why, as I live and breathe, you're ... *slurp* ... a termagant trog!'

I nodded tearfully.

The gabtroll gave me a comforting hug. It was almost as if I were back with my beloved mother Loess, and I could barely control my sobs.

'There, there,' soothed the gabtroll. '*Slurp ...* Well, you're a rare one and that's a fact ... And not turned termagant, I see ... *Slurp ...*'

I looked up, startled that she should know so much. She seemed almost to be able to read my thoughts.

'Oh, my poor, poor dear!' She shook her head.

131

'By the look of you, you were ... *slurp* ... almost due for your blooding.'

I nodded.

'Standing beneath the tap-root of the mighty bloodoak, bathing in and drinking deep of its transforming blood ... We gabtrolls are famous for our remedies and potions, but nothing we possess can match the power of the ... *slurp* ... Blooding Ceremony.'

Her strange, stalk-like eyes took on a faraway look for a moment.

'What incredible power ... *slurp* ... to transform a delicate wee creature like yourself into ... *slurp* ... a magnificent trog sister before your very eyes. Your tiny arms swelling with muscles, your legs becoming huge, your beautiful orange hair falling from your head. What an amazing sight that would be ...'

She squeezed me tight.

'And now, my little one, you will never turn termagant ... *slurp*. Oh, my dear ... *slurp* ... I'm so, so sorry. But you must promise me one thing!'

Her whispered voice became suddenly fierce and her eyes blazed.

'Never, ever reveal what you are to anyone else. *Slurp!* Or you'll put yourself in terrible danger, for there are those who would stop at nothing to get their hands on a creature such as yourself – a fabled

trogdaughter of the bloodoak. Especially ...
slurp ...'

I'll never forget how her eyes bored into mine.
'Especially where *we're* going!'

Just then, the wagon gave a sickening lurch and
came to a shuddering halt.

. CHAPTER FIVE .

THE BIDDING HOOK

The door of the slave wagon crashed open and a blinding shaft of daylight cut through the stale air. Gasps and moans around me mingled with smells and sounds coming from outside. Sizzling meat, sweat, leather, pine-resin smoke, clinking metal, mewing cries of tilder and hearty bellows of hammelhorn were all mixed together in a terrifying concoction that left me trembling with fear.

One by one, the merchandise was hauled out of the wagon by Zelt or Griddle to be greeted by excited shouts or derisory boos from the unseen crowd outside. Nothing I'd seen or heard in the terrible world up-top could have prepared me for this moment.

As the gabtroll – that dear, sweet-hearted creature – was dragged out by her manacled hands, she managed to whisper a few last words to me.

'Courage, little one!' she slurped. 'And remember! Tell no one . . . *slurp* . . . your secret!'

She disappeared out through the wagon doorway and a great roar went up, followed by a chorus of excited shouts. A short while later, Zelt Pink-Eye's face loomed over me, a leering smile plastered across it.

'Always sell well, gabtrolls do!' He smirked and grabbed my arm with his huge hands. 'Your turn now, little missy. The bidding hook awaits!'

I screwed my eyes tight shut as he dragged my trembling body out into the light and, as his grip tightened, I felt myself being raised high in the air. There was a ripping sound as my paper cloak snagged on something, and suddenly I felt myself hanging in the air. It is a sensation I will never forget – I felt sickened, vulnerable and utterly helpless . . .

Then I opened my eyes – and immediately wished I hadn't. The sight that greeted me was the most terrifying yet. I was suspended from a great jagged hook that jutted out from a gnarled iron-wood post, high above a great sea of faces gazing up at me.

There were massive ring-collared goblins with tattooed faces, battle-scarred cloddertrogs with heavy brows and twisted smiles, flinty-eyed mer-chants in high chimney-stack hats and sky pirates wearing heavy coats bedecked with glinting brass instruments. For a moment, there was a hush, before a puzzled hum grew as the crowd began muttering to each other.

Below me, a tall figure in a tattered fromp-fur coat and wide, low-brimmed hat leaned forward from a raised platform and bellowed at the upturned faces.

'And now we come to the last item. From the slave wagon of Zelt Pink-Eye and Griddle Rittblatt...'

He turned and scrutinized me. I can still remember his fat, mottled face – the stubby, upturned nose, the moist red lips and pudgy cheeks with their oiled and plaited side whiskers ... I shudder now as I did then when I recall it.

'A fine, delicate specimen of a ... a...' He seemed lost for words. 'Well, let's just say a forest-dweller. Now who'll start

the bidding at fifty? Fifty, anyone?' He scanned the faces in the crowd.

I looked down at the upturned faces gawping up at me – my own face flushed with a mixture of shame and growing terror.

'Funny little thing, ain't she,' someone near the front commented, elbowing the short, stocky goblin by his side and sniggering.

'Wouldn't last five minutes on furnace duty by the look of her,' opined someone else, who was dressed in thick, stiff clothing.

'No, and not much use at chopping logs, neither,' said his neighbour with a rueful shake of his head.

'Forty?' suggested the auctioneer. 'Thirty . . . ? Twenty? Come on, someone's got to offer me twenty.'

'I wouldn't have the first idea what to do with her,' a merchant in a tall, conical hat muttered with a sneer.

I hung my head as I swayed gently to and fro from that awful hook and wished that I'd been torn to pieces by the woodwolves just like my beloved prowlgrin pup, Blink. Anything was better than this. Just then, a thin hissing voice rang out that made my blood run cold.

'Eight.'

I searched the crowd. A tall, gaunt figure in a tricorn hat with glowing sumpwood burners attached to it was staring at me through small gold-rimmed spectacles. His eyes were of the clearest, iciest blue, and seemed to bore into me, chilling me to the core.

'Eight?' the auctioneer replied.

The figure nodded, sending two thin puffs of sumpwood smoke spiralling into the air.

'Eight, I'm bid,' the auctioneer announced. 'Any advance on eight?'

The lumpen faces stared back blankly. I willed someone – *anyone* – to bid against the terrible cold-eyed character whose stare never wavered for an instant from my face. But no one did so.

'Eight, going once . . . Going twice . . . Sold to . . . to . . .'

'Ilmus Pentephraxis,' he announced, striding through the crowd towards the front. He tossed a small purse at the auctioneer, and Zelt Pink-Eye took me down from the bidding hook and handed me over with a rueful smile.

'Such a delicate little thing,' he muttered, shaking that mottled head of his. 'Thought you'd go for more than that. You live an' learn, an' that's a fact.

So long, little one.' He turned away, and as he did so, I heard his parting words. 'Rather you than me.'

The figure in the tricorn hat ignored him, and dug his bony fingers into my arm as he marched me roughly through the crowd, muttering in his thin, reedy voice as he did so.

'Quite a bargain . . . Quite a bargain,' he repeated over and over to himself.

We made our way across the slippery mud towards the edge of the ragged, forlorn forest clearing. And it was from there, in the distance, that I saw an amazing sight. Tethered to the tops of iron-wood pines from great circular anchor rings, were great floating sky ships – the first I had ever seen. The sight took my breath away and I must have stopped in my tracks open-mouthed, for I suddenly felt my new owner's fingers digging viciously into my arm and his voice hissing in my ear.

'That's right, my little bargain! Take a good look! We're bound for Undertown, you and I, aboard that fine league ship up there.' He breathed in noisily, greedily, like a hoverworm closing in on its prey. 'You have no idea how long I have searched for a specimen like you. . .'

An evil leer spread across his face and he reached up with his bony fingers and took one of the sump-wood burners from his hat.

'A termagant trog that has yet to turn . . .' The

way he said those words
made my knees tremble,
and I felt as if I was going
to faint. 'You, my little
bargain, are unimagin-
ably valuable, did those
fools back there in the
market but realize.' He
chuckled. 'The secrets
that you can reveal under
the right – how shall I put
it? – *experimentation*, could
be of incalculable worth. I
have a workshop waiting,
bloodoak acorns, fur-
naces, blood . . .'

He traced a finger
across the line of my chin
and I could feel the sumpwood burner's heat on
my cheek, bringing tears
to my eyes.

'I shall unlock the
secrets of termagantation,
my little bargain, and you
shall help me . . . The tor-
ments shall be exquisite!'

The sumpwood burner

141

touched my skin and I let out a high-pitched scream of pain.

'Hey! *Hey!* You there!' a voice rang out. 'What do you think you're doing?'

Both of us turned to see a young sky pirate, his face flushed and his dark eyes flashing angrily, come striding towards us.

'Mind your own business, you impudent young whelp,' spat Ilmus Pentephraxis, dropping the sumpwood burner and rounding on the sky pirate. 'She is my property, and I'll treat her as I see fit—*Ooomph!*' he gasped as the sky pirate's fist crunched into his midriff.

The leaguesman folded over double, only for the sky pirate to bring a knee up and connect with his jaw. Ilmus crashed down, face first into the mud, and the remaining sumpwood burner fizzled and bubbled as it sank into the ooze.

'Come, little one,' the sky pirate said, flinging a handful of gold coins at the leaguesman. 'I've just purchased your freedom. You can't stay here – it's far too dangerous. You'd better come with me.'

I squinted up into the light through my parted hair to see a tall, handsome youth looking back down at me, his right hand outstretched. His hair was dark and wavy, his skin sallow, his eyes deepest indigo.

And he was smiling. It was the first smile I'd seen since I'd left the Great Trog Cavern. I smiled back and took his hand.

'My name's Quint,' he said as he shook my hand. 'Quint Verginix.'

. CHAPTER SIX .

THE SCOURGE OF THE WEAK

Even after all this time, I still find it difficult to describe my emotions as I set foot for the first time on the sky ship that was to become my home. The *Galerider* was a beautiful vessel, a sleek single-master with a fine prow and flying keel. She had a gabled helm at her stern and a wide, circular flight-rock platform in her centre, with meticulously weighted cooling-levers and an ornately decorated rock furnace.

Oh, how I loved that flight-rock platform with its earth buckets and rock-bellows, its cooling rods and heating tongs – tools of what was to become my trade; the trade of the stone pilot.

But, as a dazed, frightened young trog, a mere twelve seasons of the bloodoak old, I noticed none of these things. All I knew was that I was in yet another terrifying place in the world up-top, just as appalling in its own way as the bloodoak glade, the fetid slave wagon or the horrible bidding hook. I was a termagant trog, raised in the security and comfort of the underground cavern, and now I was being helped from a rope-chair onto the foredeck of a sky ship by a young sky pirate.

The wind in my face, ruffling my hair and tugging at my tattered paper cloak, was almost too much to bear. And I remember sinking to my knees and curling up into a terrified ball on the foredeck, just below the flight-rock platform.

A young girl – whom I later came to know as the wise, beautiful Maris, daughter of the late Most High Academe of Sanctaphrax and truest, most devoted friend a termagant trog could ever have – knelt beside me and stroked my trembling head. A moment later, I heard a throaty laugh and looked up to see a tall sky pirate captain smiling down at me. This was my first sight of the great Captain Wind

Jackal. He turned to his son, Quint, a look of indulgent amusement on his face.

'Another one of your waifs and strays, son?' he said. 'I swear you seem to find one in every skyforsaken Deepwoods clearing we put in to.'

Quint smiled back, but there was a serious look in his dark eyes.

'No, Father, not *every* clearing,' he said. 'But I couldn't leave young Tem Barkwater to be flogged back there in the Timber Glades, could I?'

He nodded towards a malnourished youth who was skulking in the shadows of the quarterdeck, just behind Maris. Little did I suspect that that youth was to become one of my closest and most loyal comrades.

'And as for this little one,' Quint continued, turning his attention to me. 'I'd just gone to see about those provisions, and was coming straight back – just like you told me – when I practically tripped over a brute of a leaguesman torturing her. I had to do something!'

'Slave markets are bad places, son. You can't rescue the whole world. Still, what's done is done. We'd better get out of here before you get yourself into any more trouble.' Throwing back his head, he bellowed, 'To your posts!'

All about me, the crew of the *Galerider* ran to their stations and prepared to set sail.

Captain Wind Jackal took the helm, with Quint, his son and my rescuer, by his side. The quartermaster, Filbus Queep, locked the cargo-hold doors with a large brass key which he wore on a chain around his thin neck. Spillins, an ageing oakelf, climbed to his lonely lookout point in the caternest at the top of the mast. Steg Jambles, a bluff, bearded foredecker, and his mate Ratbit, a wiry, swivel-eyed mobgnome, manned the great harpoon, while the terrifying Garum Gall – a monstrous cloddertrog with as many tattoos as my mother, Loess – sharpened his razor-edge spear on the ironwood gunwales.

And then there was Ramrock, the stone pilot,

standing above me on the flight-rock platform in his tall, conical hood, heavy gauntlets and apron, firing up the rock furnace and cooling the flight-rock. I shall never forget what happened next, not if I live to be two hundred seasons old.

Captain Wind Jackal gave the command to 'Release the tolley-rope, Steg!' and 'Full lift to the flight-rock, Stone Pilot!' and the mighty sky ship rose up from the mooring rings at the top of the ironwood pines and took to the skies. My stomach lurched and my head spun and tingled. Soon, the ragged, muddy scar in the midst of the Deepwoods that was the evil slave market was far below, and the *Galerider* was soaring off through the clouds.

The terrifying gusts of wind that filled her sails cut right through me and threatened to drive me insane. I was saved from flinging myself to destruction in a fit of sky-madness by one thing – the bright, searing rock furnace burning in its cradle attached to the mast above my head. Its heat seemed to draw me to it, acting as a counter to the horrible feel of the wind on my face.

Almost despite myself, I found I was leaving Maris on the foredeck and climbing up to the flight-rock platform to be closer to its comforting heat. There, I found Ramrock, the stone pilot, urgently going about his profession.

'Sky ship to starboard,' came the high-pitched voice of the oakelf in the caternest. 'A thousand strides and closing.'

Captain Wind Jackal raised the great brass telescope that he kept strapped to his breast-plate and gave a bitter laugh.

'Another one of those bullying league ships by the look of it, with a name to match. Crewed by the dregs of Undertown and captained by a scoundrel, no doubt. Here, take a look.'

He passed the telescope to his son.

'Sky above!' Quint exclaimed. 'He's the one I knocked out in the slave market, Father!'

'Well, whoever our little guest is, he certainly wants her back,' Wind Jackal replied. 'Why, he's brought half the thugs from the market with him!'

'Do we stand and fight, Father?' Quint asked him. 'The Knights Academy trained me well.'

'Only if we have to, son,' laughed his father. 'The *Galerider* will give the *Scourge of the Weak* a run for its league-ship money first!'

'Eight hundred strides, and closing!' Spillins shouted.

'Come on, you scurvy lot,' Wind Jackal bellowed at his crew, his hands darting over the bone-handled flight-levers. 'I need lift and speed. Ramrock, get that rock cooled. Steg, Ratbit – see to the studsail.'

'Six hundred strides,' shouted Spillins.

'By Sky, he's keen,' Wind Jackal said. 'Master Queep, defend the prow. Steg, Ratbit, the foredeck is yours!' He turned to his son. 'Watch my back, Quint, my boy. If it comes to it, they'll attack the helm first!'

'Five hundred strides!'

Maris called up to me to join her below deck, but I couldn't move. I was transfixed. My eyes were on Ramrock with his great hooded coat, his heavy boots and gauntlets, tending to the huge buoyant flight-rock as tenderly as if it were a living, breathing thing – which, as we sped across the sky, I was beginning to see that it was.

As Ramrock pumped the rock-bellows here, and prodded with the cooling rods there, the rock expanded and pressed against the rock cage with a gentle hiss, lifting the sky ship ever higher in the sky. By cooling the flight-rock, the sky ship rose; by heating it, the flight-rock sank, and I soon saw that the flight-rock platform was at the very heart of the little world of the sky ship – and, what's more, that I felt strangely at home there.

'One hundred strides and closing in fast on the port side,' Spillins called down.

I glanced round, and there – horribly close, and getting closer with every passing second – was Ilmus Pentephraxis's league ship, the *Scourge of the Weak*.

It was a heavy-prowed, twin-masted vessel, with double-rigged side sails and a sharp, evil-looking keel. Although the *Galerider* was both sleeker and more elegant, the league ship had twice as much sail and was rapidly catching her.

With the league ship fast approaching, I saw Pentephraxis at the helm, the sun glinting on his spectacles and the sumpwood burners in his tricorn hat ablaze once more. As if that wasn't enough, the decks of the league ship bristled with the fearsome faces that had stared up at me from the market place. Goblins, cloddertrogs, slavers all, and in their midst, the leering white face of Zelt Pink-Eye, a great curved bow in his hand.

'By the authority invested in me by the United Leagues of Undertown I, Ilmus Pentephraxis, order you to surrender!' the captain's thin, rasping voice rang out. 'Or take the consequences!'

'This is a free ship, leaguesman!' Wind Jackal's voice boomed out in reply. 'We recognize no authority but that of the wind and the storm.'

As if in answer, a volley of arrows and crossbow-bolts whistled through the air towards the *Galerider*. All around me, I could hear the heavy thud and splintering of wood as they embedded themselves in the hull, the mast and the decks.

'More lift, Stone Pilot!' Wind Jackal roared from the helm as his hands danced over the flight-levers.

The *Galerider* soared high as Ramrock doused the flight-rock with the drenching-levers, before wheeling round in a steep arc across the league ship's bow.

'Ready when you are, Master Steg!' the sky pirate captain bellowed.

From the prow of the *Galerider*, Steg Jambles lit the lufwood shaft of the sky ship's great barbed harpoon and sent it hurtling towards the *Scourge of the Weak*! It streaked across the sky, ripping through the spidersilk sails of the league ship, which burst into flames in its fiery wake.

With cries of fury and alarm, the crew cut free the flaming sails and hoisted new ones in their place, while the decks bristled with the crossbows and longbows of

slavers jostling for position to fire at the *Galerider* as it sped past. Another volley hissed towards us. At the ironwood gunwales, Garum, the hulking cloddertrog, gave a gurgling scream and clutched his chest as two crossbow bolts found their mark.

'Return fire!' Wind Jackal commanded.

Steg Jambles, Ratbit, Queep and Quint all raised loaded crossbows and let loose a deadly volley in reply. As I watched, ragged gaps suddenly appeared in the ranks of slavers at the balustrade of the league ship. A heavily tattooed flat-head tumbled over, a crossbow bolt buried between his widely spaced eyes, and fell towards the forest below.

The *Galerider*, in full sail, sped off into the endless expanse of treetops. The howling wind in my face made me gasp and grip the railings of the flight-rock platform in terror. I turned my face away and, looking back, saw the league ship turn and give chase. Its fresh sails billowed once more and it rapidly gained on the smaller *Galerider*.

Within moments the *Scourge of the Weak* drew within twenty strides of us, and to my horror I saw Zelt Pink-Eye raise his bow and zero in on Captain Wind Jackal at the helm. Zelt paused, and I held my breath as he trained the bow slowly along the length of the foredeck, as if selecting and rejecting each target in turn, before coming to a halt at

the flight-rock platform.

For an instant I found myself staring into his unblinking pink eye, before he let loose a great barbed arrow.

'*Annghh!*'

Beside me, Ramrock gave a muffled cry and crumpled to the deck, the arrow buried deep in the centre of his back, knocking the flight-rock levers forward as he fell.

Instantly, the rock furnace flared with a brilliant yellow flame and the flight-rock gave a high-pitched whistle as it glowed a deep red. The *Galerider* shuddered and started to go into a downward spiral.

'Ramrock!' Wind Jackal yelled from the helm. 'Do something!'

Almost without thinking, I fell to my knees on

the burning hot flight-rock platform and tore at Ramrock's lifeless body.

'Forgive me,' I murmured as I pulled the heavy gauntlets from his hands and slipped them onto my own. Then, with the heat from the rock furnace burning my face, I wrenched the great hood from his head and slid it down over my shoulders.

The change I felt within me was unforgettable. In that moment, on the burning flight-rock platform of a sinking sky ship, as I looked out of the glass eye-panels of the heavy, protecting hood, I knew that I had found my calling. Here in the midst of the hurricanes and storms of Open Sky, I could stand on this fiery platform and gaze out from the depths of my own personal cavern.

Seizing two cooling rods, I knelt down and thrust them deep into the overheated flight-rock with all the force I could muster. The effect was as exhilarating as it was instantaneous. A great hiss of steam billowed up and streamed past my hooded face, and the rock suddenly cooled and turned buoyant once more.

At the helm, Captain Wind Jackal was quick to react, like the seasoned sky pirate he was. His hands flew over the flight-levers as the *Galerider* shot up into the path of the *Scourge of the Weak*, our razor-like keel slicing the foredeck in two as we passed.

Looking down from the flight-rock deck as the *Galerider* soared away under full sail, my last view of the *Scourge of the Weak* was of the two great lumps of timber – the helm and the prow – separated from one another and tumbling towards the jagged tops of the Deepwoods trees. As it fell it scattered goblins, cloddertrogs, Ilmus Pentephraxis, Zelt Pink-Eye and all to the terrible winds.

Now, seventy-six seasons of the bloodoak later, as I stand here at lonely Riverrise, looking out over the endless Deepwoods, the fierce joy I experienced that day so long ago fills my heart. It was the day that I discovered my calling as a stone pilot and, for a long time, my profession served me well.

I sailed the skies aboard the *Galerider* with Captain Wind Jackal and then, on his passing, with his son, the brave Captain Cloud Wolf – who I'll always remember as Quint, the young sky pirate who rescued me.

After many voyages and some great sorrows, I was proud, in turn, to repay some of the great debt I owed Quint by serving his son, Captain Twig, who

I came to love with all my heart. The voyages we undertook together were some of the most amazing of my long life.

The last time I saw Twig was on this very spot, here at Riverrise many seasons ago, when I used all my knowledge of sky flight to send him hurtling back to the great floating city of Sanctaphrax, to save the Edge from destruction. I know he succeeded, because the spring here at Riverrise flows once more with its life-giving waters, and I wait by the lake it feeds for Twig to return.

I am alone, here with my sadness, the sadness of never having turned termagant, and – more terrible than that – the sadness of losing my dear, dear Twig. It is a sadness that, if I'm not careful, will sink me like a fiery flight-rock sinks a sky ship.

But it must not, because I must wait here at Riverrise. Just in case he returns . . .

THE END

THE STONE GARDENS

NEW SANCTAPHRAX

SCREE TOWN

OLD UNDERTOWN

TH

THE DEEP WOODS

THE TWILIGHT WOODS

THE EDGELANDS

The Edge.

THE THIRD
BARKSCROLL

THE SLAUGHTERER'S QUEST

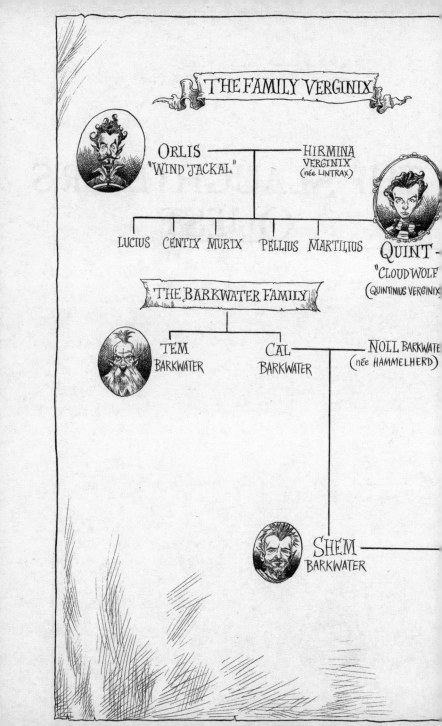

THE FAMILY VERGINIX

ORLIS — HIRMINA
"WIND JACKAL" VERGINIX
(née LINTRAX)

LUCIUS   CENTIX   MURIX   PELLIUS   MARTILIUS   QUINT -
"CLOUD WOLF
(QUINTINIUS VERGINIX

THE BARKWATER FAMILY

TEM   CAL — NOLL BARKWATE
BARKWATER BARKWATER (née HAMMELHERD)

SHEM —
BARKWATER

THE FAMILY PALLITAX

LINIUS PALLITAX
(MOST HIGH ACADEME
OF SANCTAPHRAX)

YENA PALLITAX
(née VESPIUS)

MARIS VERGINIX
(née PALLITAX)

TWIG
(ARBORINUS VERGINIX)

SINEW VERGINIX
(née TATUM)

KERIS BARKWATER
(née VERGINIX)

ROOK BARKWATER

. CHAPTER ONE .

SUPPER AT DAWN

Keris pulled back the tilder leather door-hanging and stepped out of the hot, bustling kitchen cabin. It was a beautiful wintry night, with the full moon high above the treetops. It shone down, pure and white, casting the logwood cabins into slate-grey shadow and making the dusting of frost over the village clearing sparkle like phraxdust.

But Keris had no time to admire the moonlight. The wicker basket she was carrying on the crook of her arm gave off twists of sweet-scented steam, which mingled with the clouds coming from her own mouth as she hurried through the village. She needed to hurry, or the hot spicy drink would end up tepid and tasteless.

From the kitchen cabin behind her came the clatter of knives on chopping blocks, the sizzling of large copperwood frying pans and the low rhythmic song of the slaughterer sausage-makers. The cacophony of sound meant only one thing.

The village was expecting visitors.

Keris shivered as she strode past the churning huts, with their rows of drying cheeses; the tarping stalls, with their rollers and tanning vats, which billowed acrid crimson steam as the tilder leather inside them was slowly cured; and the rilking sheds, where great shaggy hammelhorn pelts hung in clusters. But it wasn't the cold that made her fingers tremble as she pulled her own hammel-hornskin waistcoat tightly closed at the neck, but rather a surge of excitement.

Tonight, there would be a feast.

Keris loved dawn suppers in her village when visitors came. And it wasn't just the traditional slaughterer hospitality that she loved – hospitality which meant that the huge communal table in the village clearing would be piled high with steaming tilder hams, spiced sausages, hammelhorn steaks and cauldrons of rich sweetmeat soup. No, it was what came afterwards that she looked forward to so much. With the great brazier's blazing heat warming the rows of family hammocks slung from the treetops above, and the pale light of dawn casting shadows across the table and its sleepy diners, the herdmaster would climb to his feet and propose a toast.

'We have eaten well and drunk deep,' he would boom, raising his tankard of woodale high above

his spiky red head. 'Now let us feast on the tales our guests have to tell of travels from places far beyond our pastures!'

And then the stories would begin. Gnokgoblin resin-traders would describe their homes in the branches of the mighty ironwood pines amidst the giant tree-fromps on whom they depended. Cloddertrog miners would retell bawdy stories recounted on cold nights in the deep caves to keep their spirits up. And solitary oakelves would talk wistfully of the lullabee groves of their childhood, and of their lonely quests for a place to hang their wonderful caterbird cocoons.

Keris loved all their stories and would memorize and repeat them to herself or to her many cousins at day in the hammock, when they couldn't sleep. But the tales she looked forward to most eagerly and treasured above all others were the tales told by sky pirates . . .

She smiled to herself, her dark eyes flashing and the tilder-greased points of her black hair, worn long and spiked in the slaughterer-style, glistening in the moonlight. She reached the edge of the village and headed down the broad droveway towards the lower pastures. Despite the high banks of protective thornbushes that formed an impene- trable barrier on either side of the path, Keris knew that the Deepwoods lay just beyond.

She could hear it all around her. The yowling and screeching of the night creatures seemed louder than ever this bright, moonlit night. From the shriek of gladehawks and squeal of hoglets to the distant yodelling of the solitary banderbears; razorflits, weezits, fromps and quarms, she knew their every cry . . .

'The Deepwoods . . .' she murmured.

The vast, brooding forest was full of unimaginable wonders and such terrible dangers. It was a place that every slaughterer was, from infanthood, taught to both fear and respect. Like their neighbours – the woodtrolls in the villages to the east and the gyle-goblins in their colonies to the west – the slaughterers knew only too well that survival meant sticking together and never straying from the droveways and pastures they knew so well. Those who did, as Keris had been told often enough, were taking their lives in their hands.

Perhaps that was why the village laid on such bountiful feasts for visitors who came to trade their goods for the slaughterers' finely worked tilder leather and expertly cured hammelhorn pelts. Knowing the perils well, the slaughterers admired their guests' bravery in venturing so far from the safety of their own homes. Moreover, they loved the travellers' tales of hardship and bloodshed told to them, safe in the knowledge that at the beginning of the day they could retire to the comfort of their warm hammocks above the brazier fire.

'Please let it be him, please let it be him . . .' Keris repeated to herself over and over as she reached the end of the droveway and stepped into the lush, knee-deep meadowgrass of the lower pasture.

In the distance, the hammelhorn herds – great mounds of shaggy grey and brown fur in a swaying sea of silver grass – grazed contentedly in groups of a dozen or more. They were watched over by thin, wiry herders with long crooks and spiky red hair.

Keris made her way quickly to the centre of the pasture where the herds were grouped, away from the dangerous fringe of the tree-line. A couple of the hammelhorns stepped aside, lowing as they did so.

'Uncle Gristle,' she greeted a tall herder in a tooled leather cape.

He turned a grizzled face towards hers; his skin stained a deep, dark red from the smoke of the curing sheds. Keris's own complexion seemed unnaturally pale by comparison, and her spiky hair even blacker.

'Goodnight, young Keris,' he smiled, his gaze falling on the wicker basket in her hands. 'Is that my midnight fodder? You are good to your old uncle.'

He took the basket from his niece and, spreading his leather cape on the meadowgrass, motioned for her to sit before unpacking the contents of the basket. There were three tilder sausages, hot from the pan, a wedge of rich hammelhorn cheese and a hunk of moist barleybread, together with a flask of spiced winesap – still steaming.

'To keep the cold out' – Gristle winked at Keris and took a long swig from the earthenware bottle – 'and warm an old herder's heart!'

Keris watched him wipe his mouth on the back of his hand. 'Have you seen them, Uncle?' she began excitedly. 'Our visitors? Where are they from? Are they . . . ?'

'Sky pirates?' said Gristle, with a smile and a shake of the head. 'I couldn't say for certain.'

Keris sighed. Once, the sky pirates had seemed to be regular visitors, filling the sky above the village with their great sky ships, which they would anchor to the tops of the largest trees. Recently, though, their visits had dwindled. The last time they had come must have been five, maybe six, years earlier.

'Whoever they are,' he said, 'according to the

village drums, they're on their way from the woodtrolls on foot. Should be with us before dawn by all accounts, but don't get your hopes up, Keris, my dear.'

'I can't help it,' Keris admitted, frowning and biting her lip. 'Every time the village has visitors I just can't help hoping it might be . . .'

'Your father,' said Gristle, laying a hand on her shoulder and stroking the hammelhorn fleece thoughtfully. 'You know, Keris, when your mother – my sister, Sinew, Sky rest her soul – died of the fever, your father Twig took it very hard . . .'

Keris stared down at the half-eaten barleybread in front of her and swallowed hard.

'He took to brooding, going over the past, blaming himself for all sorts of things – both real and imagined – until I began to fear he'd go the same way as your poor, dear mother. He got so thin and pale . . .'

Gristle picked up the bottle of hot winesap and took another swig.

'You see, he felt he'd abandoned his crew, and that your mother's death was some sort of punishment.' He shook his head. 'Convinced himself, he did, that the only way to protect you, his little daughter, was to go back out there into the Deepwoods and put things right. Three years old, you were, Keris, and scarcely bigger than a tilder fawn when he placed your little hand in mine and asked me to look after you as if you were my own. Then he left, promising to return once he'd been reunited with his crew . . .'

'That was ten years ago,' said Keris, unable to stop the bitterness creeping into her voice.

'That's as maybe,' said Gristle, turning his grizzled red face towards the tree-line. 'But wherever your father is, you can be sure that he won't let go of the memory of you, just like he couldn't let go of his crew. And believe

me, he'll do everything he can to come back . . .'

'But how can you be so sure, Uncle?' Keris interrupted angrily, her eyes glistening with scalding tears.

How many times had she lain awake in the middle of the day going over the few memories she had of her father, together with what she'd been told of him by her uncle? How many tears had she already wept?

Fourteen years earlier, a sky pirate ship had come to the village; the *Skyraider* its name. Its young sky pirate captain – a friend of her Uncle Gristle – was sick; his crew desperate. They had left him with the slaughterers, promising to return as soon as they could. Weak with fever, he'd been nursed by her mother, Sinew. It was a long, slow recovery, but gradually, he'd got better – by which time Sinew had fallen in love with the pale young sky pirate captain and he, unlike so many others in the Deepwoods who despised the lowly slaughterers, had returned her love. When the crew had returned, Twig had sent them away, promising to catch up with them later. But he'd stayed. And stayed – delaying his departure time and again.

A year to the day after his arrival, she – Keris – had been born . . .

What memories she had of him now were no

more than fleeting images. Sitting astride his broad, strong shoulders. Looking into twinkling green eyes – the same colour as her own. Snatches of a half-remembered lullaby sung in a soft lilting voice as she drifted off to sleep in a warm hammock . . .

Her mother had died when Keris was barely a year old. And, according to her Uncle Gristle, Twig had left the village two years later.

That was ten years ago. Ten years of sharing Uncle Gristle and his family's hammock, yet feeling apart – the black-haired, pale-faced child amidst flame-haired, crimson-faced cousins. Ten years of hope every time visitors were expected – and ten years of disappointment . . .

Of course she loved the stories at the dawn suppers, and on those occasions when sky pirates had arrived in the village she'd quizzed them eagerly for news of her father, Captain Twig – but without success. The stories, though! What stories the sky pirates could tell! They told of epic voyages across the muddy wilderness of the Mire; of raids through the Twilight Woods and thrilling intrigues in the great sprawling city of Undertown and the even more extraordinary floating palaces of Sanctaphrax.

For months after every sky pirate visit, Keris's days would be filled with vivid dreams.

Yet still, even after ten years, she couldn't help feeling that heady excitement – the blooming of a hope against hope that was so powerful it caused a pain in her chest – every time the village got news of visitors heading their way. The same old questions would spring up and go round and round in her head.

This time, would it be her father returning? If it wasn't, then where was he? What had happened to him? And would she ever see him again?

'How can you be so sure my father will come back to me?' Keris repeated, softly this time, wiping away a tear on her sleeve. 'How do you know he didn't just sail off with his crew and forget all about me?'

Gristle leaned forward and broke off a hunk of the barleybread, which he nibbled, his eyes glazing over.

'Because' – he said slowly, without looking up – 'a long, long time ago, before you were born and I was just a young strip of a lad, not half-cured and still pink about the ear-tips, who thought he knew better than his elders . . .' He paused and looked up once more towards the distant tree-line of the Deepwoods. 'Your father, Twig, saved my life.'

'He did?' said Keris, astonished.

This was one story about her father that her uncle had never told before.

'I'm not proud of myself, and don't like to speak of it,' said Gristle, 'because I was foolish beyond reason.' He shook his head. 'A terrible example for young'uns like yourself, Keris.' He coughed. 'You see, I left the droveway. I wandered off into the Deepwoods . . .'

Keris's jaw dropped. It was something she herself had often thought of doing. But then, as her grand-mother had often pointed out, 'With all that sky pirate blood coursing through your veins, it's little wonder you've got the wanderlust.'

'I was curious,' he went on. 'And I thought I could scout out a new pasture, forge a new path – make a name for myself in the village. Instead, all I found was a great, fat, slimy hover worm with dripping yellow spots and a belly full of air . . .'

Keris gasped. All slaughterers knew about hover worms. They haunted the dells and glades at the pastures' edge, hovering just above the forest floor on powerful jets of air expelled through air-ducts that ran the length of their bodies. Unless an anti-dote of charlock and hempleaf was administered at once, a hover-worm bite was lethal.

'I blundered into a glade and the creature lunged at me,' Gristle told her. 'I'll never forget the sting of those tentacles embedding themselves in my ankle. The excruciating pain. Before I knew it, I was writhing in agony on the ground, calling out for help, and the hover worm was circling around me, waiting to strike again . . .'

Gristle paused and rubbed his ankle slowly, re-living the moment.

'And then Twig, your father, appeared from the depths of the Deepwoods, running full pelt in answer to my cries – only to trip head over heels over my poor swollen foot! Well, straight away, the hover worm turned its attention to him.'

Keris frowned.

'Your father was the same age as I – the same age that you are now – but tall and slim. And he was dressed in woodtroll clothes, with his hair twisted and knotted in that way that they have. But I could tell he was no woodtroll. I thought he'd turn and run – save himself. Especially as he'd dropped his knife when he fell. But not a bit of it. Twig jumped to his feet and then gave that slimy, hissing worm quite the run around, darting this way and that to avoid its lethal tentacles.

'"My knife . . . Find my knife . . ." he kept shout-ing as he did so, and luckily – despite the pain – I was able to lay a hand on it and throw it across to him. And just in time. The hover worm struck, but instead of ducking, Twig stood his ground. He raised his knife and sliced the creature from head to tail as it flew at him. The next thing, it exploded like a punctured bladder-balloon, scraps of it floating down to the forest floor all around us.

'Then it was *my* turn to feel like a bladder-balloon. You see, the hover worm's venom was in my veins by now, blowing my legs, my arms, my body and neck – even my tongue – to twice their normal size and making me float up into the air. I'll never forget the sensation, Keris – nor the look of horror on Twig's face. But he didn't panic. Instead, he seized a rope, tied one end around my foot and the other around his middle, and set off towards the village with me calling out directions as best I could as I bobbed along above his head.

'I was getting lighter and lighter, you see, and before long I was pulling us both off the ground and up towards the treetops – but he didn't let go . . .'

Gristle paused and when he resumed his story, his voice was raw with emotion.

'I'll never forget it, Keris, as long as I live,' he said, hoarsely. 'Twig was magnificent. He held onto that rope, even as we cleared the treetops and began to float off to certain death in Open Sky. He didn't let go. Just clung on tightly and hollered for help at the top of his lungs. That's how the patrol that the herdmaster had sent out to look for me found us. They lassoed his feet, dragged the pair of us down to earth and got me back to the village to give me some antidote before the hover-worm venom caused me to explode.'

He chuckled.

'There was quite a dawn supper that night, I can tell you. Singing, dancing, and Twig was the hero of the hour.' He frowned. 'Strange thing, though – following morning, he upped and left without saying a word to anyone . . . But I never forgot his bravery.

'Then, one fine night, years later, he returned as a sky pirate captain – and do you know what? Beneath his breast-plate and greatcoat, he was still wearing the hammelhornskin waistcoat my mother – your Gram-Tatum – had given him for saving my life . . .'

He paused for a moment. Then, leaning forwards, he gingerly stroked the corner of the fleece Keris was wearing.

'*This* hammelhornskin waistcoat,' he said softly.

'This belonged to my father?' whispered Keris.

She looked down at the beloved old waistcoat that she had worn for as far back as she could remember. She'd always thought the waistcoat was simply a hand-me-down, like the jackets and coats her cousins wore. She ran the tips of her fingers delicately over the soft fur. Tears welled up in the corners of her eyes. There was a painful lump in her throat.

'You see, Keris, your father doesn't let go of things,' said Gristle. 'That's why I am sure that, if he's still alive, Twig hasn't forgotten you. He didn't let go of me, he couldn't let go of his crew, and he won't let go of you . . . He'll do everything he can to come back to you.'

Keris wiped her eyes.

'Thank you for telling me the story,' she said at length, smoothing down the ruffled hammelhorn fur of her waistcoat. She climbed to her feet. 'I'd best be getting back – to help with the preparations for dawn supper.'

Gristle watched in silence as Keris turned and set off across the pasture towards the village. She looked so small and vulnerable in the silvery light of the moon. He couldn't see the tears streaming down her cheeks.

Sure enough, by the middle of the aftermidnight, the great table at the centre of the village clearing was groaning beneath the weight of heavily-laden platters. Great vats of pickled-tripweed sat next to oak barrels of woodale and large tilderskins of dark winesap. Tall gyle-wax candles, as thick as a slaughterer's arm, cast a warm glow over the feast, while the branches of the trees overhead were decked out with twinkling glow-lamps.

Surely not even a lullabee grove could look quite so magical, thought Keris, as she carried a skillet of sizzling hammelhorn steaks to the table.

Just then, from the far end of the east droveway came the unmistakable sound of hammelhorn trumpets announcing that the visitors had been spotted approaching the village. With her heart in her mouth, Keris joined Aunt Chitling and her cousins as they found their places noisily on their bench. Soon the eight sides of the great table were bustling with expectant red faces, their spiky-haired heads quivering as they all peered across the village clearing.

'Here they come!' shouted one of the younger Totters, a cry taken up by the Welkins and the Scutshaw family next to them.

Keris strained to catch a glimpse of the visitors over the bobbing heads of her companions. When she did, her face instantly fell. One glimpse was enough to tell her that whoever they were, these visitors were certainly not sky pirates. As to what they were exactly, that was much harder to say. The small group walked past the glowing brazier and approached the crowded table.

They were slight in build, shorter than the average slaughterer, with long jaws and heavily lidded eyes. Their skin was green-tinged and covered with glistening scales, and each had a tall, scalloped crest on the top of their head – a crest which seemed to change colour subtly in the candlelight. But the oddest feature of these strange visitors, it seemed to Keris as she stared open-mouthed, was their feet.

They were huge in comparison to the rest of their bodies, webbed between the toes

and with a long spike protruding from the back of each ankle, which seemed to click as they walked. They wore patched, leathery breeches, and belts bedecked with knives, barbed spears, hooks, flasks and – oddest of all – a heavy-looking pebble on the end of a long length of rope.

Their leader, who appeared older than the rest – with a larger crest, longer ankle spikes and a voluminous cloak of a dark grey leather that Keris couldn't identify – stepped forward and raised a scaly hand in greeting.

'Felfpht, chief of the north shore clan,' he announced in a soft, whispery voice, his large crest glowing a deep crimson. 'May your waters be unmuddied and your nets always full.'

He bowed, followed by his fifteen companions, whose crests all turned the same vivid colour as their leader's.

'Welcome to our humble village,' boomed the herdmaster, Rump Scutshaw, his red hair freshly greased and spiked and his broad shoulders glistening with a magnificent necklace of weezit fangs. 'Our neighbours, the woodtrolls, told us you were coming. Please do us the honour of joining us at our humble dawn supper.'

He swept his arm out in a broad gesture to indicate the magnificent feast piled high in front of him.

'We should be delighted,' whispered Felfpht, his

crest pulsating with ripples of orange and blue.

The crests of his companions did the same as they were shown to their places – eight to each side of the great table.

Keris couldn't take her eyes off these strange visitors. She shifted along the bench and tried not to stare too much as a small individual with a lower crest sat down beside her. At the head of the table – the side nearest to the brazier – Felfpht leaned over and whispered in the herdmaster's ear. Rump stood up and called for buckets of water to be brought from the troughs and given to the visitors.

When they appeared moments later in front of each of them, the slaughterers watched with astonishment – and not a little amusement – as their visitors tipped the cold, fresh water over their own heads. Keris was splashed by her strange companion, but she didn't mind, transfixed as she was by the look of contentment on his face as the water dripped from his glowing blue crest.

'Let supper commence,' announced Rump Scutshaw, and the feasting began.

According to custom, it was rude to press visitors with questions before they'd eaten their fill, so conversation was limited strictly to enquiries such as 'Can I pass you the tripweed?' or 'Another tilder sausage?' and 'More winesap, perhaps?'

Nevertheless, Keris's companion introduced

himself as Slifph and, in between mouthfuls of nibblick-cheese pie and spoonfuls of tilder stew, he told her that he was what was commonly known as a webfoot goblin – one of the webfoot clans that lived on the shores of the great lakes.

Keris was bursting to ask him more, such as where these great lakes were, how many clans were there and why that crest of his – and those of his companions – changed colour so often, and in such intricate patterns. But a stern look from her Aunt Chitling and an apologetic shrug from Uncle Gristle was enough for her to hold her tongue.

At last, just as Keris feared she was going to explode with curiosity, the herdmaster pushed back his chair and rose to his feet.

'We have eaten well and drunk deep,' he boomed, raising his tankard of woodale high above his spiky red head. 'Now let us feast on the tales our guests have to tell of travels from places far beyond our pastures!'

An expectant hush fell over the great table as Felfpht, the chief of the north shore clan of webfoot goblins, looked across at Keris's dining companion, Slifph. His crest rippled with red and orange stripes and, as if in answer, Slifph's crest did the same. Without a word being spoken, the young webfoot got to his feet and addressed the village.

'The four great lakes from whence we come lie

far from here, beyond the tree ridges of the west and the great ravines beyond that,' he began in a hushed, whispery voice. 'We are webfoot goblins of the north shore clan of the third great lake, whose waters we tend and from which come all the blessings and bounty we could wish for. Few venture to our remote lands and so, once in a spawning or so, some of us venture out into the great Deepwoods to learn something of the world beyond the lakes.

'We – my father, my brothers and I – have encountered many tribes: the white goblins of the depths, the trog hordes of the great ravines and the many tribes of the tree ridges; the flat-heads, the hammerheads, long-hairs, greys and tusked, to name but a few. We have traded for fish-hooks, fine rope twine and nets and come to you, red herders of the night, for your leather cloaks and fine pelts. We bring lake-pearls and silt-gems in return . . .'

The slaughterers nodded and raised jugs of woodale in response to this, and Felfpht, the web-

foot chief smiled, then nodded to his son to continue.

'But that is for later,' Slifph said. 'Now, I wish to
tell you of the strange sight that we witnessed in the
valley of the ironwood stands, three weeks' journey
from here. We had been trading for resin with the
gnokgoblins of the high stands, and had pitched
camp on one of the mighty branches of an ironwood pine. As dawn broke and the sun rose, a
magnificent sky pirate ship appeared on the horizon . . .'

Keris gasped, and leaned forwards.

'As it sailed over the treetops towards us, a
strange thing started to happen. The mighty vessel
listed first to one side, then to the other, shuddering all the while like a speared lake-eel. It rose and
fell, its flight-burners flaring until, low over the
trees, it crashed down into the depths of the
Deepwoods not far from our camp. That morning,
as we continued our journey, we came across the
fallen sky ship.

'Its timbers were remarkably sound and, though
ragged and splintered from the crash, its tall mast
and sails seemed in working order. But the
strangest sight, and one that I must tell you of, was
the massive flight-rock at the heart of the great ship.
It had crumbled to dust and fallen through the bars
of the rock cage, like sand escaping from a shattered

hour-glass. We found the vessel's captain . . .'

Keris let out a small cry but, spellbound by the young webfoot's tale, the slaughterers didn't seem to notice.

'He was dying, that much was clear, but he gave his name as Captain Glade Harrier of the *Edgedemon*, last of the sky ships. He told us that a terrible sickness had overtaken all the great ships of the sky, attacking their precious flight-rocks and turning them to useless dust. Many sky pirates had already scuppered their ships in a distant encampment far out in the Mire, but he, Glade Harrier, had refused to give in. Now he was paying the cost for his reckless decision. With his dying breath he looked up at me and whispered, *"The age of flight has ended"*.'

Slifph sat down and, for a moment, everyone exchanged looks of shock and surprise. The sky pirates were the greatest traders in the Deepwoods, travelling further and more widely than anyone. Now, it seems, they were no more. Little wonder that their visits had become so few and far between. And without their sky ships, they'd just be common traders like everyone else.

'My father is a sky pirate captain,' said Keris quietly, turning to the webfoot goblin. 'Do you think his sky ship has crashed like all the others?'

'That, Keris, is something that only the great clam

could answer,' said Slifph, his crest turning bright crimson. 'It dwells in the depths of the third great lake and is the most ancient of all the mighty clams.'

Keris frowned. 'And this great clam of yours,' she said. 'You're telling me that it knows if my father is still alive?'

'And whether you'll ever see him again,' Slifph replied, nodding.

'So how do I find out?' Keris asked, her voice trembling.

'Simple,' said the webfoot goblin, his crest turning a soft green. 'Come with us, and ask it yourself.'

. CHAPTER TWO .

THE TILDERSKIN SATCHEL

A small scruffy satchel of dark red tilderskin containing ten sheets of barkpaper and a stubby leadwood pencil . . . I hope this will be enough. It was all that came to hand that frosty morning three weeks ago when I left the warm snugness of my family hammock and crept away like a stealthy thief-in-the-day.

Dear Uncle Gristle, by now you will have discovered that I am gone. I hope with all my heart that you'll understand that I couldn't bear to say goodbye to you and Aunt Chitling and my cousins. I know that if I had, you'd only have pleaded with me to stay, and I wouldn't have had the strength to refuse you.

I trust by now you've found my charms and amulets. I took them from around my neck and left them, one by one, by each of your sleeping spiky-haired heads. Now you should each be wearing them alongside your own, hanging round your dear necks and close to your beloved hearts.

Think of me while I'm gone. I know your loving thoughts will help to keep me safe.

As I write these words, the barkpaper is stained with my tears, but I knew I could not set out on such a journey without at least trying to get some of it down. How glad I am now, simple slaughterer that I am, that I studied the gift of markings on bark from old Taghair, the wise old oakelf in his caternest in that lullabee tree of his. He taught us slaughterer and woodtroll young'uns alike – and I daresay he never imagined we'd use this skill to keep anything more than tally-ledgers of timber and livestock lists. Yet here I am, putting down these marks that tell of the great journey I have set out upon.

Three weeks have passed already. I can hardly believe it – and only now has there been time to put leadwood to bark. But I'm so glad I can, Uncle, for what wonders I have seen out in these mighty Deepwoods – wonders that I am compelled to record.

My webfoot companions travel swiftly and quietly on those huge feet of theirs, following the trail they left on their outward journey. I cannot tell exactly what these markers are, but on different occasions they seem to take their bearings from sniffing closely at some spot on the forest floor or, more curious still, pressing an ear up close to a mighty tree-trunk and listening intently. They speak little, but make up for this lack of speech by a strange silent communication with those crests on their heads that change colour constantly.

We sleep by night, usually in the high branches of the trees, and travel by day, which I am slowly getting used to – although I do miss the moonlight. But in the bright, colourful daylight world, I have seen some extraordinary sights. Great bell-like flowers that hum and sing in the breeze according to the level of dew collected within their mottled bowls; spiky green creatures tall enough to walk beneath, with eyes on stalks and eight stick-like legs, which feed on the leaves on the lower branches of the trees; and vast flocks of black and white birds that sometimes take all morning or afternoon to pass overhead . . .

And there has been more. So much more. But I'm painfully aware that I have only ten precious sheets of barkpaper to last me I don't know how long, so I mustn't use them all up in one sitting.

But there is one thing that I must record, for it so reminded me of you, dear Uncle and Aunt, and my beloved slaughterers. We have set up camp with a colony of gnokgoblins, high in the huge branches of an ironwood pine. It is but one of over fifty in this ironwood stand, each with its own colony. And this afternoon, our gnokgoblin guests took us up into the highest branches where I saw the giant tree-fromps that live there feeding.

They are huge creatures with shaggy white coats, long trunks and great curved claws. They cling to the tree-trunk with their razor-sharp claws and probe deep into the crevices between the barkscales with their trunks, in search of the blackbark beetles on which they feed.

The gnokgoblins climb after them and collect the golden tree resin that oozes from the deep holes made in the trunks by the tree-fromps' claws. The gnokgoblins tend and nurture these huge creatures as tenderly as you, dear Uncle, and your herders tend the herds of hammel-horn. Tonight, as my old friend the full moon rises over the ironwood stands, from my resting place on this huge branch, I can hear the rumbling snores of the tree-fromps hanging upside down from the branches high above.

It has been three long months since that magical night in the ironwood stands. The journey has been long and hard and the webfoots have been relentless in their pace. But I have kept step with them every stride of the way through the endless tree ridges with their jagged peaks and misty, dew-soaked valleys. And as we've journeyed, I've gradu-ally got to know my companions better though, like the mysterious Deepwoods themselves, I doubt I will ever discover all their secrets.

Slifph is my closest companion. Do you remember him? He sat next to me all those months ago at the dawn supper. He is one of a spawn of thirty or so hatched to one mother; the rest of our party are his brothers. We are seventeen in number, including myself. Our leader is their father, Felfpht. Back where they come from, he is the chief of the village, a cluster of huts on the north shore of one of their great lakes.

I've tried to probe Slifph and his brothers — Grulth,

Hiph and Spyve in particular – about the great clam that lives in their lake, but whenever I raise the subject their crests glow yellow and they evade my questions. Not that we have much time for fireside chats; just a few moments at the end of a long day spent climbing a tree ridge away from the gloomy, dank valleys below.

The tree ridges are home to goblin tribes too numerous to count. Most, like the fearsome flat-heads and their even more warlike cousins, the hammerheads – not to mention swarms of grey goblins and pink-eyes – move from ridge to ridge, never settling for more than a few days or weeks at a time, and engaged in constant feuding and petty warfare. Many's the night our small band has huddled together high in the branches of a copperwood or giant sallowdrop, trying to snatch much-needed sleep while below the terrible sounds of battle rang out amongst the trees.

Now, with supplies running low – tree-slugs and bark fungus our supper for the last two weeks – we have arrived in a clan village of long-haired goblins. The long-hairs are unusual amongst the warrior goblin tribes, for preferring to live in settled villages. Although vulnerable to attack, they make up for this by the size and grandeur of their defences.

The forest around this particular village has been chopped down and turned into a spike-topped barricade, surrounded by a great ditch. It is known as the Great Clearing of Threnody Battlerage, after their warrior chief *who ordered the work be done. At the centre of the village is the clan-hut, around which circle upon circle of thatched long-huts have been built. I must admit I was both frightened and bewildered by the jostling crowds, the noise and the smoke as we made our way along the central path towards the clan-hut.*

And the size of it all! Our entire village, Uncle, as well as half the lower pasture, could fit comfortably inside the great gathering place surrounding Threnody Battlerage's hut. Thousands of long-hairs – their hair spiked a little like we slaughterers wear it, yet altogether fiercer looking – had turned out to greet our little party. It seems that, on his outward journey, Felfpht had been able to warn the long-hair chief of a hammerhead raid on the village and Threnody now considers him a personal friend.

As we entered the open-sided clan-hut, I glanced up to see the grey-haired chief sitting on a throne of carved silveroak, raised high on a pile of long-hair goblin skulls, some with wisps of hair still attached. These, I was told by Slifph in a whisper, were the honoured heads of great long-hair warriors who had died in battle.

He then pointed to the roof-beams high above our heads. I looked up – and had to stifle a cry of horror. For there, hanging from the rafters, were row upon row of skeletons, the eyeless sockets in their skulls staring down at us as their bleached bones rattled against each other in the breeze. These, Slifph explained, were past chiefs of the clan, it being considered the highest

honour to hang from the clan-hut's roof-beams after death.

The sight makes me shudder when I think about it, but it was a small price to pay for a delicious supper of roast snowbird and a soft bed of summer-grass in a long-hut. We shall rest here with the long-hairs for a week. Then, according to Felfpht, when we are fully refreshed, it will be time to embark on the most dangerous part of our long jour-ney: the trog ravines.

As he whispered these words, Uncle, his crest turned a deep indigo . . .

As I write this I am shaking so badly that I can scarcely hold the *stump of leadwood pencil. Hunger is gnawing away in the pit of my stomach, and I'm not sure I have the strength for another day's journey – not that, in these dismal ravines, I can even distinguish day from night.*

The past month has been the worst of my life, and I've lost count of the number of times I wished I was back with you, Uncle Gristle, Aunt Chitling, cousins Silver, Saddle, Brisket and little Scrag, in our hammock high above the brazier. The only thing that keeps me going is the thought that if I don't, my bleached bones will end up deep down in the abyss below.

I shudder to think of it. Felfpht had warned me that the journey through the trog ravines would be difficult, but as we set off that misty morning from the village of the long-hairs, I had no idea just how difficult. As we crested the last tree ridge and paused to look down at the landscape below, it slowly began to dawn on me.

The ravines – vast fissures in the barren and rocky land, like scratches carved out by giant claws – stood in our path. There was no short way round them. The only route, Slifph assured me, was down into the depths of each ravine and up the other side; several days of hard climbing through each.

The last and the deepest of the ravines made Slifph shiver and his crest turn a whitish grey as he spoke of it. Home to the mysterious white goblins of the depths, there was no avoiding it, he said, but would say no more about it, no matter how much I pressed him.

With heavy hearts, we entered the first ravine and
clambered down over loose sheets of slate that shifted and
slid beneath our feet, making the going slow and difficult.
Finally, towards the end of the day, we reached the
bottom of the ravine, a dank, gloomy place with a small
stream running through it. We drank, and the webfoots
splashed themselves in its icy water as is their custom.

From across the stream, several massive trogs wearing
rough skins and bone earrings, and carrying crudely
sharpened stone axes, watched us suspiciously. But
thankfully, at our approach, they turned and lumbered
off into the gloom.

It was the first of many encounters with the trog clans
of the ravines – the most primitive tribes I have yet seen.
Despite their great size and fearsome appearance, they
were generally cautious and seemed content to keep their
distance as we passed through their ravines. And what
bleak, desolate, inhospitable places those ravines were, so
different from our lush, moonlit pastures and warm, welcoming village . . .

The steep, stony sides were pock-marked with cave
openings. Outside every cave was a pile of grey shells,
mottled and ridged, each one about the size of a hammelhorn calf. Slifph told me that they came from the giant
cave-lice that lived in the depths of the trog caverns and
are the trogs' main source of food in that barren place.
Judging by the number of shells scattered about outside
their caves, there seems to be no shortage of these strange

creatures – though what they might taste like, I shudder to think.

The good thing was, they seemed to keep the primitive giants well satisfied, and our small party – and our supplies – were all but ignored as we passed by. Except, that is, when we stopped for supper each night and lit a meagre fire from the dwindling supply of copperwood sticks we each carried.

Then, as we huddled round the glowing, flame-red sticks – a small bundle of which burned with an intense heat all through the night – we would all become aware of scores of pairs of watching eyes. Many was the time I'd peer up from the copper-red fire glow and glimpse a great shadowy crowd of ravine trogs standing in the darkness, transfixed.

As the days and nights passed, I slowly got used to this strange occurrence and, oddly, even began to look forward to it. You see, there was something about those great dark shapes and docile, watching eyes that reminded me of nights out in the silvery pastures, sur-rounded by grazing hammelhorns.

Six ravines we scaled in all, each one deeper than the one before. It took us twenty days – and twenty of those strange fireside nights. During the day, with the trogs keeping to their deep caverns, we saw few signs of life: the occasional rock-tilder, picking its way down the upper slopes; now and then a shaggy-winged vulpoon, circling the sky in search of carrion. Many was the time I yearned to be home.

As the dawn rose on the twenty-first day, our little party stood on the rocky lip of the last and deepest of the ravines, home to the mysterious white goblins, which the webfoots still refused to talk about. 'Better that you don't know, Mistress Keris,' Felfpht told me. 'Some things are best left cloaked in darkness.' But as I looked into the ravine, its sides falling away into an inky blackness far below, I couldn't help feeling that not knowing was far worse.

Felfpht whispered instructions for us to rope ourselves together and warned us to make as little noise as possible, though I swear my heart was beating louder than a village drum as I followed the others down the narrow, winding track, over the edge of the ravine and down the steep side below.

The further we descended, the darker it became and the more sheer the drop. Every so often, the path gave way to a mass of rocks and pebbles which, as we dislodged them, hurtled down into the abyss below. Finally it disappeared completely and we were reduced to clambering down a series of jutting ledges, one after the other.

We seemed to descend in this way for hours in the misty gloom until, at last, we reached a small stream at the very bottom of the ravine – at least, what appeared to me to be the bottom of the ravine. In fact, Slifph whispered, there were deep cracks in the ravine's floor – cracks that led further down into what were known as 'the depths', and from which, without any warning, the white goblins would soundlessly emerge in search of prey. It was, he impressed upon me, vital that we followed the path of the stream as quickly and quietly as we could through the ravine, until we reached a mound of jagged scree that marked the route of our upward climb.

What lay ahead, Slifph told me in an urgent whisper, was the most dangerous point of the entire journey. And from the sickly, mottled pallor of his crest, I didn't doubt the truth of his words. A tug on the rope interrupted our conversation and told us that the others had set off through the sluggish, brackish waters of the stream – and not wanting to be left behind in this terrible place, we hurried after them.

We walked for what seemed like several more hours and, although it must have been midday at least, the eerie darkness of the deep ravine was as impenetrable as ever. The damp and cold penetrated our clothing, even seeping through my hammelhornskin waistcoat and chilling me to the bone. Apart from our heavy gasps of exertion and the sound of our footfalls splashing through the icy stream, there was utter silence.

Then as we crept on, painfully aware of every breath and splash in the silent blackness, I felt something brush my cheek. It was faint, almost imperceptible, like brushing through a woodspider web, or against a tall blade of pasture grass. But I felt it again, and again. If they'd noticed the same thing, the others – ahead of me – made no sign of it. They pressed on through the stream, their webbed feet making surprisingly little sound considering their size. I was about to reach forward, tap Slifph on the shoulder and ask him what these strange cobwebs might be, when something cold and clammy suddenly enveloped my face.

I couldn't cry out. I couldn't even breathe. In the hideous darkness, I tried to kick out and flail my arms, but found that these too were gripped by something just as powerful. A brief twitch and snap told me that the rope binding me to my companions had been cut and – heart hammering in my chest – I found myself being half-lifted, half-dragged into the inky blackness, unable to scream or hit out.

I have never experienced anything like the blind terror of those moments in the depths of the ravine, in the grip of that terrible unseen monster . . .

Suddenly there was a blinding flash of light, and with it whatever was holding me released its grip. I fell heavily on the rocky shale and, moments later as my eyes adjusted, I saw what had snatched me.

Surrounding me was a seething, writhing mass of bony, hairless white bodies, as translucent as wood-beeswax and glistening like damp dew-slugs. The great mass retreated from the light and broke up into individuals, who stared at me with huge, black eyes, flared nostrils quivering and white tongues flicking the air. White goblins – a hundred of them, at least. Their huge hairless heads were covered in wispy tendrils that, as I watched in horror, darted out towards me, brushing my ankles and flicking at my wrists.

I took a step back and found Slifph at my side, two glowing fire-crystals in his outstretched hands. As we hastily retreated, more of the loathsome goblins clambered up out of the deep cracks in the ravine floor around us, the tendrils on their heads flicking out around them wildly like silvergrass in a storm-tossed pasture. It was at that moment I realized that the white goblins – despite their huge eyes – were all but blind, and that they were using their whiplash tendrils instead of sight in the inky blackness.

209

As we ran to join the others, their crests vivid purple with alarm, Slifph's crystals began to fade, and behind us we could hear the hissing sound of white goblin tendrils searching for us. A moment later, the light from the crystals was gone, and we were plunged again into absolute darkness. All at once, the previously silent ravine was full of hideous high-pitched shrieks and gibbering howls as the white goblins of the depths called for their kin to join in the hunt.

In this bleak and horrible place, our small band must have seemed like a rich feast for those emaciated goblins. Felfpht, though, had other thoughts. At his hushed command, we rummaged around in our backpacks for the remains of our supplies – strips of cured tilder and salted snowbird; wedges of dried hammel-horn-curd – and threw them back over our shoulders in a desperate bid to distract and slow down the terrible white goblins.

Soon, behind us, we heard snarling and squabbling as some of them fought over the paltry rations. We forged on, flailing wildly with the knives and small axes we carried, to sever the tendrils that whipped at our backs. Once I stumbled and fell to the ground, but Slifph – Earth love him – helped me to my feet and on we went. We arrived at the mound of scree not a moment too soon, and began a desperate scramble towards the light.

Of that appalling flight, I remember only the blind terror that drove us on, each of us determined not to get *left behind and fall into the clutches of our hideous pursuers. Only when those shrieks and bloodcurdling screams began to die away, and the air no longer hummed with the sound of searching tendrils, did we allow ourselves a moment to catch our breath.*

It was then that the dismal slog up the steep ravine face truly got underway; a journey that has continued, ever slower and increasingly arduous, the weaker and wearier we have become. Slifph tells me that this is the true test of our great journey, for the difficult climb out of this last ravine is the steepest and longest of all. Though it took us less than a day to descend into its appalling depths, footsore and hungry as we now are, it has so far taken us nearly a dozen to climb out of it.

As I write this on the last but one of my precious sheets of barkpaper, I can only hope against hope that these words will not be my last.

This is my final piece of barkpaper and, as I write on it, my thoughts are full of you, dear Uncle Gristle and Aunt Chitling and my darling cousins, so far away. I hope with all my heart that you are happy and well and that you think of me as you gaze into the glowing brazier fire last thing at day.

We climbed out of the terrible ravine of the white goblins into the bright sunshine and pleasant glades of a lush upland forest. I can tell by the renewed spring in my companions' steps and the happy reddish glow of their crests that we are in country they know well, and can't be too far from their distant watery home.

Now, round the campfire at night as we roast the log-grubs and barkshrooms we collect on our way, the air is full of laughter and talk of the loved ones they will soon be reunited with. I do my best to smile and share their happiness, but I find it hard – my heart as full as it is of thoughts of you, my dear slaughterers, and the little village I have left so very far behind . . .

But I must put such thoughts to the back of my mind, all tenderly wrapped and preserved, just like these barkscroll pages which I shall keep safe in this tilderskin satchel until the day comes when I can share these markings I have made with you. For now though, I must put down my leadwood pencil and face the future.

I have already glimpsed it!

Far beyond the grassy glades and treetops that spread out before our final camping place, like a vast green and blue quilt, lie the four great lakes of the webfoot goblins. There, I hope, I shall find the answer to the question with which I began this great journey. The hope of finding its answer has spurred me on through all the dangers and privations I have faced and will, I am sure, make them all worthwhile . . .

Is my father, Captain Twig the sky pirate, still alive?

. CHAPTER THREE .

MIRROR OF THE SKY

Grefphith's head, the crest glowing a bright yellow, broke the surface of the water. Ripples spread out in ever-growing concentric circles across the lake's glassy surface as he gulped in a lungful of air. A moment later, the same ripples turned to a ridged wake, as the webfoot goblin flexed his shoulders and, clutching his feeding-fork in one hand and his tether-line in the other, kicked out strongly for the shore.

There was no wind, not a breath. The third great lake was so still it more than justified the name given to it by the crested webfoot clan whose villages were clustered round its shores: Mirror of the Sky.

All four of the great lakes had been named by the different clans of webfoot goblins that lived beside them. The first lake – the smallest, yet with its great spire-clam in some ways the most unusual – was known as the Silent One. Lying at the bottom of a

bowl-shaped circle of forested hills, anyone whispering at one end of the lake could be heard by those standing at the other. It was a phenomenon of which the red-ringed webfoots who dwelt there were very proud. On long summer evenings, the clan of the first great lake could be found dancing on their stripy legs and singing to one another across its waters.

The second great lake was known as the Shimmerer by the tusked webfoot clan that lived beside it, for the lakes-skimmers and stormhornets that darted over its surface, both night and day, made the water itself seem to shimmer and glow. Although predominantly shellfish eaters, the tusked webfoots – smaller and more portly than their neighbours – were not averse to the odd stormhornet roasted over a slow fire. They carefully tended the great blackcap clam that had made its home beneath their lake's shimmering waters.

And then there was the fourth great lake – its milky waters leading it to be known by the resident white webfoot clan as the Lake of Cloud. These tall, warlike webfoots preferred to hunt in the forests around their lake, rather than fish its cloudy waters. But like the other webfoots, they carefully tended their lake's resident clams; the twins, Skeld and Skewa.

The Mirror of the Sky reflected everything around

it that bright afternoon – from the villages of stilt-raised cabins, made from woven lake-willow and roofed with meadow turf, which were grouped together on its north and south shores, to the distant ironwood stands, their jagged treetops silhouetted against the pale sky like mighty spear-tips. Even the eel-pool corrals – the great circular cork and rope enclosures which held the giant lake eels that the crested webfoot clans farmed – were absolutely motionless.

High up in the sky and honking loudly, a skein of migrating woodgeese flew overhead in a precise V-formation. Their passing was mirrored so perfectly in the placid lake, it was as though they were swimming underwater, far down in the turquoise and emerald depths.

Grefphith reached the north shore and picked up the anchor stone to which his tether-line was attached. No webfoot ever ventured into a great lake without first attaching a tether to an anchor stone and leaving it embedded in the lakeside mud. Grefphith rubbed his stone clean and secured it to his belt, before heading towards the village cluster. He'd spent the early hours at the bottom of the lake tending to the great blueshell clam, stirring up the nutrient-rich silt and laying traps for the giant lake snails.

It was hard work, but as a clam-tender, Grefphith

was proud to be one of the chosen few to care for the ancient mollusc. It certainly beat the other mundane village tasks – patching the fishing coracles, mending the nets; hook sharpening, spear grinding or feeding the lake-eels in the corrals. As a clam-tender, Grefphith had a special place round the cooking fire, and first choice from the stew-pot – after Milfphin, that is, who in Felfpht's absence was standing in as clan-chief.

That fat old excuse for a lake snail! Grefphith cursed silently.

Milfphin did nothing all day but sit on that eel-bone throne of his, being waited on hand and foot. If only his father Felfpht – the *real* clan-chief – were here, Grefphith thought, pulling on his snailskin cloak as he skirted round the reed beds on the north shore. But he had been gone this past year and more, together with Grefphith's spawn-brothers: Slifph, Spyve, Grulth, Hiph, Phlythiss and the rest . . .

Grefphith missed them. He missed their company and companionship – and their help with the great clam, for they too were all clam-tenders. Without them around to share the duties of looking after the ancient wise-one, there was only him and Milfphin's lazy, good-for-nothing sons – and *they* were usually too busy hanging round with their friends in the white webfoot clan by the Lake of

Cloud to be of much help. No, it was he, Grefphith, who ended up doing most of the work.

After what was now more than thirteen moons of toil, even though he had always tried his best, it was all getting too much for him. What was worse, Grefphith was sure the great blueshell clam itself was not happy. After all, throughout the entire time that he had been in charge of its welfare, the huge mollusc hadn't once spoken . . .

Grefphith hurried up the steep bank from the shore, past the beached coracles and fishing rafts, and onto the winding track at the top that ran between the tall, spiky bladegrass and the edge of the forest. Ahead of him, coils of brown-tinged smoke spiralled up from the cabin chimneys, where hunks of dried lake-peat burned steadily in the cooking-fires below.

As he reached the edge of the village, Grefphith found himself surrounded by webfoots of all shapes and sizes, their crests flashing and changing colour excitedly. After hours spent deep down at the bottom of the lake, the hubbub of the village cabin cluster always took a little getting used to – and today it seemed brighter and more excitable than ever.

Grefphith's crest glowed an enquiring green and blotchy orange. Everyone, it seemed, had come out to greet him.

There were his sisters, Mythwhull, Lyfph, Phlithym, Huwl and the rest; half a dozen massive spawn-nurses, each with two dozen or more young'uns tethered to the folds of their skirts, flashing their crests and pointing; there was a group of eel-farmers, their crests flecked deep purple with nervous expectation . . .

But what for? Grefphith wondered. His arrival back from the lake had never caused such excitement before.

'There. There they are.' a voice whispered, and all eyes turned towards the wooded slope behind the village cluster.

Grefphith found himself being jostled as the excited webfoots strained for a better view. Some even scampered up the sallowdrop trees or clambered onto the roofs of the cabins.

High up, just cresting the ridge of the tree-line, flickering torches could be seen. All round him, the crests of the webfoots glowed crimson and then yellow with black ripples as they speculated as to who the visitors might be. But Grefphith had no doubts. His crest glowed a deep red as he let out an uncharacteristically loud (for a webfoot) yelp of joy.

It was Felfpht, the clan-chief, together with Grefphith's brothers. It had to be! They were back, he was sure of it.

Grefphith fell into step with the great throng of

webfoot villagers heading for the edge of the village, where the north shore clan was soon joined by others. Word had spread that travellers had been spotted in the lake forests, and all sorts of web-foots – from neighbouring south-shorers to far-off fourth-lakers – had turned up to greet them.

There were webfoots from the first great lake, their brilliantly coloured red-ringed legs making up for their small, insignificant crests; lines of darts were attached to the front of their smocks for use in the long blow-pipes they carried. There were the small tusked webfoots from the second great lake,

whose heavily lidded eyes and pointed buck-teeth made them look – to Grefphith, at least – both docile and gormless. He had to stifle a snigger as a group trotted past. And then there were the tall warriors from the fourth great lake whom he would never, *ever* dream of laughing at.

Tall and rangy, with broad shoulders and low brows, the white webfoots were the fiercest of all the lake clans. They travelled everywhere with double-ended thornwood spears in their hands and coracle-shields strapped to their backs. They had obviously been the first to spot the travellers, for fifty or more had crossed the lake on their shields and now stood guard at the great waterwillow gates at the top end of the village, their thornwood spears at the ready.

'Here they come! Here they come! Here they come!' chirruped a gaggle of young'uns, tethered to a massive webfoot matron, the ones at the back straining to peek round the side of her voluminous bulk.

Grefphith – still far back on the other side of the cabin cluster – looked and, sure enough, the torches were getting nearer through the trees. He counted them. One, two, three . . . The light from the copperwood stick torches twinkled in the deepening afternoon light. Fifteen, sixteen . . .

Seventeen?

Grefphith's crest flickered with yellow ripples. If this was indeed Felfpht and Grefphith's brothers, then there was one extra. For a moment, doubt clouded Grefphith's thoughts, only to clear again as the unmistakable head and crest of Felfpht the clan-chief appeared through the trees, followed by his brothers, their crests all bright crimson in greeting.

Grefphith let out another yelp of joy. Behind him, several crested webfoot matrons tut-tutted at this unseemly show of noise – especially from a clam-tender. But Grefphith was too excited to pay them any heed. Instead, he turned on his heels and ran, full pelt, back through the village cluster.

Avoiding the main track, Grefphith cut up the maze of narrow back-alleys that zigzagged between the clustered cabins. In his haste he almost skewered himself on a hanging boathook before turning a corner and nearly falling over a couple of young'uns – not yet old enough to understand what all the excitement was about – who were playing a game of crabclaws in the middle of the path. From above him came the steady munching and crunching of the tiny stack-tilder grazing on the grassy rooftops.

As he neared the end of the cluster, an old matron – her spawning days long since behind her – who was taking the opportunity to clean the empty clan-cabin, greeted him cheerily as he passed by her window.

'Have they arrived yet, Grefphith?' she asked.

'Not yet,' Grefphith replied breathlessly.

'Well, make sure to tell them Old Mafphwyllin sends her greetings when they do,' she called after him.

'I shall, I shall,' Grefphith panted as he hurried on.

As the pathway emerged onto the lakeside clearing, Grefphith's pace quickened. Past the curing racks he hurried, the horizontal bars of sallowdrop and waterwillow bowing under the weight of drying snailskin. Past the fish-bone mills and feed-stores; past the eel-smoking cabins, the air pungent with the odour of smouldering redpine chips – a little trick borrowed from the pink-eyed goblins.

Reaching the lake's edge, Grefphith grabbed a great hanging gourd with a long hose-like spout from a post embedded in the mud, and waded in. He sank the leathery sack into the water and waited impatiently as it filled, bubbles rising to the surface in a steady stream. When at last it was full, he heaved it up onto one shoulder, his hand clamping the spout shut, and set off back the way he'd come to the great arched gates at the entrance to the village.

He arrived just in time. The stout willwicker gates had been thrown open and a contingent of tall white lake goblins stood to attention on either side, their thornwood spears forming a triumphal arch overhead. A large crowd of webfoot goblins from all the four lakes had now gathered at the gates and, panting with exertion, Grefphith had to push and jostle his way through. Reaching the front of the crowd, he encountered Milfphin, the deputy clan-chief, his podgy hands clasped

together over his pot-belly, standing just outside the boundary fence of the village, those indolent sons of his shuffling about impatiently beside him.

'Clam-tender,' Milfphin muttered gruffly as his eyes fell on Grefphith.

Grefphith snorted softly. Milfphin had never managed either to look him in the eye when speaking, or to utter his name.

'Clan-chief,' he replied, as he had done countless times since Felfpht and the others had set off — only this time adding softly, 'deputy.'

Milfphin's crest

shimmered with indignation, but he said nothing. Just ahead, emerging from the forest slope, came a small party of travellers.

'Spawn-brothers!' Grefphith shouted with joy and pushed past the indignant deputy clan-chief.

Pulling the water-filled gourd from his shoulder, Grefphith shoved it under one arm and pumped it vigorously like bellows, while with his free hand directing the nozzle of the spout towards the approaching webfoots. A jet of fresh cold lake water arched over the raised spears of the white lake goblins and fell on the crests of the travellers in a refreshing shower.

'Welcome, clan-chief,' wheezed Milfphin, his crest glowing an ambiguous pink. 'You must forgive the clam-tender's noisy outburst . . .'

Arriving at the gates, Felfpht raised a scaly hand to silence the deputy.

'There is nothing to forgive. Grefphith has greeted us with water from our lake, his anchor stone and apron still dripping from tending the great clam . . .' The clan-chief's eyes narrowed as he gazed past Milfphin to the deputy's fifteen sons, coracle shields strapped to their backs and thornwood lances in their hands. 'Whilst your sons, I see, seem to prefer the company of our white lake cousins to tending our own great clam.'

'Such headstrong boys.' Milfphin shrugged.

'Easily distracted. But your son, Grefphith, here' – he now patted Grefphith indulgently on the shoulder – 'has been looking after things in the Mirror of the Sky – and, of course, with my full support,' he added. 'Haven't you, Grefphith?'

'I have tended the wise one to the best of my ability, chief,' Grefphith whispered. 'No harm has come to it.'

'Very good, Grefphith. You have been a faithful clam-tender,' Felfpht replied, nodding stiffly. 'Clearly I chose wisely when I left you behind . . .' He turned to Milfphin's sons. 'You are free to return to the forests round the Lake of Cloud with your white lake friends,' he told them quietly. 'The sons of Felfpht have returned and shall tend the great blueshell clam from now on.'

Milfphin's bloated frame seemed to wilt at the clan-chief's words, his crest glowing a sickly green with shame and embarrassment as his sons shuffled off with their companions from the fourth lake, their thornwood spears lowered. The crowd watched them go, before breaking into quiet applause as their crests rippled with bright colours of greeting.

Felfpht's sons stepped forward and, while the crowd gathered round, embraced their brother Grefphith. Their faces were wet with a mixture of cold lake water and tears.

'It's so good to see you, brother,' Slifph whispered. 'My webs ache from walking.'

'Our lake mud will soothe them, brother,' laughed Grefphith delightedly. 'But first, what wonders from the lands beyond the lakes do you have to share with us?'

The crowd drew in their breath in anticipation as Slifph and his brothers removed their forage sacks from their belts and carefully opened them. As Milfphin and the rest of the crowd craned their necks for a better view, the clan-chief slipped away unnoticed and headed for the lakeside.

Slifph reached into his forage sack. He pulled out a dull orange block of a transparent substance and held it up for all to see.

'It looks like pinewood resin,' a tusked webfoot called out, to the tutted disapproval of the rest of the crowd.

'It *is* pinewood resin,' said Slifph, 'yet see how pure it is,' he added quickly, before disappointment could set in. After all, everyone there knew the uses of resin to waterproof their coracles and cleanse their nets. 'The resin we gather has dripped onto the forest floor, where it becomes mixed up with dirt and sand and pine-needles. This, in contrast,' he said, tilting the block so that the early evening sun shone through it, 'is perfectly clear.'

'But how?' bellowed a white lake goblin who had

remained behind, and whose own coracle looked as though it needed some work done on it.

'It was an art we learned from the gnokgoblins who dwell in the ironwood pines, far to the north,' Slifph replied. 'They share their home with giant tree-fromps, great placid creatures with huge curved claws. The goblins harvest the resin from the holes in the bark which the fromps make with their claws. When the resin begins to flow from the claw holes, they collect it in bowls – pure, clear, uncontaminated.' He waved the block of resin around. 'Like this.'

'And have you got one of these giant tree-fromps in your forage sacks, then?' a cheeky young red-ringed webfoot at the back shouted out.

A soft ripple of amusement went round the crested webfoots. Even Slifph permitted himself a smile.

'No,' he said, 'but we have one of their claws.'

Slifph's brother Grulth held up the long curved claw he'd found beneath one of the ironwood pines.

'We shall copy this design to make resin-tapping knives and then harvest our own resin . . .' Slifph gestured towards the ironwood stands behind the lake. 'After all, we have ironwood pines enough.'

The gathering of webfoots nodded and smiled, and the crests of those who had them glimmered with lilac and blue. As they watched, the other spawn-brothers reached into their forage sacks and produced small but extraordinary objects of their own.

Hiph brought out a smooth chunk of ironwood used by woodtrolls to hone their axes to a razor-sharp edge. His brother Phlythiss revealed a fistful of seeds from the woodflax plant, grown and harvested by lowbelly goblins to weave into strong cloth for their belly slings.

'Milfphin could do with one of those,' someone whispered, and a ripple of laughter went round the crowd as the deputy clan-chief glared furiously around him.

Spyve held up an ingenious harness-catch used by slaughterers; while three of his brothers revealed punnets of bright pigment – blue, yellow and crimson – easily manufactured from barks of trees according to the long-hair goblins of the tree ridges. Needles, fish-hooks, weaves for nets and shells for floats; the spawn-brothers held up each in turn and explained to the delighted onlookers how each could be copied, duplicated and put to good use by the webfoots of the four great lakes.

While the white, tusked and red-ringed webfoots in the crowd cheered enthusiastically, the crested webfoots contented themselves with beaming smiles and a dazzling display of iridescent green. Milfphin raised his head and sniffed at the air ostentatiously, then patted his flabby belly.

'My friends, it is time to celebrate this fine and

fruitful journey to the lands beyond the lakes. Everything is prepared. The cooking-fire is blazing brightly and the stew-pot is full. Let us feast and sup and give thanks for the safe return of clan-chief Felfpht and his sons.'

The crowd began to file away. But just then, as Slifph and his brothers were returning their forage sacks to their belts, one of the crested webfoots – little more than a young'un – stopped and pointed.

'You haven't told us what *she's* for?' he said.

The crowd turned and stared at the spot the young webfoot was pointing to. Grefphith gulped. There, standing by the willow-wicker gates – overlooked in all the excitement – was the bearer of the seventeenth copperwood stick torch, which still flickered with an orange flame. With her black, spiky hair and pale face, the stranger looked back at Grefphith with an intense dark-eyed stare.

'This is Keris,' whispered Slifph, 'from a village of the far-off night-herders known as slaughterers.'

She stepped forward, the crowd parting instinctively at her approach. Her dark eyes never left Grefphith's face. She stopped in front of him.

'Felfpht the clan-chief called you a faithful clam-tender,' she said softly.

As the others watched, Grefphith nodded, his crest rippling green and gold with a mixture of pride and shyness.

'The clam,' the slaughterer said, her eyes sparkling. 'It talks to you?'

Grefphith shook his head. 'Not for a long time . . .' He checked himself when he noticed the disappointment in Keris's eyes. 'Leastways, not since my father and brothers left these thirteen moons since.'

'Come!' Milfphin's voice cut their conversation short. 'The stew-pots await!'

The webfoots turned and streamed through the village towards the great cluster of lake-willow cabins, with their meadow-turf roofs. Keris, Grefphith, Slifph and

their spawn-brothers were swept along with them. By the time they had all crowded into the large oval hall at the centre of the cluster of cabins, the celebrations were in full swing.

A series of curved tables had been put up around the edge of the hall, each one looking towards the centre, where a vast bubbling cauldron dangled from a hook above the cooking-fire. The air was laced with pungent lake-peat smoke, overlaid with the mouth-watering smells of blatt-prawn and bloaterfish, lake-eel and rock-oyster, brieve and moonfin, and herbs from every corner of the Deepwoods, brought back and cultivated by generations of crested webfoots who had set out on foraging journeys of their own.

'Let's sit down here,' Grefphith said, ushering Slifph and Keris into a space at a table on the far side of the hall.

In front of them, on a raised platform, the village band was playing on reed-pipes, shell-horns and gut-string fiddles – strange, haunting music that made Keris suddenly so homesick, it was all she could do not to weep . . .

'Come on,' she heard Slifph saying, his voice breaking into her thoughts of her Uncle Gristle, Aunt Chitling and the cousins. 'Tuck in while it's still hot.'

She looked down to discover that her bowl had been filled with steaming fish-stew by one of the webfoot matrons, who were waddling back and forth between stew-pot and tables, ensuring that everyone had enough to eat. And it wasn't only the bowl that was now full. Her goblet, too, was full to the brim with a deep golden liquid that smelled curiously like the spiced winesap she would take to her uncle out in the hammelhorn pastures. How long ago that now seemed . . .

'To my spawn-brothers,' Grefphith said, his crest glowing crimson as he raised his goblet high. 'And our new friend, Keris.'

'To Keris,' chorused Slifph and his brothers in unison. Keris smiled bravely and sipped at her drink. She was about to thank her new friend and offer a toast of her own, but was interrupted by something going on at the other side of the hall.

The voice of Milfphin, deputy clan-chief, was sounding oddly high-pitched and querulous, and rose in volume as the band abruptly stopped playing. 'But I don't understand,' he blustered. 'It can't be true . . . No outlaker has ever . . . I mean, this must be some sort of misunderstanding . . .'

'There is no misunderstanding.' Clan-chief Felfpht's soft voice rose an octave as he strode to the centre of the hall, lake water dripping from his scaly chin and the tips of his lop-ears. 'I have come from the Mirror of the Sky and the great blueshell clam has heard of our new arrival . . .'

He turned to Keris.

'And it wishes to talk with you.'

. CHAPTER FOUR .

THE GREAT BLUESHELL CLAM

'The great blueshell clam has spoken!' Grefphith's voice was hushed with awe and his crest glowed an excited amber as he guided Keris out of the cluster of lake-willow cabins and towards the lakeside. Behind them, in the hall, Keris could hear the clan-chief and his sons in debate with the furious Milfphin.

'An outlaker being taken to the great clam,' he was protesting. 'This is an outrage!'

'She has journeyed far to see the wise one,' Slifph's voice rang out in reply.

'And the great clam wishes to speak with her,' clan-chief Felfpht repeated, to murmurs of approval.

Outside in the moonlight, Keris and Grefphith the clam-tender hurried along the lakeshore. Keris could hardly contain her excitement. At last, after all she had been through, she was to meet the great clam. Close by, a colony of reed-toads croaked, their deep rumblings interrupted by the shrill cry of a blackheron flying low over the lake. Past the rest of the cabin cluster the pair of them went; past the beached fishing rafts and tarred coracles and beyond, picking their way between the rows of sallowdrops and weeping willoaks that lined the shore. Over their heads, the moon broke the horizon and rose in the sky, huge and golden, reflected in the mirror-like surface of the lake. They stopped at a place with no trees behind them, where a tussock of grass jutted out over a small curved beach.

Keris noticed footprints in the mud leading into the gently lapping waters of the lake.

'This is the place?' she said, her heart suddenly thumping in her chest.

Grefphith's crest glowed blue in assent. He padded on his great webbed feet over the soft lakeshore mud to a post from which hung a great leather gourd, similar to the one he'd filled with water to greet his brothers. Unhooking it, Grefphith reached into the forage sack that hung next to the anchor stone on his belt and drew out a handful of small, sponge-like mushrooms.

As Keris watched, intrigued, the clam-tender carefully poured the mushrooms down the long tubular spout of the gourd. Then he placed the gourd under one arm and pumped it like a pair of bellows. Almost at once, there was a loud hissing

sound, and the gourd's leathery folds stretched until it was twice its original size.

Grefphith motioned to Keris to join him at the water's edge, where he strapped the gourd securely to her back.

'We webfoots can breathe the waters of our lake, but you outlakers need a little help,' he told her, handing Keris the spout and indicating that she should place it in her mouth.

She clamped the end of the spout between her teeth, noting the taste of woodmint that filled her mouth as she did so. Carefully, Grefphith placed a small carved ivory clip over Keris's nose.

'Breathe through your mouth,' he told her. 'The silt-fungus will have absorbed enough air for your dive to the lake bed and back, but your time with the clam will be short . . .'

'But how will I be able to talk with this in my mouth?' Keris asked in confusion, taking the spout out of her mouth for a moment.

The clam-tender smiled and placed his anchor stone firmly in the lakeshore mud. 'You'll see,' he said. 'Now, when you're ready, place your hands on my shoulders and I'll swim for the both of us.'

Grefphith turned to face the lake with his back to her, and Keris did as she was told. The webfoot's scaly skin was cold to the touch and she felt the muscles in his shoulders give a sudden ripple.

Then, before Keris knew it, they had dived into the mirror-like surface of the lake and were plunging down into the clear depths suffused in bright moonlight. She breathed in cool, minty air. Behind her, on her back, she could feel the gourd expand and contract with each breath. With every kick of his powerful legs and great webbed feet, Grefphith propelled them both, faster and faster, through the crystal-clear water.

To Keris's left, a shoal of silver fish swam towards them, their fins flashing in the moonlight that sliced down through the water, before darting off to the left, a huge, brown fish with bulging eyes and a jutting lower jaw in hot pursuit. A nattertoad – all gaping mouth and kicking orange legs – swam past them at an angle, its target a great translucent stormhornet larvae, whose shapeless bodies writhed and wriggled in the shadows of the great plateleaf lilies up above.

Apart from the shallow streams that ran through the lower pastures of her home, Keris had seldom been in water before, and the sensations – coldness, wetness and the constant pressure coming in from all sides – unnerved her. Yet she felt safe with Grefphith. And as she relaxed and her grip on his shoulders loosened slightly, the webfoot began pointing things out to her – a frondy ball of pink weed that, as they came closer,

revealed itself to be thousands of feeding watershrimps clustered together; a ten-legged creature with a body like a balloon, which sucked in and spat out water as it propelled itself across the lake; striped lakeworms and spotted waterscorpions. And far far below them, where the lakegrass swayed like barleyrice in a gale, she saw a long line of giant lake snails, their pearly shells gleaming as the moonbeams struck them, plodding sedately across the silty bottom of the lake.

All at once, Grefphith pointed

downwards. His crest throbbed deepest indigo with lines of silver as he kicked out even more strongly. Keris tightened her grip on his shoulders as they swooped down towards the lake bed far beneath them. The next moment, she felt the lake water bubble and swirl about them as, instead of being propelled by Grefphith's steady kicks, they were suddenly being shot forward by a far greater force.

With his crest bright orange, Grefphith clamped his arms to his side. Keris clung on tightly. Faster and faster the two of them went, hurtling through the water like . . . like . . .

Keris smiled to herself as the lake rushed past her in a blur of blue and silvery white.

Like flying!

Oh, Father, she wondered, was this what it was like on the bridge of a mighty sky pirate ship, speeding across the sky?

Down into the depths of the lake they raced, leaving the moonlit water behind. Ahead of them, yet getting closer with every passing second, the dark waters of the lake bed were illuminated by an eerie blue glow. And as they drew closer, Keris realized where the light was emanating from.

It was pouring out of a magnificent, ridged bicuspid shell.

The lower half was fused to the rocky lake bed,

while the upper half gaped open. A hundred or more strides high it was, and twice that in breadth. To Keris it looked like a vast grinning mouth – a mouth that was sucking them inexorably closer and closer on a great swirling current of water. And as they hurtled towards it, she was suddenly over-whelmed with a cramping fear that they were about to be swallowed up. Closer to the great gaping maw they came, closer and closer and . . .

With a great creaking groan, the two huge halves of the vast clam slammed shut. The swirling current instantly ceased, the blue light was extinguished, and Keris and Grefphith found themselves floating gently down to the lake bed, their eyes filled with the orange afterglow of the clam's dazzling light.

Grefphith motioned for Keris to let go of his shoulders and indicated a flat rock in front of the giant clam for her to perch on. Then, as she waited in the gloom, Grefphith swam off, feeding-fork at the ready, to deal with the line of giant lake snails they had spotted earlier. In the distance, the huge creatures seemed to sense his approach and began to scatter in clouds of muddy sediment. On her stone perch, Keris waited, the gourd on her back ris-ing and falling with each breath.

What now? she wondered. How long would she have to wait? Grefphith had said her time with the clam would have to be short. Should she do something? Tap on its shell perhaps?

In front of her, the clam remained resolutely shut, the join between the two shells now a zigzag line without even the hint of a crack. High above, the surface of the upper shell was like a vast garden, home to countless flowers, ferns, and towering tree-like plants that swayed in the ever-shifting currents of water, just as the massive trees of the Deepwoods forest did in the air far above. And as she sat there, Keris watched intrigued as dim shafts of moonlight from far above struck the striped fish and tusked eels which swam in and out of the fronds; at the rock lobsters scut-tling along the ridges of the great blue shell – and on an ungainly crea-ture with twelve spindly legs and a disc-shaped head

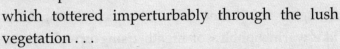

which tottered imperturbably through the lush vegetation . . .

All at once there was a tremendous rumbling sound followed by an unearthly creaking. The fish all round darted for cover in the underwater vege-tation. The rumbling became louder and stronger, vibrating through the rocks beneath her feet and stirring up the mud once more. The water itself seemed to tremble.

At last! thought Keris, gripping the sides of the flat rock with a mixture of excitement and fear.

As the two shells of the giant clam slowly parted, the dazzling blue light shone out once more, flooding the lake bed all round with its intense radiance and pouring into Keris's wide, unblinking eyes. Slowly and sedately, the clam yawned open, to reveal a vast interior of mottled blue pleats and folds.

And there, nestling deep at the centre of the gaping clam, was a pearl. A huge, opalescent pearl. Flawless and spherical, it was the source of the light which was bathing Keris in its intense blue glow.

Keris was mesmerized and transfixed. Unable to stir herself and pull away, her senses were completely overwhelmed. Now there was nothing but the pulsating blue light, filling her eyes, her mouth and ears, seeping through her pores, banishing any thought of time or place.

It was as if she was dissolving. Her conscious thoughts faded; her sense of herself disappeared, like warm bubbles of breath rising up and being carried away on the lake currents.

She was no longer Keris the slaughterer girl, far from home and full of questions.

Instead she was now the great blueshell clam,

sharing its memories of the very start of its long existence . . .

A tiny insignificant speck, she was, being blown through the great empty void on strong currents, for ever. Back and forth, journeying restlessly through the endless tracts of Open Sky. On and on, gathering speed and power . . .

An intense and pulsating brightness. Tiny yet inexpressibly powerful until . . .

There was a blinding flash and great black storm-clouds swirled up overhead. There was a crash of thunder. And then came the sensation of falling, falling down towards the thirsty earth.

Then blackness. Everything quiet, muffled. Trickling slowly through rock, deep below the surface of the earth. Moving through cracks, over crevices, into pools – gathering speed, gaining momentum. Flowing faster and faster with the underground springs, this way and that. Becoming part of a mighty current blasting its way through the earth; powerful, surging, then . . .

Everything suddenly stopped.

Stuck fast to this very rock. Rooted, immovable, down here on the lake bed. After so long, finally at rest.

At last, all that pulsating power turned itself into growth. The speck got bigger – a wonderful feeling . . .

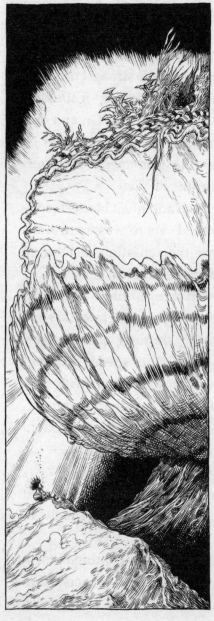

My shell formed, the currents flowed back and forth over my blue surface, the nourishing silt swirled beneath. The rock anchored my great blue shell.

And time passed . . .

Now I am huge. Down here in the calm depths, I can sense the world above me. It seeps into the lake water, eddies up through the lake bed; it flavours the silt. I can taste it. I sift through it all as I lie, rooted to the rock; tasting, sensing, knowing . . .

The coming of creatures, the slow growth of the forest, the storms passing overhead – I can sense them all.

Far off, the acrid taint of Undertown; the deathly must of the Mire that tinges the lake water; the flashing spark of stormphrax and the glow of the Twilight Woods; they ripple imperceptibly through the currents. Always changing. And I – the great blueshell clam – detect them. I can taste the migration of tilder and hammelhorn, feel the tramp of goblin tribes, sense the movement of clouds over the glassy surface of the lake overhead.

I am the first, the most ancient. I am the beginning of life. A speck from Open Sky that fell from the Mother Storm and took root here on this rock far down in the depths of this peaceful lake.

Now you, Keris – another tiny speck of life – have come to the great blueshell clam to find answers. You, Keris, are a speck that clings to life but has no place to root itself. Lost, far from the silver pastures and smoky brazier fires, you are seeking your roots. I can sense it . . .

You are seeking your father.

Yes, little one, the great blueshell clam can sense him. Out there, far beyond the four great lakes, is the trace of your father; one who has been touched by the Mother Storm. A tiny speck of life himself, but a strong one . . .

And there is someone else. Yet another speck of life. Connected to both of you. Faint, yet acrid, and glowing like the spark that starts a great forest fire, this speck of life has changed the forests all round her with her fierce intensity. This speck of life is changing the world.

The great blueshell clam can sense it.

It can sense something else, too. The time has come, as the clam always knew it would; the time to reach out into this world.

You, my little one, must reach out with me . . .

Keris's mind was filled with a cascade of dazzling images, one after the other, fleeting yet crystal clear.

'Yes,' she nodded, 'I understand.'

All at once the clam slammed abruptly shut and, like the blast of a hurricane or the thrust of a mighty waterfall sweeping a dam aside and gushing forwards, a powerful surge of water struck Keris full on, tearing her away from the blue light.

Ever faster she sped, twisting and turning in the dark water as she hurtled through the moonbeam-shot depths up towards the surface of the lake, before shooting out of the water like a leaping gladesalmon.

Gasping and spluttering, Keris came crashing back down into the lake. Great waves rippled out across the placid surface. On her back, the gourd deflated with a wheezing sigh as Keris pulled the breathing spout from her mouth and gulped in a lungful of fresh night air. A moment later, beside her, Grefphith's crest broke the surface of the water and his smiling face greeted her.

He reached out for Keris, who clutched gratefully to his arm, and together – following the long tether-rope – the two of them swam slowly back to shore where his anchor-rock nestled in the lakeshore mud. Crawling onto the grassy bank, Keris turned to Grefphith.

'The clam spoke to me,' she said softly. 'The answer I seek lies far from here in a place called the Free Glades. I must . . .' She frowned, for the web-foot was staring back at her, his mouth open and his crest pulsating with surprise. 'What?' she said. 'Grefphith, what *is* it?'

'It's incredible,' he said, looking her up and down. 'In all my time as a clam-tender, I've never seen anything like it . . .'

Keris looked down – and then she noticed. Her entire body – skin, hair, clothes – was covered in a fine layer of sparkling silt. It was powdery and pale in the moonlight, with slightly lighter streaks that had collected in the crook of her arm and the cracks of her knuckles. She licked a finger and ran it across her arm, and turned back to Grefphith.

'It won't come off,' she said.

. CHAPTER FIVE .

THE SILVER PASTURES

The ancient spindlebug turned his great angular head, lifted his lantern and peered down the new tunnel being dug to his left. Everything was coming along nicely, he noted with a satisfied clicking sound. The new contingent of spindle-bugs might be young, but what they lacked in size and strength, they more than made up for in enthusiasm.

Working in shifts, they had already excavated two large chambers and, following the detailed plans he'd drawn up, constructed a broad central tunnel. Now the transverse tunnels were being dug. These winding walkways would not only connect the completed chambers on this level, but would also link up with the existing cellars, caverns and galleries of the earlier excavations, transforming the old underground colony into a vast and thriving hive of industry where milchgrubs, nightspiders and chookbats would soon join the indigenous

slime-moles, and be farmed. Already, the new fun-gus beds had been seeded and the spongy toadstools that had sprouted were beginning to emit the glowing pink light that would soon make all lamps and lanterns unnecessary.

The spindlebug trilled with excitement. If this rate of progress continued – and there was nothing to suggest that it would not – then, by his calcula-tions, the Gardens of Light should be completed in far less than the five years he'd originally planned for.

It was all most gratifying, Tweezel thought, as he made his way across one of the new viaducts, passed a group of young spindlebugs, newly-arrived and trilling with an excitement that matched his own. After all, this was what the Free Glades was all about – welcoming new arrivals and building a new life for them in peace and har-mony.

Not that they'd had any idea of what they were starting when he, Tweezel, and the young mistress – Earth and Sky protect her – had first gathered up those urchins and alley-strays from the streets of Undertown and led them out into the Deepwoods in search of a better life. Almost four decades had passed since that small party, some three hundred strong, had stumbled upon the broad, grassy lake-side slopes of what was to become their new home.

At first they had all lived in the small burrows that, under Tweezel's supervision, they'd dug beneath the Ironwood Stands next to the central lake. Then, with the help of the small colony of oakelves they'd encountered on Lullabee Island on the North Lake, the older orphans had begun building simple log cabins. Ten years had passed in the blinking of a translucent spindlebug's eye, and that little settlement on the shores of the North Lake had turned into New Undertown.

Word had spread quickly, and by the time the Free Glades celebrated the dawn of its second decade, there had already been a great influx of new blood. Trappers, traders and fisherfolk came; gab-trolls with wagons laden with herbal remedies and cure-alls; mobgnome tinkers, red dwarves and black dwarves . . . In short, all those who found it difficult to fit in elsewhere found a welcome in the Free Glades and an offer to settle there permanently.

All, that is, apart from the slavers. Occasionally they would turn up, together with their terrifying packs of white-collar wolves, in search of victims for their foul trade. At these times, Tweezel remembered proudly, those urchins and alley-strays – now grown vigorous and strong in the pure Free Glades air – banded together and sent them packing with their tails between their legs.

Tweezel paused to watch a gang of young spindlebugs. They were moving a great mound of earth from one side of the excavated hall to the other, exposing the pillar-like roots of the ironwood pines on one side and shoring up the walls on the other.

'Very good,' he trilled, before moving on.

It was as the Free Glades moved into its third decade that the place really began to expand, he remembered. Word spread about this curious settlement at the heart of the Deepwoods, home to those who wanted to live in peace and harmony with their neighbours, no matter who they were, and increasing numbers decided to see the wonderful place for themselves.

Entire clans began to arrive. Cloddertrogs from various parts of the Deepwoods congregated at the cliff sides to the east of New Undertown. They set up home in the system of caves; some turned to mining, others to brewing. A while later an entire colony of gyle-goblins – grossmother and all – established a new home close by, together with a small band of waifs, who planted a thornwood enclosure on the eastern shores of the North Lake. At the same time, in the Ironwood Stands at the opposite side of the glades, two separate clans of gnokgoblins formed colonies in the ironwood pines; while beneath them – down among the roots

– spindlebugs came from far and wide to join Tweezel.

The population of the Free Glades was by now more than ten times its original number and bustling with trogs, trolls and goblins, fourthlings and waifs from all four corners of the Edge. They had little in common with one another, save one important thing – that all-embracing desire to live their new life in peace and harmony.

Tweezel sighed, causing the lantern light to flicker momentarily. Unfortunately, there were always others who hated peace and harmony, choosing instead to make war and enslave others. The Free Glades had reluctantly been forced to defend its freedoms, always trying to find peace if possible, but not at the cost of a Freeglader's liberty.

So it was that the Freeglade Lancers, the Cloddertrog Guards and the Librarian Knights had come into being – each full of brave Freegladers prepared to lay down their lives in defence of their home.

And just as well, thought Tweezel, for these were dark days in the Edgelands – dark days indeed, judging by the tales new arrivals to the Free Glades brought with them.

The floating city of Old Sanctaphrax, it seemed, was no more. In its place, a new Sanctaphrax was developing – but with a crazed tyrant, rather than professors, ruling over it. Shrykes had apparently been accorded special status for helping to construct a road across the Mire, while an army of goblins – under a bullying scoundrel by the name of General Tytugg – had reportedly enslaved the inhabitants of Undertown.

It sounded incredible. Yet the sudden influx of refugees from Sanctaphrax and Undertown spoke of little else.

In this latest wave of incomers, academics of every type turned up. Professors, alchemists, librarians – the latter carrying barkscrolls and treatises that they had rescued from the barbaric book-burning Guardians of Night who had taken over Sanctaphrax. They built the Academy of Lake Landing and brought their knowledge and love of learning to the Free Glades. Even in these dark times, the Free Glades had proved itself to be a shining beacon of hope – just as the young mistress, Earth and Sky protect her, had always intended it should.

Now, Tweezel noted with satisfaction, work on his beloved Gardens of Light was moving on apace. Soon the great caverns would match his dreams, with vaulted ceilings and swooping colonnades; arches, bridges and winding stairways, and everything bathed in the rose-coloured glow of the nourishing fungus – dreams he had had not just for decades, he realized with a chuckle, but for centuries . . .

As he turned a sharp corner, Tweezel could see bright daylight streaming in through the end of the tunnel ahead of him. After the subdued glow of the caves and tunnels, it seemed dazzlingly bright. He blew out the flame in the lantern he'd been clutching and proceeded briskly along the narrow corridor. Then, fifty strides or so along, he paused briefly at a small chamber to his left, where a solitary spindlebug was hunched over a leadwood desk, a pot bubbling on a small brass burner before him.

'Sisal,' the old spindlebug greeted him as he entered the small chamber. 'How's it coming along?'

'Pretty well,' Sisal replied. 'I've been stirring it for over an hour now, and it's just beginning to turn colour. The trick is not to let it catch on the bottom.'

'Excellent, excellent,' said Tweezel, clicking with excitement. He put down the lantern and leaned forwards for a closer look. 'When do you think you'll have some ready?'

Sisal paused in his stirring, lifted a spoonful up into the air and let the hot liquid pour back down into the pot. It was thick and viscous. He looked up.

'Any minute now,' he said. 'When it forms a long stringy line rather than a liquid trickle, it's done.'

He stirred the pot vigorously for a couple of minutes more, taking care that none of the liquid splashed over the side. Then, with another spoonful, he let the liquid run back down again. This time it did what he'd described. Instead of pouring, it formed a long rope-like twist that seemed to unravel rather than trickle.

'Done,' Sisal announced.

'Outstanding!' Tweezel exclaimed, reaching forward and picking up the pot by the handle. 'And if those librarians at Lake Landing aren't impressed, then . . . then' – he clicked, momentarily at a loss for words – 'then I'm a jack-stacking leafhopper!'

He crossed the chamber to a low shelf, where a series of logs of various woods were piled. He swept them all into a sack. Then, with the pot clamped in the claws of his left hand and the bulging sack slung over his shoulder, Tweezel left the chamber, headed down the corridor and emerged into the bright sunny afternoon outside. He paused for a moment, wisps of steam coming from the pot, and gazed across the lake.

It was so beautiful at this time of day, he thought; when the sun was past its highest and turning that rich yellow colour that changed everything beneath it to gold. He never tired of the view. The sun gleamed on the pointed minarets and jutting buttresses of the half-completed academy, already looking so self-assured at the end of Lake Landing in the centre of the shimmering golden lake. Beyond it, the circle of thorn-bushes the waifs had planted – fringed with gold – had grown almost as tall. And behind that, its rooftops and crenellated towers peeking over the top, was New Undertown.

'So much we have achieved,' he muttered to himself proudly. 'Yet we cannot afford to be complacent.'

He turned his head, eyeing the thick dark forest that surrounded them. To the north and east, the Free Glades had spread out into the woodland a little. The felled trees were used for buildings, while the newly cleared land was planted up with barleyrice, sour-cabbage and glimmer onions. But the forest was resilient. It took time and effort to keep it at bay if it wasn't simply to grow back and swallow up the new fields and pastureland.

No, thought Tweezel, the Deepwoods should

never be underestimated. And nor should those who dwell within it.

Far to the east, he saw that the blue sky was stained once again with brown. It was, he knew, smoke from the Foundry Glades – a terrible place by all accounts, where the worst type of leagues-men had established factories and forges which, if rumours were to be believed, were operated by slave labour. Moreover, according to a growing number of visitors to the Free Glades, others were also establishing more permanent settlements in the forest: goblins from various tribes and clans who had abandoned their nomadic ways and settled down in villages in loose alliances with each other.

Tweezel shook his head sadly. It wasn't peace these Goblin Nations sought, but merely a more effective way of waging war. Just like the leagues-men of the Foundry Glades, they would have to be closely watched.

The old spindlebug was a good watcher. He'd had plenty of practice . . .

Born more than two centuries ago, he had spent his earliest days in a gyle-goblin colony – until the slavers had come, that is. He'd lived in the Deepwoods, he'd lived in Undertown, and in Sanctaphrax – as servant to the Most High Academe, no less. Now he was back in the Deepwoods. Full circle.

But his long life was far from over. After all, there was so much still to do. Take this sticky liquid in the pot he was carrying, for example. If it lived up to his hopes and expectations, who knew what it could lead to . . . ?

Above his head a bevy of white ravens flapped across the darkening sky, cawing raucously.

With the pot swinging and his antennae trembling, Tweezel strode around the banks of the Great Lake. Once, he remembered, the entire shoreline had been fringed with long, waving speargrass that had grown down to the water's edge. Now there was a track which ran all the way round – narrow and muddy in places, paved with wooden boards in others. Tweezel was passing a small stand of woodsap trees when he first noticed the bunch of librarians ahead of him, their robes fluttering in the soft breeze.

'Nearly there,' Tweezel muttered under his breath and increased his pace.

As he approached, his feet clattering over the boardwalk of the academy at Lake Landing, the academics turned and looked at him. Parsimmon, the young yet ambitious Chief Librarian, glanced up at the sun. Tweezel looked at the gnokgoblin uncertainly.

'My dear sir,' said Tweezel a little breathlessly. 'Sirs,' he added, including the others. 'Humblest

apologies for my late arrival.'

Parsimmon's leathery face broke into a smile. 'You're not late, old fellow,' he said. 'We were early. Early,' he added, 'because we are so keen to see what you have to show us.' He gestured towards the pot. 'Is that it?'

Tweezel nodded.

'Then let us go to the Long Hall and examine this varnish of yours,' said Parsimmon, and some of the librarians turned to go.

'Actually it might be better if we remained outside,' said Tweezel. 'Perhaps if we went out onto the jetty. If you have no objections . . .'

262

'None, whatsoever,' said Parsimmon, and he strode out onto the wooden landing.

On the great platform at the end of Lake Landing, the librarians sat down in a line on a long, rough-hewn bench, while Tweezel prepared a small demonstration. He pulled the logs from the sack and laid them out beside the pot.

'I'm sure I don't have to tell academics like your good selves that there are three orders of Deepwoods timber,' he began. 'In the third order are leadwood and copperwood – wood that is stable at every temperature. In the second order are lufwood and bloodoak among others. These woods fly when burned. Then,' he said, picking up a pale brown log, 'we have timbers from the first order.' He smiled. 'The most interesting order.'

The librarians frowned and glanced at one another. Had the old spindlebug really gathered them all together to talk about wood?

'This is sumpwood,' Tweezel continued, undeterred. 'Not only the most common wood of the first order, but also the most stable. A well-seasoned piece of sumpwood is twice as light as air. Of course, we have been using sumpwood for years – buoyant chairs, floating lecterns and the like. But, since the slightest change in humidity or temperature destabilizes the timber, this use has been limited to within buildings only.' He placed the log

263

of wood down, and picked up the pot. 'My varnish will change all that.'

The librarians leaned forwards, their interest aroused. A couple of them sniffed the air as the curious spicy fragrances seemed to waft across from the pot.

'This varnish,' Tweezel announced, 'is the result of many months of patient experimentation. It will seal in the buoyant properties of sumpwood, while still allowing it to "breathe". This means that this first-order timber will remain stable in all but the most extreme temperatures, but can never overheat. For this reason, instead of being used solely for furniture in properly heated rooms, sumpwood can now be used out here in the open air.' He paused dramatically. 'For flight.'

As one, the librarians gasped. The significance of Tweezel's discovery was not lost on them. Reports of stone-sickness and the end of stone flight were everywhere. No sky ship had been seen for several years or more. Disconsolate sky pirates now packed the taverns of New Undertown with tales of doom and destruction. If Tweezel's varnish could make wood float, then a new age of flight might just be possible.

'Show us, Tweezel,' said Parsimmon, his voice both encouraging and excited. 'Show us what this varnish of yours can do.'

Tweezel held the sumpwood log in one claw and applied a coat of steaming varnish with a broad brush with the other. Then, waiting a few moments, he released it. The log rose a few feet on the gentle breeze, then hovered unsteadily above the spindlebug's translucent head.

'Bravo!' the librarians shouted.

'Tweezel, you're a genius,' Parsimmon cried out.

But the spindlebug raised a hand to silence them. 'That was my first varnish,' he said. 'Produced from one hundred per cent slime-mole glue. Simmered for two hours. One coat applied.' He picked up the second small log. 'Whereas this varnish has been supplemented with oakpepper . . .'

'*That's* what I could smell,' one of the young librarians whispered to his neighbour.

'And I have applied three coats to the upper surfaces, two to the lower . . .'

This time, the log rose swiftly and hung motionless in the air before a gust of wind moved it smoothly and steadily towards Parsimmon's beaming face.

'Even better!' a librarian exclaimed.

'We're going to be able to produce skycraft to rival anything powered by flight-rocks,' another said excitedly.

'In theory,' Parsimmon broke in. 'But let's not get ahead of ourselves. Tweezel's varnish is indeed remarkable, but there is a long way to go before we can claim to have solved the problem of wood flight.'

Tweezel nodded in agreement, and was about to explain some experiments he'd attempted using hanging-weights on the logs, when the unmistakable sound of a prowlgrin bark made everyone turn. Half a dozen Freeglade Lancers on prowlgrinback approached, escorting a group of tired-looking individuals. The captain of the guard, Ferris – a tall, broad-faced individual with a tattered ear – pulled away from the others and trotted over to Parsimmon.

'Excuse the intrusion, sir,' he said gruffly. 'Wasn't sure where else to take them.'

'That's quite all right, captain,' said Parsimmon. As one of the more learned individuals in the Free Glades, he was used to new arrivals being brought to him. 'What have you got this time?'

'Group of webfoots,' said Captain Ferris. 'And a slaughterer girl.'

Parsimmon turned and watched them approaching. There were some webfoot goblins living in the Goblin Nations; small, frightened creatures, easily bullied and often enslaved. But these glowing-crested strangers looked nothing like them. As for slaughterers, so far as he knew, the Free Glades had none. He frowned.

'Is the slaughterer hurt, captain?' he asked, seeing the figure slumped over the saddle of the
nearest prowlgrin.

'I'm afraid she stepped on a poisonthorn in the
Silver Pastures. Nasty wound on her heel,' the captain reported. 'And the infection is spreading by the
look of it . . .'

'I am Grefphith,' said the taller of the webfoots
holding the prowlgrin's bridle. 'These are my
brothers: Slifph, Hiph, Spyve and Grulth. We
have travelled far from our home in the Great Lakes
with this slaughterer, Keris, who has been told to
journey here by our great clam. She is injured,' he
said, his crest glowing a shimmering yellow. 'Can
you help her?'

'Allow me,' said Tweezel, bending down and
plucking Keris from the saddle. 'I shall tend to her
in the Gardens of Light. She will have the best of
care!'

With that, he set off at a galloping pace, back
along the lake path towards the Ironwood Stands in
the distance.

'Your friend is in safe hands,' Parsimmon said.
He spread his arms wide open. 'In the name of the
librarians of the Free Glades, I welcome you.'

Grefphith nodded briefly, then stared at the
varnished log still hovering above the chief
librarian's head.

'This wood's buoyancy is quite amazing,' the webfoot exclaimed, one hand instinctively going to his forage sack.

'Indeed,' nodded Parsimmon. 'It has been coated with a special varnish.'

'Varnish, you say,' said Grefphith, fascinated.

'Derived from the secretions of slime-moles,' Parsimmon explained. 'According to Tweezel the spindlebug.'

'Fascinating, fascinating,' Grefphith whispered.

'Of course,' Slifph observed, 'an expertly carved piece of wood could infinitely improve the properties of the varnish . . .'

Parsimmon nodded thoughtfully.

'Indeed,' said his brother Hiph. 'We recently visited some woodtroll villages whose inhabitants were masters of woodworking.' His crest glowed an inquisitive pale green. 'Do you have any woodtrolls living in these parts?'

Parsimmon shook his head. 'None,' he said, then added thoughtfully, 'though it might be an idea to invite some to settle here in the Free Glades . . .'

'And of course, after the varnish and the wordworking, you're going to need sails and ropes,' suggested Spyve, turning to his brother Grulth, who nodded. 'Slaughterers are the best ropemakers and sail-riggers I know of,' he added.

'Slaughterers,' Parsimmon repeated softly. 'Yes, we could do with some slaughterers . . .'

He stared out across the lake with a faraway look in his eyes, before shaking his head and gesturing to the webfoot goblins beside him.

'Come, friends,' Parsimmon said. 'While Tweezel the spindlebug tends to Keris's needs, you must join us in the academy for supper. You look as though you have journeyed a long way.' He smiled. 'Come and dine with us. And afterwards, I should like to discuss an idea I have just had that might very well interest you . . .'

As the librarians and the webfoots made their way to the refectory, the sun was already setting behind the Ironwood Stands, their jagged treetops glinting as though tipped with shards of gold and silver. High in the branches, the giant tree-fromps grunted and squeaked as they foraged for black-bark beetles and plump resin-grubs, while the gnokgoblins who now tended them lit communal fires and set their stew-pots and cauldrons to bubble.

'Almost there, little one,' Tweezel murmured as he proceeded down the tunnel into the Gardens of Light. 'You're going to be fine. Trust me. Old Tweezel will see to you.'

But Keris – her spiky hair limp and her face flushed with fever – did not respond. She could not.

Still unconscious, the only sound that came from her lips was a low and rasping breathing. Tweezel's heart tugged with pity, and he was taken back to a time, so so many years ago, when he had carried Linius Pallitax, Most High Academe of Sanctaphrax, from the blazing building of the Palace of Shadows. He, too, had been unconscious; his breathing low and rasping . . .

'Rest here, little one,' whispered Tweezel, pushing everything from the couch in his study-chamber and laying her gently down.

Then, taking care not to let her slip to the floor, he removed her hammelhornskin waistcoat and hung it over the back of the chair. With his arm at her shoulders, he laid her head back on the cushion, lit the lantern and inspected her leg.

It was a mess – swollen, purple-black where the infection had spread, and hot to the touch. What was more, it, like the rest of her skin, was covered with a fine layer of blue silt that shimmered in the light.

'Curious . . .' he murmured as he turned away and began sorting through the bottles and jars on the wall-shelves. 'Poultice to draw the poison. Hyleberry leaves, wood-juniper salve and a cold compress . . .'

With single-minded efficiency, Tweezel tended his patient. He delicately applied the thick cream

to the taut, shiny
skin of her leg and
wrapped the whole
lot up in a length of
bandage. He placed
the cold compress
against her forehead
and, to ensure
that her temperature
dropped, smeared on
her lips a little of
the sweet-smelling
wood-juniper salve –
which, even in her
unconscious state,
Keris tasted with the
tip of her tongue.

And when he had
done everything he
could, and there was
nothing else to do but
wait, Tweezel sat
down beside the
couch and watched
the young slaugh-
terer's face, willing
her to get better.

Her fever ebbed

and flowed. One moment she was crimson and sweat-drenched, the next, leaden-cheeked and sunken-eyed, her teeth chattering so much Tweezel feared they might chip.

He lay a woven blanket over Keris and was about to place her hammelhornskin waistcoat on top of that when one of his claws became snagged in the lining. As the material ripped, there was a soft clatter as a small disc-shaped object that had been concealed inside the inner folds of the waistcoat tumbled to the floor.

'Oh, how dreadfully clumsy of me,' the spindle-bug muttered as he bent down to inspect exactly what it was he had discovered.

He stared at the little disc for a moment, non-plussed. Then, with the lantern held close, he picked it up, flipped it over in his hand – and cried out with surprise.

'It can't be!' he cried, and his great glassy head shook from side to side in disbelief, his antennae trembling. 'It can't be,' he repeated. 'But it is . . .'

He turned back to Keris, searching her face for clues. Her breathing was coming a little more easily now.

'That's it, little one,' he whispered urgently. 'Rest, and recover your strength just as soon as you can, for there is someone very special I want you to meet.'

. CHAPTER SIX .

THE LULLABEE GROVE

The coracle lurched from side to side as Keris turned and looked back over her shoulder. Behind her, at the end of a small wooden jetty, stood the spindlebug. The light from the full moon shone through his transparent body, revealing the dark blood pumping through a latticework of arteries, the great bowed curve of his ribcage, the mighty buttress of his hip-bones, the arch of his spine and, deep within his great chest, his huge heart, rising and falling with a steady beat.

'Farewell, Mistress Keris,' the spindlebug's ancient voice boomed out across the dark waters of North Lake. 'And sweet dreams.'

Taking care not to make any more sudden movements, Keris slowly turned her back on Tweezel and gripped on tightly to the wooden bench-seat. Around her in the small boat, half a dozen cowled figures rowed in a silent, steady

rhythm. The coracle glided across the gently lapping water, leaving the lights of New Undertown
twinkling in the distance behind them.

Ahead, emerging from the mist that hung
above the surface of the water in languid swirls,
Lullabee Island – home to the Oakelf Brotherhood
– was just coming into view. Keris glimpsed the
shoreline. It was fringed with the great bulbous
lullabee trees, each one giving off a strange and
hypnotic turquoise light. She shivered with a
mixture of excitement and trepidation. The glowing lullabee groves looked even more wonderful
than she'd imagined . . .

That morning it had been all she could do to stifle a cry of horror when she'd opened her eyes.
There, staring down at her, was a great glass-
bodied insect, its huge angular head cocked to
one side.

'Feeling better, Mistress Keris?' it had trilled in
a quavery, yet kindly voice.

'W . . . who are you . . . ? And . . . h . . . how do
you know my name?' she had stuttered, bewildered.

'I am Tweezel the spindlebug,' said the insect,
holding out a great glass claw for Keris to shake.
'Your webfoot goblin friends sought my help,' he
explained gently. 'You stepped on a poisonthorn
in the Silver Pastures. You've been very sick.'

'I did?'

Keris tried to clear her thoughts. She remembered the great sea of silver grass they had come to, and the excitement she'd felt when she saw the crests of Grefphith and the others glow orange.

Not far now, she'd thought, running out into the glorious, sunlit grasslands, her spirits soaring at the sight of the great herds of tilder and hammelhorns grazing in the distance. Then she'd felt the pain – sharp, stabbing, and unbearably intense as it shot up from her ankle. She must have fainted . . .

'It was touch and go for a while,' the spindle-bug was saying. 'The poison had made your leg swell and you were burning up with fever. I did what I could. A wood-juniper salve for the fever, a hyleberry and darkroot poultice for your leg – and then I sat with you through the night . . .' The spindlebug's eyes glistened. 'And you, Mistress Keris, did the rest.'

Curious, Keris leaned forwards. Her left leg was heavily bandaged from the ankle to the knee.

'I think it's time we took a look at that,' Tweezel told her. 'If you'll allow me.'

He bent down and gently unwrapped the bandage with his great claws. Keris watched curiously as the last strip of material pulled away, leaving a pale green paste on her skin. Tweezel delicately turned her ankle to the left, to the right, then up and down, before pronouncing himself satisfied.

'The poison is gone,' he said, and clicked with pleasure. He handed her a soft cloth and placed a bowl of warm water beside her. 'There,' he said. 'You can wash the poultice off now.'

As Keris wiped away the green paste, the fruity smell of hyleberry making her mouth water, Tweezel retired to the other side of the chamber. The poultice washed away easily in the warm water, but beneath it the tiny grains of sparkling silt still clung to the skin, as they did to the rest of her.

Ever since that extraordinary night when she'd emerged from the third great lake, Keris had sparkled with the gritty particles that no amount of washing seemed to shift. She placed the cloth in the bowl of water and looked up. Tweezel was standing over her, with the hammelhornskin waistcoat clasped in his claws.

'Is this yours?' he asked quietly.

'Yes,' she said, reaching out and taking the waistcoat from him. She held it to her cheek and felt the fur brush against her skin, soft and re-assuring. 'It was my father's. It's all I have of his to remember him by . . .' Keris's eyes suddenly filled with tears. 'He was a sky pirate captain, you know.'

Tweezel nodded, his enormous eyes staring into her own.

'Captain Twig,' Keris said, her voice thick with emotion. 'Captain Twig Verginix . . .'

She paused as she noticed the small rip in the green felt lining of the waistcoat. Tweezel followed her gaze.

'My fault,' he told her. 'Clumsy old creature that I am. My claw, you see . . .'

Keris smiled and wiped away a tear. 'I left my village to search for news of my father. So long ago it now seems. The great blueshell clam sent me here to the Free Glades . . .'

Tweezel's antennae quivered and his enormous eyes seemed to grow even bigger.

'I have heard tell of the great clams of the far-off lake country,' he trilled. 'Like the magnificent caterbird of the Lullabee Groves, they are ancient ones, their memories going back to the earliest of times . . .'

Keris nodded as she remembered the great blueshell clam's voice in her head.

'So the great clam sent you here, Mistress Keris, to the Free Glades,' Tweezel muttered, turning away and gathering a small teapot and two cups onto a tray. He turned back and looked her sparkling body up and down. 'Now it is all beginning to make sense . . .'

'It is?' said Keris, slipping on the familiar old waistcoat and sitting up in the sumpwood bed.

'I must take you to the Lullabee Grove,' said Tweezel, returning with the laden tray and setting it down between them. He poured two cups of hot, aromatic tea from the pot and handed one to Keris. 'But first I have to tell you a story . . .'

Keris took a sip of the tea. It was sweet and comforting, and filled her with a warm glow. Tweezel held up a small, round disc of lufwood between two curved claws.

'A story,' he continued, 'about a young lad I first met years ago in the floating city of Sanctaphrax, when I was the butler to the Most High Academe, Linius Pallitax, Sky rest his soul.'

Keris stared at the miniature painting on the lufwood disc. It was of a handsome dark-haired youth in glistening armour, tall towers rising in the distance behind him. As she gazed at those features – so strange and yet so familiar – the hairs on the back of her neck stood on end.

'Quintinius Verginix was his name, and this is his portrait,' Tweezel said quietly, his eyes fixed on Keris's face.

'Verginix,' Keris breathed, aware of a painful lump in her throat.

'He grew up and married my master's daughter, Maris. They voyaged the skies as sky pirates, and had a baby son.' He shook his head solemnly. 'But then disaster struck and they were forced to leave him in the care of woodtrolls. Maris was unable to forgive herself – and never spoke again. I nursed her through a long illness and then, when she left Undertown for the Deepwoods in search of her son, I went with her. Quint set sail in his sky ship in an attempt to forget his own sorrow and I never saw him again. Until now.'

Tweezel turned the disc over several times, and peered closely at the painted image on its surface.

'This is a portrait miniature from a sword hilt.' The spindlebug paused. 'Passed down from father to son.'

Keris gasped.

'I found it last night,' he went on. 'It was sewn into the lining of your hammelhornskin waist-coat.' He looked up. 'It can mean only one thing, Mistress Keris. Quint found his son. He must have given him his sword when he knew – or thought he knew – he was dying . . .'

'And my father?' Keris asked, trembling.

'I would imagine he understood well enough that a pirate's sword would be of little use to his slaughterer daughter, so he took the portrait from the hilt and sewed it into the one thing she'd treasure always . . .'

'My hammelhornskin waistcoat,' Keris said,

finishing the spindlebug's thought for him. 'And my father?' she repeated, searching the spindlebug's glassy features for clues. 'Is he still alive?'

'The answer to that,' Tweezel said, holding out a claw and helping Keris to her feet, 'lies on Lullabee Island, in North Lake. Come.'

With the spindlebug showing the way, Keris left the chamber and stumbled through the series of underground tunnels and caverns, her eyes wide with amazement. The sheer scale of the lofty, pink-drenched halls took her breath away. And when Tweezel began to outline his plans for the place, explaining how the varnish he had invented would help to introduce the second age of flight, Keris shook her head in amazement.

'And here I am,' she murmured, 'at the very start of it all.'

As they emerged from the tunnel on the far side of the ironwood glade, the spindlebug took a narrow track that wound its way through the trees, between embedded boulders and clumps of tasselled yellow butterblooms. He walked purposefully, pushing low-hanging branches and thorny creepers out of the way, allowing Keris to follow unimpeded.

In front of them, the waters of the South Lake glittered in the mid-morning sun, cool, clear and inviting. Unlike the Great Lake and North Lake, South Lake had no settlements clustered round its shores. As they reached a low, rocky bluff jutting out over its waters, Keris suddenly paused.

She was aware of an extraordinary tingling sensation all over her body. And, as she gazed out over the still waters of South Lake, it seemed to become more intense. It was as if her skin was on fire. Behind her, Tweezel let out a trill of wonder.

'Why, Mistress Keris!' he exclaimed. 'It's as I thought. You're covered in clamdust. Go, the water is calling to you . . .'

Suddenly, Keris could bear it no longer. With a sudden surge of energy, she launched herself off the rocky bluff and high out over the shining lake water, before plunging down beneath the surface with a tremendous *splash*. Bubbles rose and burst, marking the spot where she had disappeared. Ripples rolled out in ever-widening concentric circles . . .

'That's right,' the spindlebug whispered, his heart thumping inside his glassy thorax. 'The lake will wash you clean.'

But Keris couldn't hear him. With powerful strokes of her arms and kicks of her legs, she was diving down deeper and deeper into the lake.

Below her, great underwater pastures of lake-grass swayed in the currents. Fish darted this way and that, their fins and underbellies flashing silver and gold. And all the while she swam, Keris herself gave off a stream of tiny sparkling specks. From her arms, her legs, her fingers, they came; from her cuffs and her hem. Sparks that twinkled like con- stellations of stars as they floated off into the indigo depths of the lake. Slowly the burning sensation was soothed, and then dis- appeared.

At last, with the glittering specks of lights all spent and her lungs aching, she

soared back up to the light far above her. Her head burst through the surface of the lake and she gulped at the warm, fresh air.

'Mistress Keris!' she heard. 'Mistress Keris.'

Treading water, she twisted round. The great spindlebug was standing at the edge of the lake, beaming down at her benevolently.

'Does that feel better?' he asked.

'Oh, yes,' she called back. 'Wonderful.'

With that, she flipped over onto her front and began swimming towards him, her arms and legs pushing the water back behind her. Overhead, a pair of snow-white woodcranes flapped across the pale blue sky, while from the surrounding forest – wilder and less explored than the other lakes – the sounds of hunting woodwolves and the anxious whooping of quarms echoed through the trees.

Emerging from the water, Keris looked down at her arms and legs. For the first time since her meeting with the blueshell clam, they had been washed clean and were free of the sparkling silt. Beside her, Tweezel gave a knowing chuckle.

'Why, Mistress Keris, do you know what you've just done?' he asked.

Keris shook her still dripping head. 'All I know,' she said, 'was that when I saw the water, I just had to dive into it. My skin was on fire . . .'

Tweezel chuckled. 'You've brought a great gift

to the Free Glades. A gift that generations to come will thank you for.'

'I have?' said Keris, astonished.

'Yes,' said Tweezel, taking her hand and guiding her back to the path. 'You have seeded the South Lake with life. One day, it shall have clams growing in its depths. And who knows, maybe one day – generations from now – a giant clam of its very own!'

'You think so?' said Keris, amazed. 'That's why the blueshell clam sent me here?'

'I'm sure of it,' said the spindlebug thoughtfully, gazing across towards the Great Lake and the North Lake in the distance. He smiled. 'Amongst other things . . .'

They continued down the path, leaving the wild shores of the South Lake for the eastern side of the Great Lake, with its pastures and farmland. What with the breeze blowing and the sun beating down, by the time they approached the shores of the North Lake and New Undertown, Keris's hair and clothes were bone dry.

As they reached the bustling market stalls and timbered cabins on the northern lakeshore, Keris spotted a group of familiar and brightly glowing crests bobbing up through the crowds.

'Grefphith! Slifph!' she shouted, waving wildly. 'Over here!'

'Keris! You've recovered!' shouted Grefphith, hurrying towards her down the dusty street, followed by the other webfoots, their crests all flashing a joyful orange and blue.

'Thank you, kind sir,' cried the webfoots, each one bowing to the spindlebug in turn. 'Thank you for helping our friend.'

'It was my honour,' said Tweezel, proudly. 'And she has repaid the Free Glades a hundredfold already by seeding our South Lake with clamdust!'

'You mean . . . ?' exclaimed Grefphith and his brothers. 'There will be clams in the lake!' They did a delighted jig in the middle of the street, their great webbed feet kicking up a cloud of dust that made several passers-by sneeze, and many more stop and gawp.

'Well, that settles it,' said Slifph, slapping his brother Grefphith on the back. 'As soon as we've taken Parsimmon's invitation to come and settle in the Free Glades to the woodtroll and slaughterer villages, we're coming back here ourselves!'

'You're going back to my village?' Keris exclaimed excitedly.

Grefphith nodded. 'Do you wish to return with us?' he asked, taking her hands in his own as his crest switched from bright purples and reds to a soft, pale orange.

'I can't,' said Keris, her eyes glistening. 'At

least, not yet. There is someone Tweezel says I must meet first. But perhaps you could give my Uncle Gristle this . . .'

She unbuckled the dark red leather satchel containing ten slightly crumpled pieces of barkpaper, each one covered in tiny writing, and thrust it into Grefphith's hands.

'Here,' she said. 'And give him – and them all – my love.'

The crests of all the webfoots glowed a curious turquoise and yellow – a combination of colours Keris had never seen before.

She said goodbye to each of the webfoots in turn – then looked away before any of them noticed the tears welling up in her eyes. The five webfoot goblins – packs on their backs and knobbled sticks gripped in the hands – set off back the way they'd come, waving as they went. Tweezel waved back. And, when she was confident that they were far enough away not to see that she was crying, Keris turned and waved too.

'Fare you well,' she whispered, and though she knew they couldn't possibly have heard her, she noticed their crests change once more to the same rippling turquoise and yellow colour.

The webfoots passed the Parley Hall and disappeared round a corner at the far end of the street. Keris did not move. She stood rooted to the spot, staring ahead at the place she had last seen them – until Tweezel took her gently by the arm.

'Come along now, Mistress Keris,' he said. 'There is still much to do.'

They walked up from the lakeside and through the streets of New Undertown that bustled with life. Gabtrolls rubbed shoulders with clod-dertrogs; mobgnomes, gnokgoblins and fourth-lings of all descriptions filled the alleys and squares. As they approached a busy crossroads, Keris noticed a lop-ear and a gyle-goblin who would normally have had absolutely nothing to do with one another, standing at the far corner, deep in intimate conversation.

The Free Glades would be a fine place to settle, she thought, a place where everyone lived in peace and harmony.

She followed the spindlebug into a large tavern called the Lufwood Inn. Despite the lamps on the lufwood-stump tables and torches clamped to the walls, the tavern was far darker than outside, and it took a while for Keris's eyes to grow accus-tomed to it. As they slowly did so, she looked round to find herself in a huge, low-beamed hall, bedecked with sweet-smelling clusters of Deepwoods flowers. Great bunches of herbs and garlands of foliage hung from every beam. The air was rich and intoxicating and a large stove in the corner gave off a soft turquoise glow.

Tweezel, too, looked around for a moment, his own eyes growing used to the light. A young fourthling in a patched apron appeared and smiled good-naturedly.

'Master Tweezel, what can I do for you?' He smiled, his dark eyes flashing as they met Keris's.

Despite herself, Keris found herself blushing.

'Ah! Young Shem Barkwater, isn't it?' the spindlebug trilled. 'I'm looking for Brother Tredegar . . .'

'You'll find him in his usual spot by the stove, log watching, Master Tweezel. Can I get you or the young lady anything to drink?'

'Not just now, thank you, Shem,' said Tweezel, crossing the tavern to the stove, where a small group of oakelves sat warming their ears in front of the stove.

Keris followed behind, but not before the young tavern-keeper had winked at her and given her a dazzling smile.

At their approach, the seven oakelves turned
and gazed past the spindlebug at Keris with their
pitch-black eyes. Keris felt her knees give way,
and she reached out to steady herself. Taghair –
the kindly old oakelf hermit who lived in the
clearing near her village – had eyes like theirs.
Deep, dark and full of wisdom. His solitary gaze
was unsettling enough, but seven pairs of oakelf
eyes . . .

The oakelf nearest to her rose and took her by
the arm, and Keris found herself looking back at
her own reflection in his eyes. For what seemed
to Keris an eternity, he said nothing. Then, with a
trace of a smile, the oakelf said, 'Come, there is
someone waiting to meet you.'

With that, the others rose, pulled their hoods
over their heads and followed in a procession
behind Tweezel, Keris and Brother Tredegar, out
of the Lufwood Inn.

The coracle bucked and bobbed as it reached the
shore of Lullabee Island. A moment later, there
came a soft grinding sound from the bottom of the
small boat as the hull scraped up over the gravel.
Brother Tregedar jumped out, seized the rope and
tethered it to a wooden stake sunk into the ground.
Keris looked up and her eyes widened.

The pale turquoise glow she'd seen above the

island was much brighter here. The air was suffused with the pulsating blue-green light and, as the breeze came wafting towards her, she heard a faint music – slow and keening – which filled her thoughts with longing.

The oakelves nimbly climbed out of the coracle, the last one reaching out and helping Keris ashore. Then, with Tredegar leading the way, a flickering lantern in his raised hand, and the others following, they set off through the trees. The path was winding and uneven and, despite the full moon, shot with confusing shadows. Yet the further they went into the island's interior, the brighter the turquoise light became and the easier it was to see.

After a short walk, they emerged into a clearing fringed by the largest lullabee trees yet. Vast knobbly trunks they had, and branches that seemed to be reaching up towards the moon. From the foliage that grew in dense clusters at the end of every limb, there came the eerie turquoise glow – a gleaming light that illuminated both the tiny sparks hovering in the air around each leaf and the long, sock-like cocoons that hung down from the broadest branches.

They came to a halt and Keris craned her neck back and marvelled at the great cocoons hanging above them. Then, suddenly, the strange lilting music of the trees grew louder and the turquoise

glow at the centre of the grove became more intense.

A cocoon – huge, intricately woven and twinkling with tiny sparks – slowly began to descend towards Keris, until it stopped in front of her, inches from the forest floor. Scarcely daring to breathe, Keris peered into the soft velvety darkness within the cocoon.

A hand emerged – old, frail and milky white, its palm upraised. From behind Keris, Tredegar reached forwards and placed the lufwood portrait in the outstretched palm.

The hand withdrew.

For a moment, nothing happened. Then the hand appeared again and cupped Keris's face in a soft, silken touch. It traced the line of her brow, the slope of her nose, her lips, her chin, as if comparing her features to those in the portrait.

'I am Keris Verginix,' whispered Keris. 'Daughter of Twig.'

She felt the hand tremble as she spoke the words and there was the sound of a half-stifled sob from within the cocoon. Then the hand beckoned to her.

Close beside her ear, Tredegar's gentle voice – little more than a whisper – sounded.

'Step forward, Keris, daughter of Twig; granddaughter of Maris, founder of the Free Glades. Those who sleep within a caterbird cocoon share the dreams of the caterbird . . . The answers you seek lie within.'

Keris looked at the dark shape in front of her. So this is what she had travelled so far for. Here on this strange island, in this mystical lullabee grove, was her grandmother, sitting in a great woven cocoon of glister-silk from which a mighty caterbird had hatched. The caterbird was, like the great blueshell clam, one of the ancient ones, and saw everything on its endless flights over the mighty Deepwoods. Now she was about to share its dreams.

Keris climbed into the velvety darkness and a warm embrace. She felt two arms envelop her, wet tears drip on her neck and gentle sobs tremble through the body holding her close. She reached out in the comforting darkness and returned the embrace.

'Grandmother,' she whispered, hot tears of her own coursing down her face. 'Will I see my father, Twig?'

She closed her eyes as a great wave of relief and tiredness washed over her, and her breathing slowed. In the darkness, as Keris drifted off to sleep, a voice whispered tenderly beside her ear.

'Yes.'

THE END

THE FOURTH
BARKSCROLL

THE BLOODING OF
RUFUS FILATINE

THE
FREE GLADES

THE SLAUGHTERERS
CAMP

THE IRONWOOD
GLADE

SOUTH
LAKE

WOODTROLL
TIMBER YARDS

THE GREAT LAKE

LAKE LANDING

WAIF GLEN

NORTH
LAKE

LULLABEE
ISLAND

NEW
UNDERTOWN

CLODDERTROG
CAVES

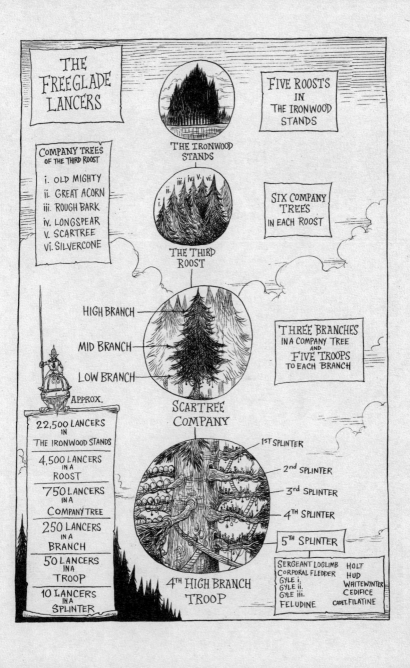

THE FREEGLADE LANCERS

FIVE ROOSTS IN THE IRONWOOD STANDS

THE IRONWOOD STANDS

COMPANY TREES OF THE THIRD ROOST

i. OLD MIGHTY
ii. GREAT ACORN
iii. ROUGH BARK
iv. LONGSPEAR
v. SCARTREE
vi. SILVERCONE

THE THIRD ROOST

SIX COMPANY TREES IN EACH ROOST

HIGH BRANCH
MID BRANCH
LOW BRANCH

SCARTREE COMPANY

THREE BRANCHES IN A COMPANY TREE AND FIVE TROOPS TO EACH BRANCH

APPROX.

22,500 LANCERS IN THE IRONWOOD STANDS

4,500 LANCERS IN A ROOST

750 LANCERS IN A COMPANY TREE

250 LANCERS IN A BRANCH

50 LANCERS IN A TROOP

10 LANCERS IN A SPLINTER

1ST SPLINTER
2ND SPLINTER
3RD SPLINTER
4TH SPLINTER
5TH SPLINTER

4TH HIGH BRANCH TROOP

SERGEANT LOGLIMB
CORPORAL FLEDDER
GYLE i.
GYLE ii.
GYLE iii.
FELUDINE
HOLT
HUD
WHITEWYNTER
CEDIFICE
CADET. FILATINE

. CHAPTER ONE .

THE NAMELESS ONE

The creature threw back its massive head and let out a thunderous roar. The sound – a mixture of guttural rage and savage pain – boomed through the Deepwoods. It made the earth tremble and the treetops quiver, while those for whom the great forest was home cowered and cringed with fear.

Colonies of long-armed weezits, feasting high up in the sallowdrop trees, abruptly abandoned the succulent fruit and scattered in howling gangs of fright-spiked fur. Bright flashes of iridescent blue, leaping from branch to branch, revealed themselves to be groups of fleeing lemkins, the smaller ones clinging to the backs of their elders in clusters of three and sometimes four. On the forest floor, a huge herd of tilder – their long snouts flared, and emitting the characteristic whooping call of alarm – stampeded through the forest glades like Edge-salmon leaping a cliff fall. In their wake, the sunlit air was filled with thousands of translucent wind-

spinners, torn from their tendril-grip in the long glade grass and now spinning upwards to the safety of the forest canopy far above.

Sucking in the air in huge, wheezing breaths, the creature continued its frenzied zigzag charge through the forest. It barged into trees, shrubs and bush-clumps, knocking them effortlessly out of its way. And as it battered a churned-up, stump-splintered path through the Deepwoods, shafts of sunlight broke through the shattered canopy, piercing the shadows and illuminating the creature's massive form.

Huge, muscled shoulders bunched at a thick-set and misshapen head, with no discernible neck between. A gigantic belly, pitted and encrusted with boils and pustules, ballooned over relatively short but immensely solid-looking legs, the size and thickness of copperwood tree-trunks. But more remarkable than these – or the yellow tusk-fringed mouth, or the tiny bloodshot eyes, black ringed and glistening – were the creature's arms.

They were gigantic, the knuckles of the great clawed hands at their ends grazing the forest floor as it ran. It was with these arms that the creature smashed its way through the forest, with great scything blows that brought sallowdrop and stinkwood trees crashing to the ground and splintered clumps of shadowbushes and moonshrubs.

The creature paused. As it did so, the unwelcome sunlight glinted in its bloodshot eyes and on the raw fleshy wounds which ran in green-fringed stripes across its shoulders. It glistened on the dripping yellow tusks as the furious creature threw back that huge ugly head and howled once more, a curdled mixture of pain and rage.

A moment later, in a flurry of dust and fallen branches, it was off again, pounding blindly through the forest. It stumbled over a knot of roots and crashed hard against a tall, slender lufwood sapling. Roaring with rage, it wrapped its great arms around the pitted trunk and uprooted the entire tree, then threw it over its immense shoulders. It landed with a heavy crash in a shower of twigs and leaves.

High up in the very topmost branches of a mighty ironwood pine, far above the forest canopy, a prowlgrin and rider emerged from the shadows cast by the great black fir-cones clustered at the tree's summit. The prowlgrin delicately padded along the branch, its large sensitive toes telling it instinctively that the tree-limb would take its weight. It paused at the very tip of the branch and waited, expertly balanced, for instructions.

The prowlgrin's rider was dressed in the distinctive uniform of the Freeglade Lancers; a crested copper helmet with neck and cheek-guards, a white tunic emblazoned with a red banderbear head, finely tooled wood-armour of rich sumpwood and forest elm which protected arms and legs and, most distinctive of all, a thick lance of seasoned iron-wood clasped in a gauntleted hand. Only the collar gave away the fact that, despite appearances, this rider was not quite a Freeglade Lancer. It was solid green, and marked its wearer out as a cadet who had not yet been blooded in battle.

The rider reached down and patted his prowlgrin mount.

'Steady, Lyrinx, lass,' he whispered. 'I hear it, too. Seems to be coming this way.'

Far below, the great bellowing roar of the creature sounded again.

'*Gather, brothers,*' a soft, whispery voice sounded in the cadet's head. '*The glades are threatened . . .*'

The cadet gave a twitch of the reins he held in one hand. In response, the prowlgrin launched herself from the ironwood branch and out over the green forest canopy below. They fell for what seemed like minutes, but was in fact, as the cadet well knew, mere seconds, as the treetops raced up to meet them. Suddenly – like breaking the surface of a green forest pool – they plunged through the leafy canopy and into the depths of the forest below. The prowlgrin's great toes fastened onto a branch as her huge rear-legs braced to cushion the landing.

From branches all round came the gentle creak and leaf-rustle of other landing prowlgrins. Two, three there were. Eight, nine, ten – prowlgrins and riders, clustered in the branches of the surrounding trees.

'*All here, sergeant,*' the whispery voice sounded in every head. The speaker – a tiny waif called Cedifice – gazed at the others with his enormous pale grey eyes, his veined wafer-thin ears quivering. 'Whatever it is, I can tell from the sound of its footfalls, it is enormous,' the waif whispered. 'And it appears to be in pain.'

As if in answer, another howl sounded in the distance, and the waif's prowlgrin – a sleek white beast with a long, knotted beard – shifted uneasily on his branch.

'I can discern no coherent thoughts, Sergeant.' Cedifice's huge ears trembled and the waif winced uncomfortably. 'Only rage . . . And pain. But one thing I can tell you,' the waif concluded, 'is that the creature is heading for the southern fringes of the Free Glades.'

Sergeant Hulm Logglimb tugged at the stump of the ear he'd lost at the Battle of Lufwood Mount many years earlier, and looked around at the expectant faces of his lancers. He was a short, stocky gnokgoblin, battle-scarred and wily, who never asked his lancers to do anything that he wouldn't do himself. For that, they loved and respected him.

'Well, brothers,' he began, tapping his lance on the tree branch as he weighed up his words. 'Seems like there won't be time to call out the rest of the troop, so it's going to be all down to us in the Fifth Splinter to head this creature off before it reaches the Glades. What do you say?'

'I say, yes, sergeant!' the cadet responded enthusiastically. 'Lyrinx and I can scout ahead of the splinter and . . .'

'It's not for you to say anything. You're still just a cadet,' said the first of three short, large-nosed gyle-goblins, each of them mounted on a frisky white and grey prowlgrin.

The gyle-goblins admitted to no names individually and were known by the rest of the lancers simply as 'the Gyles'. Draped over their saddles, they each had an elaborate cloak of expertly woven leaves and berry branches which, when worn, rendered them virtually invisible in the forest canopy. Their job was to scout for the splinter.

'The Gyles are right, Rufus, old son,' said Lancer Felludine. He turned to Sergeant Logglimb. 'As for me, sir, I say let's do it.'

Gaddius Felludine was a large, heavy-browed fourthling. He was ungainly but powerful, and when roused to anger a fearsome fighter. A lancer of few words, Felludine never spoke of his past, yet it was common knowledge that he had left a troubled and difficult life behind him. After many long years

310

of searching he had found acceptance in the Free Glades. He was a frequent visitor to Waif Glen, where the wounds of his past were gradually being healed. Grateful to the Free Glades, he had no hesitation in laying down his life for the place he loved, and his fellow lancers knew it.

'Thank you, Gaddius,' said the sergeant. He looked up at the three lancers perched on the branches above him. 'And how about you?'

All three were, like himself, gnokgoblins. There was Lance-Corporal Degg Fledder, heavy-lidded and cautious, always looking before leaping, but a skilful lancer. And then there were the twins, Hudflux and Holt. The pair of them were cheerful and happy-go-lucky, always ready with a joke or an encouraging word – and both were deadly accurate with a crossbow.

'We're with you, sergeant,' all three replied, suddenly serious as yet another chilling howl echoed up from the forest below them.

'It's getting closer, whatever it is,' said the final lancer in the splinter, a young mobgnome by the name of Tam Whytewinter.

Like his comrades, he wore a collar of white and green chequerboards that denoted that he'd been blooded in battle, fighting alongside the others in his splinter. In Whytewinter's case, his boards had been earned just a few months ago in a nasty skirmish to the south of the Goblin Nations with a roving band of skulltrogs. He'd been wounded in the leg – an injury that still bothered him, though he was always careful not to show it.

'Rufus can ride with me, sergeant,' Tam said. He smiled at the cadet. 'I'll keep him out of trouble! He's far too young to earn his boards just yet.'

The others laughed. Everyone knew that Tam and Cadet Rufus Filatine were practically the same age – and were also the best of friends. In fact, it was only a nasty case of bark-croup that had kept Rufus back at the roost when the company had been called out to deal with the skulltrogs. Otherwise, he would not still be wearing the plain green collar.

'*Patience, Rufus,*' the waif's whispery voice sounded in the cadet's head. '*Your time will come soon enough.*'

Rufus Filatine, his face flushed and unhappy-looking, gazed across into the kindly eyes of Cedifice the waif. Small and physically weak the waif signaller might be, Rufus acknowledged, but Cedifice was a vital member of the splinter. He sent messages, listened out for sounds of danger and, most importantly of all perhaps, spread words of comfort and understanding amongst the group with his telepathy.

'Well, what are we waiting for?' said Sergeant Logglimb, raising his lance and giving the time-honoured battle-cry. 'FREEGLADER!'

'FREEGLADER!' the ten lancers of his splinter replied, their prowlgrins taking off at a gallop and leaping through the treetops after their leader in the direction of the terrible sound.

The Gyles sped on ahead, their white and grey prowlgrins faster and even more nimble than the others.

'Tell them to distract the creature,' Sergeant Logglimb called to the waif. 'We'll ride round and come in from the south.'

'Sir,' the waif whispered back.

'Load those crossbows,' the sergeant called over to Lance-Corporal Fledder and the gnokgoblin twins, who nodded grimly.

'And Gaddius, keep that lance handy,' he said. 'You two . . .' He glanced over his shoulder to make sure Tam and Rufus were following on their prowl-grins. 'Make sure you cover our backs.'

With that, the sergeant urged his own great orange prowlgrin on faster through the trees, the gnokgoblins and large fourthling following close behind. Up ahead, the sound of trees crashing to the forest floor grew suddenly louder.

'You heard what he said,' said Tam, pulling up his prowlgrin, Nixus, and watching the five lancers advance through the trees ahead.

'I know, I know,' said Rufus bitterly, following his friend's example.

Lyrinx halted next to Nixus on the broad branch of a pewterbark tree. Together, the two lancers surveyed the forest floor below.

'*Here it comes,*' Cedifice's voice sounded in their heads. '*It's ignoring the Gyles' slings.*'

Sure enough, up ahead, Rufus could just make out the buzzing sound of the small pebbles being catapulted at the creature by the gyle-goblins in their efforts to distract it.

'*The sergeant says to strike your fire-crystals . . .*' The waif communicated their leader's instructions.

In the treetops in the distance, Rufus saw five pin-points of light suddenly flare up as the lancers lit brushwood torches.

Of course, fire! he realized. The deepest fear of any primitive creature. His hand reached for the two crystals in the small pouch at his belt and he turned to pull a brushwood bundle from his saddle pack.

'Tam, Rufus,' came the voice. '*Don't light your torches yet . . .*' The waif passed on Sergeant Logglimb's command. '*We're going to try and turn it before it reaches you . . .*'

Tam and Rufus exchanged glances. As the junior members of the splinter, they knew their role was to stay in reserve – but it was frustrating nonetheless.

Rufus leaned forward in the saddle and scanned the horizon. He could see the torches flaring in the treetops – yet the sound of crashing and splintering trees seemed to be getting closer still.

'*Hudflux! Holt! To the left! Fledder, higher! Double back behind! . . .*' The waif's voice, still a whisper, was tense and urgent. '*That's it . . . That's it . . . Sergeant, look out!*'

Up ahead, there was a deafening howl and Rufus saw a great copperwood tree rise up, then topple back with a crash. Beside him, Tam gasped. But looking up, Rufus saw that his friend's gaze was not on the forest in front of him. No, rather, he was staring down at the forest floor below them. He looked down too, and gasped with horror.

Back from a day's foraging, a party of half a dozen woodtrolls – an old male, three females and a couple of young'uns – were making their way towards the Free Glades. They were carrying baskets and barrels of oak-mushrooms, wood-toadstools, pine-nuts and bark-gourds carefully on their heads and, although from the looks on their faces it was clear that they could hear the commotion ahead of them, they didn't seem to realize the danger they were heading towards.

Rufus twitched the reins and Lyrinx bounded down through the branches to the forest floor.

'Rufus, wait . . .' Tam called after him, but the cadet ignored him.

The woodtrolls were in danger and he had to warn them.

Lyrinx landed on the ground ten strides in front of the small party, and Rufus was about to call out to them when all at once the woodtrolls came to a sudden halt. Their eyes as large as lufwood saucers, the woodtrolls tossed their barrels and baskets of carefully gathered produce to the forest floor, spun on their heels and fled for their lives.

'Rufus! Watch out!' Tam's voice called out from above.

Too late, the cadet swivelled round in his saddle and caught sight of what the woodtrolls had glimpsed over his shoulder. He swallowed hard.

Coming towards him through the forest, its red eyes boring into his own, drool hanging in heavy gobbets from a snaggle-tusked mouth, was the most enormous creature Rufus had ever seen. With a roar of rage, it shot out a great curved claw, forcing Lyrinx to leap out of the way with a yelp of terror.

The movement caught Rufus off-balance and sent him crashing to the earth. He looked up to see the terrifying creature towering over him. It howled with rage. He screwed his eyes shut and clawed at the Deepwoods dirt, his body tensing for the blow he was sure was about to fall.

Above him, the creature's furious howling seemed suddenly to catch in its throat and turn to a spluttering gurgle. Hardly daring to look, Rufus raised his face from the rich, peaty loam of the soil and looked up. The mighty creature stood before him, motionless. Its great arms were spread wide, the chipped claws glistening strangely in the sunlight. There was a look of dazed shock and confusion plastered across its misshapen features.

Then Rufus saw it. Protruding from the creature's barrel-chest, just above its great bloated belly, was the tip of an ironwood lance glistening with blood. With a soft sigh, the creature pitched forwards and crashed to the forest floor with a great thud.

Frozen with shock, Rufus found himself inches from the creature's contorted face, staring at his own horrified reflection in a single glazed red eye.

Sergeant Logglimb appeared a moment later, his

prowlgrin Pheddix panting with exertion. He dismounted and climbed onto the massive creature's back. Then, with a grunt of effort, he slowly pulled his ironwood lance from the body and stood looking at its dripping point ruefully. Rufus climbed shakily to his feet, his heart still hammering away beneath his rib cage.

'I didn't want to do that,' said Sergeant Logglimb quietly. He fixed Rufus with his unblinking gaze. 'But you gave me no choice, cadet.'

Rufus stared back at the sergeant, his face flushing with colour.

'I . . . I wanted to warn the woodtrolls . . .' he began, but the expression on the sergeant's face stopped him.

'Lancer Whytewinter did that from the treetops,' he said. 'You, on the other hand, put yourself in harm's way – and forced me to kill this unfortunate, demented creature.' The sergeant shook his head slowly and climbed down, lance in hand. 'This is no way to earn your boards, Rufus.'

The cadet hung his head in shame and bit his lip. 'I'm sorry, sergeant . . .' he mumbled.

He felt Logglimb's hand on his shoulder.

'That's all right, cadet,' he said, his voice suddenly gentle and compassionate. 'We shall not speak of this again.'

Rufus nodded and, looking up, saw that the rest of the splinter were arriving. They gathered round the body of the strange creature, their eyes wide. Beside him, Tam handed his friend back the reins of his prowlgrin.

'Are you all right?' he asked.

Rufus nodded, and patted Lyrinx's soft orange fur. 'Sorry, lass,' he whispered in her ear.

All eyes were on the dead creature. Cedifice was walking round it, his huge ears quivering.

'Sergeant,' he said at last. 'Look at these marks.'

Sergeant Logglimb turned to the waif, who was pointing to deep wounds on the creature's shoulders.

'These aren't the wounds of an accident . . .' The waif shook his head and inspected the green-fringed stripes, before turning back. 'No, these are rope burns, sergeant.'

'Rope burns?'

'Made by some sort of tight-fitting harness.' Cedifice frowned thoughtfully. 'This creature, whatever it was, has been ill-treated. These wounds alone must have been torment, not to mention these . . .' His ears trembled as he pointed to small criss-crossing scars on the creature's arms and legs. 'Whip marks. No wonder the poor thing was driven half out of its mind.'

'I've never seen a creature like it,' said Corporal Fledder, shaking his head.

'Nor have we,' agreed the gyle-goblins, their leafy cloaks rustling.

Lancer Gaddius Felludine stroked his beard thoughtfully. 'What do you suppose it is?' he asked.

'*I* know,' said Rufus, stepping forward. 'At least I know what my father and the other librarian academics call creatures like this . . .'

'You do?' said Tam, turning to his friend.

'Yes,' said Rufus quietly. 'They call them the nameless ones.'

. CHAPTER TWO .

THE SKIRMISH AT WOODED CRAG

Rufus pushed the hair from his eyes and, half standing, inched the rough-hewn grooming-stool forward. Lyrinx purred appreciatively and nuzzled the side of her broad head against Rufus's shoulder, glancing up at him through one large blue eye as she did so.

He unsnagged the thick hair of her beard, picking out the twigs and burrs that had got tangled there, he massaged her twisting tail, and he used the curry-comb to brush her orange coat till it gleamed. Rufus patted her, ruffled her fur and gave her a tit-bit of dried offal, which she swallowed gratefully.

'Come on, Lyrinx, girl,' he said softly. 'Let's see to those toes of yours.'

With a low growl, the thrumming sound rising from deep down inside her throat, the prowlgrin shifted her balance to one side and extended her left foot. Rufus, who was perched on the grooming-stool, gently placed the foot on the length of thick

cloth which lay across his lap and inspected each toe closely.

'Oh, what's this?' he said, tutting sympathetically. 'That doesn't look too good, does it?' He took his knife from his belt and, squinting with concentration, removed a sharp piece of ironwood bark which had become wedged beneath one of the broad, ivory-coloured nails. 'That's better,' he said soothingly, 'isn't it, lass?'

Then, resheathing the blade, he picked up his whetstone – a small, porous pebble shaped rather like the hull of a miniature old-fashioned sky ship – and, taking care not to go against the natural grain, began rubbing it along the prowlgrin's nails. Slowly he filed away the ridges and notches on the surface of each nail until they gleamed ivory white.

As he worked, the prowlgrin gently leaned her great round body against him and waited patiently. The feet of a prowlgrin are incredibly sensitive, and it was testament to the trust between rider and beast that Lyrinx allowed Rufus to handle her toes without flinching.

'Good girl,' Rufus whispered encouragingly. 'The hard part is over. Now for the bit I know you enjoy . . .'

Rufus unhooked a spatula from the side of his grooming-stool, picked up the bucket at his feet and began stirring the thick, pale yellow liquid it contained. As he did so, the rich, woody aroma of the oil was released, making Lyrinx emit a deep, rumbling purr of appreciation.

All prowlgrins loved darkelm oil, even those that hadn't been tamed. Herds of wild prowlgrins would gather in the spreading boughs of the massive darkelm trees, shuffling and stamping in a strange undulating dance until their feet were drenched in the oil that seeped through the spongy bark of the tree. Not only did the prowlgrins find it irresistible, but the darkelm oil coated and protected their delicate feet, keeping them in excellent condition.

The head groom organized regular forays into the surrounding forests to keep the prowlgrins of Scartree Company – all seven hundred and fifty of them – well supplied with the precious oil. Each prowlgrin had two grooms assigned to feed and groom him or her, but Rufus preferred to oil Lyrinx's feet himself.

'Here we go then,' he said, plunging his hands into the bucket and then proceeding to rub it into the creases, the knuckles and the soft leathery pads of Lyrinx's left foot. 'That's better, isn't it?' he whispered as Lyrinx closed her eyes dreamily and gave a deep, growling purr.

Nothing, Rufus knew, was more important than caring for your prowlgrin's feet. They were so sensitive they could detect the slightest of movements. At night, while perching, a trained prowlgrin would alert their rider to any tremor or vibration they detected which might indicate approaching danger. And by day, while out riding, the same toes could tell in an instant which branches could support them and which would break under their weight. In prime condition, those toes would carry both rider and mount safely through the very topmost branches of the forest in exhilarating gallops. An untended blister or a neglected splinter could spell disaster out on patrol.

'Good girl,' Rufus whispered. 'Good, good girl.'

All around them, the vast ironwood pine buzzed with activity. On the great broad branch where he sat oiling Lyrinx's paws, the other lancers of the Fifth Splinter were also hard at work.

Lance-Corporal Degg Fledder – a white oakapple flower pinned to his forage cap at a jaunty angle – was sharpening the long straight sabre that was standard issue to all lancers. As he worked the blade to a razor-sharp edge, he smiled to himself and hummed the latest catchy tune that was doing the rounds of the New Undertown taverns. Further along the mighty ironwood branch, the looming figure of Lancer Gaddius Felludine sat surrounded by grappling-hooks, water-bottles, saddlebags and other bits of kit. The big fourthling tutted and muttered darkly as he attempted to sew a patch onto an old pair of breeches with clumsy fingers.

'Sky blast it!' he exploded with exasperation. 'Groom! Groom! Has anyone seen a groom?'

Strictly speaking, all the grooms reported to the head groom – a punctilious mobgnome with a sharp tongue and an obsessive eye for detail – and had responsibility only for the prowlgrins who roosted on the other side of Scartree, in the western branches of the mighty ironwood pine. But here where the lancers lived, on the eastern side of the tree, its branches filled with hammocks and equipment, weapon-stores and armoury-benches, the grooms often found that their services were in high demand.

'What is it, Gad?' said an exasperated-sounding gnokgoblin in the flat felt cap of a groom, hurrying along the branch, an offal bucket clutched in each hand.

'You couldn't patch these, could you, Higg?' said Gaddius, looking up and showing the groom his hopeless efforts to repair the breeches. 'Only, they're my favourite pair.'

'You choose your moments,' said Higg the groom. 'Can't you see it's feeding time in the roost?'

He swung a strong-smelling bucket beneath the lancer's nose. Further along the branch, the three gyle-goblins – who were expertly repairing their camouflage capes with carefully-woven twigs and leaves – all laughed out loud.

'That bucket smells sweet as oakapple-blossom, Higg – compared to Gadd's breeches!' one of them called.

Hudflux and Holt, the gnokgoblin brothers, looked up from the crossbows they were dismantling and greasing, and chuckled.

'Yes, yes, very funny,' growled Gaddius, draping the breeches over the groom's outstretched arm and tucking a thornwood needle and waxed thread into his apron. 'I'll buy you a tankard in the New Bloodoak, Higg.'

'Make it two,' said the groom, as he hurried back along the branch and descended a wooden walkway that spiralled round the trunk towards the western side of the tree. In the distance the barks and growls of hungry prowlgrins could just be heard.

'All right, lass,' said Rufus, patting Lyrinx's great round side. 'Off you go and enjoy your supper.'

With an excited yelping growl, the prowlgrin leaped off the branch and disappeared into the dappled branches below. Rufus stood up, swung his grooming-stool onto his shoulder – then paused. Spread out all around him in the gigantic tree, the seven hundred and fifty lancers of Scartree Company were going about their evening's work.

Rufus smiled happily as he listened to the sounds that in the year that he'd served as a lance-cadet he'd grown to know and love.

There were anvil-clangs and hammerblows as swords were forged, axes honed and lances sharpened. There was the squeak of turning cogs and the rasping hiss of mighty bellows. There was the clash of swords and crunch of maces as the lancers practised their skills, fencing and fighting – as well as the sudden cries of delight or derision as a crossbow bolt either struck a bullseye or missed the target completely. There was the gruff babble of numerous voices; song, laughter, barked commands – as well as the rhythmic rumble of all those weary lancers, curled up in the hammocks suspended from the eastern branches, fast asleep after a long day's patrol.

Coupled with the sounds, the air was filled with smells. High up on a branch of the mighty pine, Rufus breathed in. Aromatic smoke from the hanging braziers mingled with the scent of frying tilder and toasting oakbread as it rose up. From the middle of the tree where the five mid-branch troops were cooking supper before going out on night patrol, there was the odour of scorched metal – and the fumes from the leather-tanning vats from the low-branch troops, who were busy repairing and refitting equipment damaged or lost on recent patrols.

To the west, faint traces of acrid offal and the woody tang of dung drifted up from the roost branches of the prowl-grins, while all around the distinct musty smell of exhausted unwashed bodies floated across the hammocks full of the high-branch lancers getting what sleep they could before dawn patrol.

The company of lancers who lived in Scartree were divided into low-branch, mid-branch and high-branch troops, every troop divided again into splinters – each one occupying their particular place in the mighty iron-wood tree. The Fifth Splinter was situated at the top of Scartree, where the weather was keenest and the views were best – and Rufus loved it.

He looked out from the broad branch where the Fifth Splinter – the fourth outfit of five that comprised the high-branch of Scartree Company – were settling down for the night. All around, the other ironwood trees of the roost bustled with activity. Old Mighty, Great Acorn, Roughbark, Longspear and Silvercone each also held a company of lancers some seven hundred and fifty strong. Together they made up the third roost.

There were five roosts in all, their dark silhouettes just visible in the gathering dusk, offering refuge, in total, to over twenty-two thousand lancers in the vast Ironwood Stands that towered over the dark waters of the Great Lake. Twenty-two thousand lancers to patrol the forests around the Free Glades and warn of danger. Twenty-two thousand to ride their prowlgrins into battle and die, if they had to, defending this wonderful place.

And he, Rufus Filatine, was a part of it all. He touched the red banderbear badge stitched to the front of the white tunic he wore, and felt a surge of pride and excitement.

'Lost in thought, green collar?'

Rufus turned to see his friend, Tam Whytewinter. His smiling face, lit by lamplight now that the sun had set, was framed by the great circular darkness of the troop store – a knot hole in the huge trunk of the tree, so big it looked like nothing so much as a deep cave. It was full of supplies of all kinds. Everything from pickled pine-nuts, sumpwood armour polish, dried tilder hams and blood sausage in huge spirals, to wood grog (for medicinal purposes only), whetstones, flagons of darkelm oil, caskets of dried charlock, smoked hyleberry and desiccated thousandfoot. Tam held up a caddy full of aromatic oaktea.

'Fancy a brew?' he said. 'The pot's just coming to the boil.'

Rufus nodded. 'Nothing I'd like better, old veteran,' he said.

Tam laughed and disappeared inside the knot hole. A moment later there was the clink of an ironwood spoon in pewter mugs and the aroma of freshly brewed oaktea, the splash of creamy hammelhorn milk and the sweet smell of woodhoney. Tam reappeared with two steaming mugs grasped in his hands.

'Here we go, green collar,' he said, striding along the branch and placing the mug down beside him.

Tam's slight limp, Rufus noticed, seemed no better.

'Thanks, old veteran,' he said. 'How's the leg, by the way?'

'Fine, green collar,' Tam replied. 'And thanks for asking.'

Tam lowered himself down onto the branch,

wincing as he did so. Then, legs outstretched, he wrapped his hands round the warm mug and took a sip of oaktea. He glanced over at Rufus, who was sipping his own tea.

'Actually, Rufus,' he said quietly, suddenly serious and unsmiling, 'it's not fine . . . It's not fine at all.'

'Is your leg hurting?' said Rufus.

'It's not my leg so much as . . .' Tam paused and, with a jolt of shock, Rufus realized that his friend was trying very hard not to cry. 'As . . . as . . . this.'

Tam's hand went to the green and white chequerboard collar he wore. For a moment the pair of them were silent, and Rufus was painfully aware of the other lancers exchanging glances, making their excuses and climbing into their hammocks suspended in the shadows below the branch. When the last of them – the waif Cedifice, who preferred to sleep in a corner of the knot hole rather than a hammock – had said goodnight and left them alone on the branch, Rufus put down his mug and turned to his friend.

'Do you want to talk about it, Tam?' he asked.

Tam didn't look at him, but continued to stare into the depths of his own mug, his eyes blank and expressionless. At length, he breathed in and shook his head.

'You were laid up with the croup,' he said quietly.

'I wish to Sky that *I* had been . . .'

'But you earned your boards, Tam,' Rufus interrupted. 'You were blooded . . . !'

A single tear trickled down Tam's cheek and fell into his oaktea.

'Yes,' he whispered. Two more tears plinked into the mug clasped in his hands. 'I was blooded . . .'

For a moment he was silent again. Then, when he started speaking, the words came thick and fast – though his voice betrayed no emotion.

'We left you coughing in your hammock, Rufus, and set off for the southern fringes just as the moon was rising. It was a bright clear night, but the forest shadows were crisp and deep and we made good progress. Nixus was as excited as I was, growling beneath his breath and bounding expertly through the high branches like a prowlgrin twice his age. Reports had come in . . . Perhaps you don't remember them, Rufus – you were running quite a fever at the time. Reports of skulltrogs moving into the forests beyond the slaughterers' camp. A slaughterer herder had spotted a large group of them from his skycraft at a place called Wooded Crag.'

Rufus listened closely. Tam was right. He'd known nothing of those reports.

'Apparently, it looked like they were preparing for one of their feasts.' Tam shuddered. 'Sergeant Logglimb said we had to get there and drive them off before they started. Once these creatures from the depths of the Deepwoods get a taste for blood, he said, they get settled in and make everyone's life a misery. A few well-placed copperwood fire-darts, a whole load of shouting and they'd turn heel and flee, he said, primitive creatures that they are . . .'

Tam swallowed hard.

'And that's what you did, didn't you, Tam?' said Rufus, searching his friend's face for signs of emotion. 'The sergeant reported back to old Marshal Wooden-Leg himself. Fifth Splinter sent those skulltrogs packing – and you earned your boards for being in action. A skirmish, he called it . . .'

'Yes, a skirmish,' said Tam. He put down his mug and turned to Rufus, his face drawn and blotchy. 'Do you have any idea what that simple word actually means, Rufus? A skirmish? Not the mighty war for the Free Glades, or the epic Battle of Lufwood Mount, but just a skirmish – a small forgotten little skirmish? Well, do you?'

'Tell me,' said Rufus, his mouth suddenly dry.

'We arrived at Wooded Crag too late,' Tam continued, staring at Rufus with red-rimmed eyes. 'The skulltrogs had captured a party of low-bellied goblins and . . . and the feasting had begun. Twenty skulltrogs there were, the size of banderbears, clothed in ragged skins, the skulls of previous victims jangling at their necks . . .' He swallowed hard. 'Covered in blood as they competed with each other in tearing their captives limb from limb. The rocks, the trees, the dusty earth; everything was splattered in blood and entrails. Up above, we paused in the top of a copse of copperwoods and looked down.'

'"It's begun," said Sergeant Logglimb, "and they won't give up now until we make them stop – at the end of an ironwood lance." Simple as that. Cedifice then called out the order to form up, lances at the ready, and we charged. The hideous creatures didn't know what hit them. The Gyles took one each at the first leap; Gaddius and Fledder, three, while the twins ran through eight between them. As for Sergeant Logglimb . . .'

'And you?' asked Rufus, softly.

Tam looked down. 'One,' he said. 'Nixus leaped high off the branch, and then down we came, my lance braced and steady, my stirrups forward, heels back. Just like in practice, Rufus. Except this wasn't practice . . .

'He looked up at me, the skulltrog. Deepset eyes, blood-smeared face, all pitted and scarred. And huge great yellow fangs. Bared. Snarling. I felt my lance jump in my hands . . . Jar at my shoulder. Then just sort of slide in.

'The sound, like a bursting woodsap. All fleshy and wet . . . I'll never forget it . . .

'The skulltrog groaned, its stinking breath blasting in my face as my lance slid through its body and it lurched towards me. The last thing I remember before Nixus hit the ground and leaped again, was the glistening yellow eye of the skulltrog staring into mine, inches away from my face for a split second. I'll never forget it, Rufus. Never. It was a dead stare. The spark of life had been extinguished – and I . . . I had extinguished it.

'The lance slipped from my hands, greasy with blood, and Nixus and I were up in the treetops, back with the rest of the splinter. Below us – in amongst the barely distinguishable remains of the low-belly goblins – lay twenty skulltrogs, each one run through with ironwood lances. I knew that we . . . that *I*, had to do it. That now the forests round the Free Glades would be safer. But I felt no joy or elation. Just a sick feeling in the pit of my stomach, and a sadness that won't seem to go away.

'Cedifice spoke to me, told me it would pass, and as we rode back in the early light of dawn I thought he was probably right. Then, just as we reached Scartree, I felt a pain in my leg and, looking down, realized I'd been wounded. I'd been so wrapped up in my thoughts that I hadn't even noticed. It was only a scratch. One of the skulltrog's fangs must have caught me as Nixus leaped clear. It's nothing really – only it won't seem to heal. Just aches and aches, and keeps reminding me of that dead eye staring into mine . . .'

'Here, let me take a look,' said Rufus.

Tam pulled off his tilder leather boot and revealed a livid wound cut deep into his calf, oozing with yellow pus. He winced.

'Oh, it doesn't look too bad, old veteran,' Rufus lied to his friend, forcing his voice to sound cheerful and unconcerned.

'Thought earning my boards would be the happiest day of my life . . .'

Rufus reached into the leather bag at his side and dug around, before pulling out a pot of hyleberry salve that worked wonders on Lyrinx's feet.

'Instead, green collar, old friend,' said Tam, fingering his chequerboard collar, hardly noticing as Rufus applied the sweet-smelling ointment to the wound, 'it's only brought me nightmares . . .'

The sound of the wooden leg on the timber boards of Lake Landing Academy was unmistakable. *Tap-tap-tap*, it went, the sound growing louder and louder until, at last, the doors to the Great Lecture Theatre slowly opened.

'Come in, Marshal Heg-tugg,' said the High Master of the Academy, Xanth Filatine.

He was standing by the great window of the academy's magnificent lecture theatre, hands clasped

THE LOST BARKSCROLLS

behind his back, looking out across the lake. The sun had just set and the surface of the water was mirroring the red and orange sunset. Silhouetted against the sky were half a dozen librarian-knight apprentices riding their flimsy skycraft. They were coming in to land on the jetty after an arduous afternoon of flying practice.

'Greetings, High Master,' said the elderly flat-head goblin. He was dressed in the white tunic and chequerboard collar of the Freeglade Lancers. His wood armour was pitted and scratched, his boots scuffed and worn, but the ornately stitched bander-bear badge of gold on his threadbare tunic announced his high rank. Marshal Heg-tugg, or old Wooden-Leg, was High Commander of the Freeglade Lancers of the Ironwood Stands, all twenty-two thousand, five hundred of them. Together with the librarian knights, it was his job to organize the protection and defence of the Free Glades. Which was why – wooden leg or no wooden leg – he had come running when summoned to Lake Landing by the head of the librarian knights, Xanth Filatine.

'So, what have we here? . . .' The marshal stopped and gazed up in astonishment.

There, suspended on a floating cradle of buoyant sumpwood, the light from the great window casting it in vivid light and shadow, was an imposing

338

gigantic creature. In death, the librarians had gently and reverently restored what dignity they could to the Deepwoods monster, for they cherished and studied all aspects of the mysterious forests. The filth and debris had been carefully removed, wounds examined and cleaned, mouth, ears and nostrils gently probed, and the tortured features arranged into a mask of peaceful slumber. And as they'd worked, they had noted and catalogued everything, building up a treatise on this never-before-seen creature that had blundered out of the forest depths.

'My lancers told me it was big, but I had no idea . . .' said the old marshal in awe.

Xanth Filatine turned from the window, a barkscroll treatise in his hand, and joined the marshal in the middle of the Great Lecture Theatre. As the sunset faded, its rose and golden glow was replaced by the warm light of half a dozen globes which hung from the arching timbered ceiling. Xanth stroked his thin straggly beard, once bright russet but now flecked with grey.

'It is what can only be described by us librarians as a nameless one,' he told Marshal Heg-tugg. 'So far as we can tell, creatures as huge and primitive as this one originate in the very darkest depths of the Deepwoods beyond the forest of thorns, beyond the Nightwoods and perhaps even further than Riverrise itself. Life in those regions is often in its earliest state. According to some theories, it is as if it has only recently evolved from the life-bringing "seeds" of the Mother Storm . . .'

'Yes, well, I'll leave such matters to you, High Master,' said the marshal, tapping his wooden leg on the timber floor impatiently. 'What concerns me is, how did it get here? And should we, in the Free Glades, be concerned about it?'

Xanth looked down at the barkscroll treatise in his hand.

'Our librarian knights on their treatise voyages have reported sightings of such creatures skewered on the razor-like barbs of the thornforest,' he said, 'but none has ever found a path through. Until now. But it is such a rare occurrence that I don't think we need to be concerned.' He unfurled the barkscroll. 'What *should* concern us, however, is the treatment this poor, primitive creature evidently received once it had found its way here.'

'Treatment?' The marshal stared up at the creature hovering above, seemingly sleeping peacefully, its massive arms folded over its great distended belly.

'Indeed,' Xanth said sadly. 'According to my librarians' findings, there is evidence of this creature being harnessed and whipped. Scars across its back and legs, and rope burns across the chest and under its arms. It was, we think, harnessed and forced to pull some sort of heavy burden.'

'Have you any idea what?' asked the marshal.

'It's puzzling,' said Xanth, scratching his close-cropped head.

He crossed the floor of the lecture theatre to a floating lectern bobbing on the end of a chain and pulled it down towards him. A moment later, he returned with a small ironwood tray.

'These tiny specks were found beneath the creature's toenails.'

He held the tray up to the light from the globes above. As he did so, the golden glow that fell on the glittering scrapings abruptly diffused, sending shafts of dazzling light shooting off through the air in every direction.

'There's only one substance in all the Edge that does that,' said Marshal Heg-tugg. 'Phraxdust.'

'From the Twilight Woods,' said Xanth thought-fully. 'Perhaps the creature strayed there . . . But that is not where it was harnessed and enslaved.'

'No?' said Heg-tugg.

'No,' said Xanth. 'We found the nameless one's body spattered and smeared with this.'

He picked up a clod of dried mud from the tray and rubbed it between his finger and thumb, then inspected them. There was a dark, oily stain across his fingertips. He held it up to his nose and sniffed. His brow creased with concentration.

'Rocksulphur,' he said slowly. 'Swarf. Pitch.' He sniffed again. 'Charcoal-grits . . . You can still smell it in the soil.'

'So far as I am aware, one place alone has earth as foul and contaminated as that,' said the marshal, shaking his head. 'And that accursed place has been deserted ever since the war for the Free Glades . . .'

'My thoughts exactly,' said Xanth. He remem-bered that terrible war only too well. The furnace masters with their war-machines, the glade-eaters, had invaded the Free Glades aided by the massed armies of the Goblin Nations in an effort to enslave the Freegladers. 'Yet these findings suggest it might be deserted no longer.'

Just then, there was a creak from the other side of the hall as the handle turned, and the door to the Great Lecture Theatre opened a fraction. A face appeared in the crack.

'I'm sorry, Father,' came a voice. 'Am I too early?'

'Oh, Rufus, it's you,' Xanth replied. 'No . . .' He turned to the marshal. 'My son, Rufus. He's dining with me tonight. I see all too little of him since he joined those lancers of yours.'

Rufus entered the imposing lecture theatre and shut the door quietly behind him. His eyes fell on the eerie sight of the huge body suspended from the ceiling, the pools of golden lamplight making its curves and crevices look like a statue carved from a great slab of dark wood. How peaceful it looked, he thought. Not at all like the horrific monster he'd encountered in the forest.

Rufus turned and realized he was in the presence of old Wooden Leg himself, Marshal Heg-tugg of the Freeglade Lancers.

'Marshal,' he said, touching his banderbear badge with his right hand. 'Lance-Cadet Filatine, of the Fifth Splinter, Fourth High-Branch Troop, Scartree Company, Third Roost. Servant of the Free Glades.'

'Marshal Heg-tugg of the Ironwood Stands,' said the marshal formally, touching his gold badge with his right hand. 'Also servant of the Free Glades.' He smiled. 'Fifth Splinter, you say?'

Rufus nodded.

'You're making quite a name for yourselves. Weren't you the splinter involved in that skirmish at Wooded Crag?'

Rufus blushed and fingered his green collar. 'I missed that one myself, but yes, the Fifth Splinter was there.'

The marshal exchanged looks with the High Master of Lake Landing before patting the young lancer on his green-collared shoulder.

'Well, it just so happens that your father and I might have a mission for the Fifth Splinter, Fourth High-Branch Troop of Scartree Company . . .'

'You might?' said Rufus, intrigued.

'Yes,' said the old marshal. 'A mission to the Foundry Glades.'

. CHAPTER THREE .

THE DEATH-CHEATERS

'*Open formation*,' Cedifice the waif's voice sounded inside every head. '*Advance at the gallop!*'

Lined up in an orderly row at the southern fringe of the Free Glades, it was the order they'd all been waiting for. The lancers of the Fifth Splinter, Fourth High-Branch Troop, Scartree Company, twitched the reins of their prowlgrin mounts. As one, the great beasts launched themselves high into the air with their powerful back legs.

Rufus clung on tight to the curved saddle roll, braced his legs in the stirrups and waited for his stomach to catch up with him. Lyrinx landed on a branch high in the forest canopy and leaped instantly for another, then another. Leaning forward in the saddle, Rufus pressed himself down as low as he could as his prowlgrin broke through the smaller branches and leafy twigs of the canopy. He felt his ironwood lance judder and buck under his arm as it sliced through the foliage.

They broke through into the bright sunlight. Above the forest canopy now, Lyrinx's feet were a blur of motion as the prowlgrin sped over the leafy tops of the trees at full gallop. Rufus could see the rest of his splinter spread out on either side of him – orange and grey blurs in a sea of green.

Tree-cresting it was called, and it was exhilarating. Up there in the crystal air, leaping from branch to branch, the rider had to entrust his life to the skill of his mount. It was a heart-thrilling, soul-stirring experience. In fact, according to those few lancers who had also piloted a skycraft, galloping across the forest canopy on the back of a prowlgrin – with the lurch and thud of every soaring leap – was more intoxicating than any flight.

Rufus straightened in the saddle and quickly checked his equipment. Broadsword buckled firmly at his side, kitbags secured behind the saddle, knife strapped to his calf – thankfully everything was in its place. When breaking through the upper canopy, it was easy for a whipping branch or thrashing twig to snag any piece of equipment that was not firmly fastened down.

'*Keep formation,*' Cedifice reminded them all.

Rufus looked around. Lyrinx had pulled ahead of the others and he tugged lightly on the reins to check her. The prowlgrin slowed slightly and the gyle-goblins – their camouflage cloaks streaming out behind them – drew level on one side. Beyond them, was the large figure of Gaddius Felludine and his prowlgrin, Dendrix, bounding over the treetops, together with Lance-Corporal Fledder and the gnokgoblin twins, Hudflux and Holt, on their own smaller but no less powerful prowlgrins.

Glancing to the other side, the reassuring figure of Sergeant Logglimb drew level, his ironwood lance – recently sharpened and oiled – glinting in the sunlight. And directly level with him came Cedifice on his own mount, Sulix; snow-white and blue-eyed, the swiftest of all the prowlgrins in Scartree Company.

Beyond them, Rufus noticed Tam and Nixus out on the left flank, speeding ahead.

'Keep formation, Tam,' Cedifice reminded him.

Glancing over his shoulder, Tam raised a hand in acknowledgement and reined Nixus in until they were in line with the others.

Up here, tree-cresting over the top of the Deepwoods, high above the thickets, briars and dense undergrowth of the forest floor, the lancers could travel further in one hour than those on foot could manage in a week. And the denser and more impenetrable the forest below, the easier the prowlgrins found it, galloping over the closely packed treetops.

Lyrinx's nostrils flared as she exhaled bursts of air that felt as hot as steaming oaktea against the knuckles of Rufus's hand. Beneath him, Rufus could feel the prowlgrin's great round body expanding and contracting as she filled her lungs with rasping gulps of air. The creature's huge legs flexed and thrummed as the sensitive toes of her feet, splayed wide, sped over the uppermost branches of the trees, causing them to buck and sway in their wake.

Flocks of screeching berry-finches and brightly coloured skullpeckers rose from their perches and scattered before the line of lancers like river spume on an Edgewater current. And from the treetops all around, the forest echoed with the hoarse cries of weezits, the barking alarm-calls of fromps and the squealing of agitated quarms. Tree-cresting might be a speedy way of crossing the vast tracts of the Deepwoods, Rufus realized, but it was also one of the noisiest, alerting everything and everyone in the forest below to their presence.

After an hour or so, and with Lyrinx beginning to tire beneath Rufus, the order came through.

'*Form line.*' Cedifice's voice, as calm and resonant as ever, sounded in Rufus's head. '*Mid-branch canter.*'

Rufus pulled the reins gently to the left and Lyrinx leaned over, one eye peering down through the canopy of leaves as she slowed. Then, following Sergeant Logglimb who was up in front, and with the gyle-goblins falling in behind, Rufus and Lyrinx dropped down into the dappled depths. Rufus stood in the stirrups as they fell, then took the jolt as Lyrinx landed on a broad branch far below.

Ahead of him, Sergeant Logglimb, Cedifice and Tam urged their prowlgrins along the branch in a line. Behind Rufus, the tree juddered as the Gyles, the twins Holt and Hudflux and Lance-Corporal Fledder all landed, their sweating prowlgrins blowing noisily. Rufus twitched the reins and Lyrinx set off in large bounds after the prowlgrins in front.

They snaked through the middle branches of the trees in a sinuous line, like a hunting hover worm, a ripple running along the column now and again as one prowlgrin jumped after the other from tree to tree. Slower, but far quieter down here in the shadow-filled branches – apart from the odd silver-backed quarm whooping at them as they passed – the lancers made steady progress. In the saddle, although Rufus trusted to his prowlgrin to make the leaps from branch to branch as sure-footed as ever, he still had plenty to do.

Peering ahead, he ducked and swivelled as overhanging branches and foliage sped past in a blur. The air filled with the sweet smell of bruised pine needles and crushed leaves. Occasionally, an acorn-laden sprig or leafy bough would catch Rufus a glancing blow to the helmet or arm, but the long hours of 'branch practice' in the training slings back at the Scartree had served him well.

Deeper into the forest they cantered, Tam at the front of the line, calculating their direction from the sunlight hitting the tree-trunks, heading further and further south. Finally, as the shadows lengthened, the light faded and the forest filled with the echoing calls of night creatures, Sergeant Logglimb gave Cedifice a nod.

'*Splinter, halt!*' The waif passed on the order. '*Make roost for the night.*'

The Fifth Splinter reined in their prowlgrins and came to a halt in the spreading branches of a dark-elm. The prowlgrins immediately started purring and thrumming their feet on the glistening branches beneath them.

'Perfect spot,' announced Sergeant Logglimb, dismounting and patting his prowlgrin, an orange giant called Pheddix. 'Go ahead, boy, oil those toes of yours. You've earned it.'

'*Time to rise, Fifth Splinter!*'

Roused to wakefulness by the sound of the waif's voice in his head, Rufus sat up and yawned sleepily. His muscles ached from the exertions of the previous day's ride, but it was a pleasant feeling and he felt well-rested – despite a night filled with dreams of ducking branches and leaping from tree-top to treetop. He rubbed the sleep from his eyes and saw Cedifice and Sergeant Logglimb perched on an upper branch of the darkelm, peering out into the distance, already busy calculating the route of that day's gallop. Above their heads, the bright blue sky twinkled between the dense foliage of the over-head canopy like a mass of jewels.

'Come on, out of those hammocks, you idle lot!' boomed Hulm Logglimb's deep voice. 'Before a rot-sucker has you for breakfast.'

Rufus threw himself enthusiastically into the morning routine of the deep patrol. He groomed Lyrinx and fed her with the rations of dried offal from his forage bag. He rolled up his hammock and strapped it securely to the saddle, and checked over his equipment for any damage caused by twigs and branches. Then he joined the others at the hanging-brazier, where the Gyles and Degg Fledder had prepared a breakfast of cobbley – a lancers' favourite, consisting of fried woodyams, wild mushrooms, kaleaf and chopped rashers of smoked tilder. It was washed down with oaktea. Half an hour later, with their provisions packed and their stomachs full, the Fifth Splinter set off again.

They started at a brief gallop, but soon dropped down to a mid-branch canter for the rest of the morning and into the afternoon. Then, as the sun dropped lower in the sky, the forest began to thin, and they descended first to the lower branches and then to the forest floor itself.

'*Single file,*' Cedifice whispered inside Rufus's head. '*Close order. No talking.*'

The prowlgrins bunched together and padded through the forest. Around them, the mottled-barked, sickly-looking trees with their twisted branches and patchy leaves thinned out further and the soft dark earth began to give off an increasingly stale and dank odour as the prowlgrins' toes sank into it.

As they trotted on, and the gaps between the trees widened, Rufus noticed that the sounds of the forest creatures that had surrounded them ever since they'd set out on patrol the morning before had died away. Now the forest was eerily silent, apart from the snuffling breaths of the prowlgrins, who had grown nervous and skittish.

Finally Sergeant Logglimb raised his lance and pointed to a clump of bleached trees with yellow, diseased-looking foliage just ahead.

'*Roost the prowlgrins and dismount,*' Cedifice relayed the order.

Tam and Rufus exchanged worried looks as they urged their jittery prowlgrins up into the branches after the others. Moments later, they landed on a white-barked branch, dismounted and peered out through the yellow leaves.

The scene before them was one of utter desolation. They were in a tree on the very edge of what, Rufus realized, was the old Foundry Glades – the Foundry Glades that had risen up many years ago, around the time that the Free Glades themselves were beginning. But the two places, Rufus knew from the records of the librarians, could not have been more different.

What had started as a single forest forge in a small glade, set up by Hemuel Spume to provide passing goblin tribes with pots and pans, had developed into a sprawling mass of glades, full of roaring furnaces which voraciously consumed the trees all round them. Before long, the Foundry Glades had destroyed vast swathes of forestland and become one great, polluted blot on the face of the Deepwoods.

Where the Free Glades represented freedom, the Foundry Glades had embraced slavery – at one point forcing even those most noble of creatures, the banderbears, into a brutal life of forced labour. Where the Free Glades existed in harmony with their surroundings, the Foundry Glades destroyed the forest and poisoned the earth. Where the Council of the Free Glades decreed that the land belonged to no one, but that the fruits of the land belonged to everyone, the handful of black-hearted furnace masters who ruled the Foundry Glades were interested only in exploiting their fellow creatures for profit . . .

In short, whereas the Free Glades had always been a beacon of shining light that shone for all the poor, the weak and the downtrodden who wished to start a new life, for any who ended up in the rank mills and dark forges of the Foundry Glades the light of hope was snuffed out for ever. Just reading about the place on those long evenings in his father's study at the academy at Lake Landing, had been enough to cause Rufus childhood nightmares. Now, here he was, on the very edge of those infamous glades. Swallowing hard, Rufus stared down.

At the centre of the great clearing were row upon row of foundries crouched in the dead earth, their blackened chimneys – some cracked, some fractured, some reduced to ugly stumps – pointing to the sky like broken fingers. Some of the forges still had piles of stripped logs outside them, unburned and abandoned. To the right were the slave-huts with their open sides and central pillars, the chains and manacles that had deprived so many of their freedom still hanging from rusting iron rings. And far ahead, beyond the forges and foundries, was a huge ruin of a building: the Palace of the Furnace Masters.

Once it had been a magnificent edifice with a castellated roof, elegant twisting chimneys and mullioned windows. Like everything else, however, it had been abandoned. Now there were tiles missing from the roof and black cavities where the windows had been; the chimneys were broken and stubby, while the ornately carved Counting House at its western end had collapsed into a ramshackle heap of beams and rubble.

The power of the evil furnace masters had been smashed once and for all after the catastrophic defeat of their giant war-machines during the war for the Free Glades. Hemuel Spume, their leader, had perished when his glade-eater had plunged into the depths of the North Lake in sight of New Undertown, and the slaves of the Foundry Glades had been freed and given a new life in the beautiful Free Glades. Rufus's father, Xanth, had fought in that war along with his best friend, Rook Barkwater, a legendary Freeglade lancer.

'What a terrible place,' whispered Tam, peering over Rufus's shoulder, his face ashen white.

'Gather round, Fifth Splinter,' Sergeant Logglimb ordered in a quiet voice.

Rufus and Tam joined Hudflux, Holt, Lance-Corporal Fledder, Cedifice and Gaddius on the higher branches of the tree, where the sergeant surveyed the scene. The Gyles remained with the nervous, jittery prowlgrins and began camouflaging them carefully with spider-silk nets.

'The prowlgrins are spooked, so we're better off on foot,' said Logglimb, his voice calm and measured. 'Fledder, take the twins and scout out the furnaces to the east. Cedifice, Gaddius and I will search the slave-huts on the western fringe. You two . . .' He turned to Tam and Rufus. 'Think you can handle that tumbledown ruin in the middle?' He nodded towards the Palace of the Furnace Masters.

'Yes, sergeant,' Rufus replied, and nudged his friend.

'Y . . . yes, sergeant,' replied Tam, his face, if anything, even whiter than it had been a moment before.

'Good,' said Logglimb, unsheathing his sword. 'Remember, we're scouting for any sign of recent activity – footprints, churned-up earth, campfire ash . . . Anything. And listen out for Cedifice at *all* times.'

The lancers nodded.

Sergeant Logglimb touched the banderbear badge on his tunic with his fist. 'Freeglader,' he whispered.

'Freeglader,' the lancers of Fifth Splinter replied.

'*Move out!*' Cedifice gave the silent command.

The lancers, their swords unsheathed – except for Hudflux and Holt, who carried their crossbows at the ready – climbed silently down the tree and spread out into the eerie, deserted Foundry Glades.

Rufus and Tam made their way between the mounds of slag and piles of blackened timber that fringed a rough track, beaten flat by countless slave feet and rutted by heavy carts that hauled timber and ore-laden rock. The heavy silence was broken only by the crunch of their footsteps on the polluted earth and a soft wailing sound caused by the light breeze whistling through the black mouths of the open furnaces and out of the rusting chimneys above.

'It's as if the dead are whispering to us, warning us . . .' Tam began, his eyes dark and haunted-looking.

Rufus put a reassuring hand on his shoulder. 'It

doesn't help to think like that, Tam,' he said softly. 'Not in a place like this. We've got a job to do . . .' He nodded towards the Palace of the Furnace Masters up ahead.

As they approached it, they could see that the once magnificent building was even more of a ruin than it had first appeared. The metal-panelled doors at the entrance hung off their hinges, the mullioned windows had all been smashed, while the gaping cracks that ran down the outside walls were so deep that it looked as if the entire building could collapse at any moment.

'Come on,' said Rufus, trying to sound braver than he felt. 'Let's scout it out.'

With Rufus in front and Tam following reluctantly behind, limping slightly as he climbed the steps that led into the main hall, the pair of them went in. There was a pungent smell of damp inside and they had to pick their way carefully through the debris-strewn hallway to avoid falling through the rotting floorboards and ending up with a broken leg, or worse, in the cellars below. Room by room, they checked the ground floor. They were full of ornate furniture, opulent wall-hangings and fine carpets, all rotted and mouldering away to dust.

'All that pain and suffering,' said Rufus, reaching out to a mottled green-tinged tapestry that crumbled like a dry leaf at his touch. 'For this . . .'

They left the ground floor and headed up a creaking staircase to the first floor, which was huge. Carved pillars supported a high ceiling, beneath which row after row of dusty desks with empty inkwells and abandoned quills were neatly arranged. The meticulous columns of expenditure and profit recorded on barkscrolls had rotted to piles of brown mulch beneath each desk.

'Much good it did them,' said Tam, scattering a pile of rotten ledger-scrolls with the toe of his boot.

They carefully climbed another wobbly staircase and, taking the corridor to the left, ended up in an even more opulent part of the palace. They entered a vast hall with rugs on the floors, silver-theaded tapestries on the walls and intricate ceiling mouldings overhead, decorated with gold. Even though the missing tiles meant that rain had got in, rotting the carpets and eating into the plaster, the former grandeur of the place was unmistakable.

'This must be where Hemuel Spume himself lived,' said Rufus, looking around with horrified fascination, 'while his slaves outside died in their hundreds from overwork and foundry croup.'

'What do you think's in there?' wondered Tam, pointing to a small, rounded door at the end of the hall. 'His treasure room perhaps?'

The pair of them crossed the tiled floor, their footfalls echoing round the high ceilings as they went.

Rufus grasped the door-handle, half-expecting the room to be locked. With a soft creak, though, the door opened and they found themselves in a small tiled room. There were shelves set into an alcove, crowded with row upon row of bottled unguents and salves, thick with dust, and in the centre of the room a copper cauldron with pipes, pressure gauges, dials and levers sprouting from its rusting sides.

But that wasn't what made Rufus and Tam recoil in horror . . .

Staring back at them, his knobbly oversized skull just visible over the rim of the cauldron was the skeleton of a waif. Rufus approached and peered inside. The sides of the cauldron were blackened and scorched, and marked with deep scratches from the waif's puny hands as he had fought to

climb out. The waif's empty eye-sockets peered up at him, his jaws fixed in a silent scream; his rigid arm-bones reaching out in a desperate pleading gesture.

'What do you suppose happened to him?' Tam wondered, appalled.

'We'll never know,' said Rufus, turning away. 'Come on, Tam, let's get out of here.'

Back outside, they paused for a moment in the gathering gloom. Rufus spotted Hudflux and Holt in the distance, skirting round the looming shapes of the foundries, crossbows in hand. On the other side of the glade, Logglimb, Gaddius and Cedifice emerged from a long slave-hut and entered another.

'Look!' said Tam. 'Round there, behind the palace . . .'

Rufus followed his gaze. Deep ruts – recent, by the look of them – led away behind the ruins. They followed them and found a wide courtyard with stables leading off it on three sides. Several contained ornate carriages, their axles broken, now lurching on their sides like stricken hammelhorns. But the main stable – huge and cavernous as a barn, with great pillars supporting its thatched roof – was empty. Rufus and Tam entered it.

There was thick, fresh straw on the floor and a large bucket of sallowdrop fruit. Heavy chains with manacles at the ends hung down from the roof beams, and there were large metal rings bolted to the floor. There was blood splattered on two of the walls – brown, dried, but clearly recent – and a broken, splintered drinking trough that appeared to have been flung with some force at a third . . .

'Come on, Tam,' said Rufus. 'We'd better report this to the sergeant . . .'

His words were cut short by the sound of Cedifice's voice, whispering inside his head.

'*Fifth Splinter!*' he said. '*Disappear.*'

Rufus turned to Tam who, like all the other lancers in the Foundry Glades, had been alerted by the same warning. Without a word, they followed the waif's order.

Tam rolled into the shadows in the corner of the stables, burying himself in a thin covering of straw. Rufus ran to one of the pillars and shinned up it into the roof rafters where he froze, still as a statue.

Moments later, two figures appeared below him in the stables. One was a tall black-plumed shryke with piercing yellow eyes and long curved beak, gleaming ebony black. Around her feathered neck she wore a necklace of shiny whetstones, worn smooth from honing her razor-sharp talons. Below the necklace, she wore a belt slung over one shoulder, from which four small silvery globes hung on thin silver chains. Her long robe was black and faded and appeared to be made up of a number of tunics stitched together, each bearing the grubby white emblem of a screaming gloamglozer. In her claws she gripped an evil-looking flail, which she cracked impatiently.

'So much for your theory, Squive,' she screeched hoarsely. 'Good riddance, I say.'

The shryke's companion took a step forward into the stables. Rufus looked down from the rafters. The creature was tiny, with blotchy red skin and a round, bloated body supported on thin, spindly legs. His small eyes were set wide apart on either side of a round, low-browed head with a sharp, beaklike nose jutting out over a huge lower jaw. He looked like a cross between a Mire raven and a halitoad – yet the pointed, tufted ears on either side of his head were the sure sign that he was one of the rare, seldom encountered, goblin types; a red dwarf.

So rare in fact were these creatures that Rufus had only ever seen drawings of the tiny goblins in the treatises in his father's library at Lake Landing. Like so many of the strangest, least-known creatures, they came from the Nightwoods, far beyond the thorn forests.

'Pity,' the red dwarf wheezed. His voice had the hooting quality of a nightowl. 'Thought the sallow-drops might tempt it . . .'

The shryke kicked the bucket over and the soft fruit tumbled out across the floor, one rolling towards the corner where Tam lay concealed beneath the straw. Suddenly the light in the stables seemed to dim. Rufus glanced over towards the entrance and almost rolled off the rafter he was clinging to. Behind the shryke and the red dwarf, there was a crowd of silent, sepia-coloured figures. The hairs on the back of Rufus's neck stood on end.

The figures were dressed in a wide variety of clothes of all styles, but all faded and rotting and the same inky brown colour. Some wore old-fashioned sky pirate coats with battered breast-plates and broken parawings. Others had goblin capes of half-rotted animal pelts, or the conical hats of merchants, or tattered traders' aprons. One even wore the rusted armour of an ancient knight academic, hundreds of years old.

But it wasn't so much their clothes that told Rufus where they'd come from, but their faces. They were horrific. Sunken, shrivelled, half rotted away – teeth, noses, ears, sometimes jaw-bones were missing or hanging hideously by a thread . . . They were the faces of those poor sky-cursed souls who had become lost in the Twilight Woods.

Occasionally, a figure might stumble accidentally out of those terrible woods and find their way to the Free Glades, half-crazed and in search of forgotten

memories. With their hauntingly blue eyes and silent demeanour, survivors of the treacherous Twilight Woods were known – behind their backs, and in horrified whispers – as death-cheaters.

Few, if any, Freegladers envied them. Rufus's father had spoken of one he'd once met, an old sky pirate who'd spent his remaining days silently in the corner of a tavern in New Undertown. Rufus shuddered. He'd never seen a death-cheater before – and now here were fifty of them standing below him, their dank, rotten odour rising up in the rafters and making him want to gag. He bit his lip and looked away.

'We'd better get back,'

hooted the red dwarf. 'The armourer will be expecting us.'

'You heard him,' screeched the shryke, clacking her flail at the death-cheaters. 'Back to the armoury, you stinking sacks of bones!'

She tossed them hunks of raw meat dipped in phraxdust, the tempting morsels with which she had lured them from the Twilight Woods, and which ensured that their immortality would be prolonged just long enough to do her bidding. With low, moaning sighs, the chewing death-cheaters turned and shuffled out, their weapons – scythes, ancient cutlasses, goblin spears and sling-shots – rattling and clinking like ghostly wind-chimes as they went.

'Come, Squive, best not to keep the armourer waiting,' the black-plumed shryke squawked.

She held out a taloned claw. The tiny figure of the red dwarf leaped up onto it and perched there like a brooding halitoad as the pair of them left the stables.

Up in the rafters, Rufus tensed, waiting for Cedifice's orders. Outside, he could hear the death-cheaters tramping along the track from the Palace of the Furnace Masters, back through the Foundry Glades. Balancing on the roof beam, he gently parted the thatch above his head and peered out. He saw the horrific band making their way towards the forest fringe, the tall figure of the black shryke bringing up the rear.

The shambling figures began disappearing into the darkening forest, only for the shryke to stop suddenly and look about her, beak held high, as if sniffing the air. The red dwarf seemed to lean up and say something and, as Rufus watched, transfixed, the shryke cackled and screeched, 'Better safe than sorry!'

She reached for one of the metal globes hanging from her belt and unhooked it. Then, with a great arcing movement of one feathered arm, she hurled it at the clump of trees at the glade's edge.

Rufus saw a flash of blinding light followed by a loud crack, and to his horror a ball of vivid yellow flames engulfed the trees.

With a cackle of hideous laughter, the shryke disappeared into the forest. For a moment, all Rufus could hear was the sound of blood pumping in his head and his own rapid breathing. Then Cedifice's voice broke through into the shocked blankness of his mind.

'Fifth Splinter! Muster!'

. CHAPTER FOUR .

THE ARMOURER

The lancers of Fifth Splinter stood before the blazing tree, open-mouthed. The diseased foliage fizzed and sparked, blackened tree limbs snapping off and shooting high into the sky as the flames ignited the buoyant sap within. From close by, the high-pitched yelping barks of panicked prowlgrins filled the air, along with the stench of charred wood and burned flesh. Cedifice the waif wrung his hands together, the veins in his paper-thin ears vivid in the hideous yellow light.

'The Gyles,' he whispered. 'They're dead.'

Sergeant Logglimb turned to Rufus and Tam, his face impassive. 'See to the prowlgrins,' he said simply.

Rufus and Tam broke away from the rest of the splinter and dashed towards the yelping, which was coming from a clump of trees to the left of the inferno. Rufus arrived first, bent down and clasped his hands together to give Tam a hoist up to the

lower branches of the closest tree, then scampered up after him. They climbed quickly, neither speaking, until they reached the upper branches of the stunted copperwood where – fur camouflaged against the yellow and orange leaves – there were five cowering prowlgrins.

'Steady, there,' Rufus whispered. 'It's all right. Everything's all right now.'

As he was pulling himself up onto the roost branch one of the prowlgrins leaped forwards, his huge mouth wide open to reveal rows of razor-sharp teeth. Rufus licked his fingers and reached out his hand. The prowlgrin breathed in. Instantly, his mouth closed and the snarls and growls turned to a deep, throaty purr. Beside him, Tam did the same to the terrified prowlgrin next to him.

'That's it,' whispered Rufus in a soothing voice. 'Steady, now. We're here . . .'

He reached out and traced a finger round the flaring nostrils of the third beast, and then the fourth. Tam reached the fifth and turned back to his friend.

'Lyrinx, Nixus . . .' he said, the relief plain in his voice as their own prowlgrins nuzzled against them, purring contentedly.

'Luxus, Dendrix and Dex,' Rufus identified the other prowlgrins on the branch. 'Which means . . .'

'*The other five prowlgrins perished with the Gyles,*'

Cedifice's voice sounded in their heads. '*The splinter has lost half its mounts.*'

Rufus and Tam climbed onto their prowlgrins, gathered the reins of the three others and leaped down the copperwood. As they did so, from over to their right, there came a creaking, splintering sound followed by a loud *whoosh* as the blazing tree – its bubbling sap now buoyant – tore itself out of the ground by the roots and shot up into the darkening sky like a shooting star.

'Sky rest their souls,' muttered Gaddius Felludine, unbuckling his helmet and cupping it in his great hands.

'Listen up,' Sergeant Logglimb barked.

The order went some way to concealing his own sense of loss. The gyle-goblins had been with him ever since they'd enlisted, fresh-faced and honey-fed, straight from their colony. The three of them had turned into the best trackers in Scartree Company and had served the Free Glades well in hundreds of patrols and skirmishes.

There was the occasion at the Battle of Lufwood Mount when he would have lost his life to a blood-frenzied shryke had it not been for the Gyles' deadly lances; and the time the three of them had laid a trap for one of the great lumbering war machines known as glade-eaters, during the Battle of New Undertown, and set it ablaze. He swallowed hard.

And then also to have lost his beloved Pheddix . . .

'*Sergeant Logglimb.*' The waif's soft voice sounded inside the sergeant's head.

He looked round, momentarily unsettled, to see the rest of the splinter – seven lancers and five prowlgrins – staring back at him.

'We . . . *um,*' he murmured, gathering his thoughts. 'Yes, we're going to have to double up. On the prowlgrins.'

He turned to the corporal, his eyes glistening, but a stony expression set hard on his face. 'Degg, I'll ride with you on Luxus,' he said gruffly. 'Gaddius and Cedifice, you can ride together on Dendrix. Holt, you take your brother on Dex . . .'

The lancers nodded grimly and climbed onto the prowlgrins, their long ironwood lances clasped firmly in their fists. Sergeant Logglimb turned in the saddle and shook his own lance menacingly.

'We're going after that murdering shryke and her stinking death-cheaters. Whatever that weapon was that killed the Gyles and our brave-hearted prowlgrins, I for one won't rest until I've prised it from the dead claw of the bird-creature . . .' The sergeant turned his glittering eyes on the two young lancers. 'Tam, Rufus,' he said. 'I want you to ride on those prowlgrins of yours, faster than you've ever ridden before. You must get back to the Free Glades, and raise the roost . . .'

'The whole roost?' gasped Rufus.

That was all six companies – over four thousand lancers . . .

'Yes, the whole roost,' said Sergeant Logglimb. 'And as quickly as you can . . .' He paused and smiled grimly. 'Something tells me we're going to need all the help we can get.'

A strong wind had got up in the Foundry Glades. It came hissing through the stunted trees at the fringes of the clearing, whipping up the acrid-smelling dust and soot into angry swirls as it went.

'*Splinter, move out!*' Cedifice's voice sounded. '*Good luck, Tam. Good luck, Rufus.*'

The deep orange and brown prowlgrin, Dendrix, went first, leaping up into the tree-line with Gaddius Felludine and Cedifice on its back. Holt and Hudflux, on the skittish, blue-eyed Dex, followed. Luxus – heavyset and a paler orange – hesitated. Degg Fledder in the saddle was keeping a tight grip on his reins. Behind him, Sergeant Logglimb leaned down and cut a deep notch into the bark of a darkelm tree at the eastern edge of the glade. Then, resheathing his knife, he turned round.

'Tam, Rufus. You're to get back here with the third roost as fast as you can, then follow our tracks.' He tapped the trunk of the darkelm tree. 'I'll make them good and clear.' He touched the banderbear badge on his tunic with his fist. 'Freeglader!'

'Freeglader!' Tam and Rufus replied as Degg twitched Luxus's reins.

The great prowlgrin gave a low whinny and leaped up into the broad low branches of the neighbouring tree. Then the next. And the next. A moment later, the prowlgrin and his two riders were swallowed up in the forest, leaving the young lancers alone in the gloomy Foundry Glades.

Rufus glanced over at the notch the sergeant had carved in the tree; one end wide, the other tapering to a point. It was the simplest and most commonly used of tracking-marks – short, wedge-shaped cuts in the trunks of the smoother barked trees like silver oak and young lufwood. The point of the mark indicated the direction to follow. But there were other ways of leaving tracking-marks. Lots of them – and Rufus had learned them all.

One of the huge, ball-shaped nodules of a lullabee, for instance, could be sliced off in the direction to be followed. Ironwood pines – the lower bark too hard for a knife even to scratch – were often turned into makeshift signposts by embedding carefully pointing twigs into the seeping resin; while a length of a long, frondy branch of the sallowdrop tree could be intricately knotted to give detailed information to those who knew how to read the signs – direction of journey, number of party, rough time of day of passing by . . .

And down on the forest floor itself, there were other signs that could be left. A carefully placed pinecone on a flat stone, for example. A twist of tilder-grass. A re-positioned log . . . Whatever the method, the theory was the same. A lancer of the Free Glades could use tracking-marks to quite liter-ally make the forest talk to his fellow lancers. It was a skill prized even more highly than lancework – and, as he turned away, Rufus remembered with a jolt that the Fifth Splinter had just lost three of its most accomplished 'forest talkers' in this terrible place.

'Come on, Tam,' he called over to his friend. 'Let's get out of here.'

They travelled without easing up for the best part of three hours. It was hard going. Not only was the wind against them, but it was getting stronger with every passing minute. As late afternoon drifted into early evening, the darkening sky began to curdle. Banks of black and violet cloud, heavy with rain, rolled across the sky in waves. Huge raindrops began to drum steadily on the leaves of the forest canopy around them. Rufus pulled his green collar up round his ears and set-tled down low in the saddle as, beneath him, Lyrinx gave an excited bark and increased the pace of her treetop gallop.

There was nothing a prowlgrin liked more than a rain storm. In the wild, whole herds of prowlgrins would be gripped by the frenzy of the howling wind and driving rain, leave their perches and go galloping off through the storm-lashed forest. They were made for it. Thick oily fur kept them dry, hooded eyelids shielded their eyes, while the spongy pads beneath their feet and the clawed grip of their paws ensured there was no danger of the creatures slipping.

Rufus gripped onto the saddle as tightly as he could, his lance strapped securely behind him like the mast of a skycraft. The rain was blinding and, with the dense black clouds closing overhead, night was falling fast. Behind him, Rufus could hear Nixus panting and blowing as he kept pace, Tam urging his prowlgrin on. Suddenly, in front of them, night turned to dazzling day as a flash of lightning cut down through the sky.

'Sky blast it!' Rufus cursed, reining in Lyrinx, and hastily turning in the saddle to unbuckle his iron-wood lance.

Wind and rain, a lancer could cope with; hail, sleet – snow, even. But lightning . . .

Lightning was a different matter. Lightning was swift, unpredictable and deadly – especially up here, tree-cresting over the forest canopy with a lance sticking up behind you like a lightning rod.

'Rufus!' Tam's voice rang out, just before the crack of thunder broke overhead. 'Forest floor!'

Rufus leaned forward, his face inches from Lyrinx's blowing nostrils, and tugged hard on the reins. In answer, the prowlgrin plunged down into the dark forest below, Rufus feeling the tree's leafy limbs whipping past him like grabbing fingers as the two of them fell. Lyrinx landed on a branch and gripped tight as lightning flashed across the sky high above them. Moments later, Nixus landed on a branch to the left.

Tam winced as he dismounted and pulled the oiled tilder leather blanket from his saddle pack. Rufus watched him. As if reading Rufus's thoughts, Tam shrugged, pulled the blanket over his shoulders and settled down on the branch between his prowlgrin's feet. Great raindrops splattered around them and the thunder – now directly overhead – seemed to make the whole forest tremble.

'Lightning,' Tam said simply. 'Get some sleep while we wait it out.'

Rufus nodded and, neither unbuckling his sword nor unstrapping his helmet so as to be ready to leave at a moment's notice, pulled his own oiled blanket from his pack. He settled himself between Lyrinx's feet, the great round body of his prowlgrin shielding him from the rain which dripped down through the forest canopy. He listened for a while to

the sound of the heavy
raindrops splashing onto
Lyrinx's back, and to her
soft rumbling breathing,
before falling into a heavy
dreamless sleep.

Rufus opened his eyes. He
sat bolt upright and
looked around. There was
nothing. It was like staring
at a white woollen blan-
ket. The forest, the tree,
even the branch he was
sitting on, were enveloped
in a thick, impenetrable
bank of fog.

'Tree cloud,' murmured
Rufus, slamming his fist
against the branch in frustration. Above him, Lyrinx
awoke with a start, a low
growl rumbling in the
back of her throat.

'Rufus, are you awake?'
Tam's voice sounded
through the swirling
whiteness.

Rufus got to his feet and stretched with a dispirited groan. Not only was the fog impenetrable, it was also freezing. He felt chilled to the bone and it was all he could do to stop his teeth chattering.

'Yes, I'm awake,' he said miserably. '*Now* what are going to do?'

They both knew the problem they faced. The thunderstorm had drenched the warm forest floor with icy rain, causing great banks of freezing fog to rise up and envelop the trees. This tree cloud could, with a strong prevailing wind, be blown up into the sky in a couple of hours. Alternatively, in the still dank air, tree cloud could smother the forest for days with a blinding blanket of white. This forced even experienced lancers down to the forest floor, where they'd have to inch their way forward through the fog at a slime-mole's pace.

'You heard the sergeant.' Tam loomed up suddenly through the whiteness onto Rufus's branch. He crouched next to his friend, grimacing with pain, the dark circles beneath his eyes made darker by the extreme pallor of his skin. 'We've got to get back to Scartree and raise the other companies – the whole roost – as fast as we can.'

'Are you all right, Tam? Is your leg playing up? Let me take a look . . .' Rufus began, putting a hand on Tam's shoulder – only to have it shrugged off.

'There's no time for that. We have to go on; take our chances tree-cresting . . .'

'In this cloud?' Rufus was shocked. 'But Tam, haven't you noticed? There's not a breath of wind. If we tree-crest in this, we won't be able to steer the prowlgrins. They'll be jumping blind to whatever branch is within reach.' He shook his head. 'We could end up miles off course . . .'

'Do you think I don't know that?' said Tam irritably. Rufus could tell he was in pain. 'But we have no choice. You said it yourself, Rufus, there's not a breath of wind. This tree cloud could last for days. We've got to try to run through it.'

Rufus nodded. 'You're right, of course,' he said, trying to sound cheerful. 'We'll have to take a chance. The sergeant's depending on us.'

'Let's move out. And we'd better use tethers or we'll lose each other.' Tam smiled, handing Rufus one end of a long length of barkrope, before disappearing back into the fog.

There was a rustling of leaves, followed by Nixus's bark. Rufus climbed onto Lyrinx's back and fastened the rope to the saddle.

'Ready?' Tam called through the blanket of white.

'Ready,' replied Rufus.

He heard Tam's prowlgrin kick off from the branch above, and urged Lyrinx on with a twitch of the reins. The prowlgrin flexed her powerful legs and flared her nostrils, both eyes swivelling upwards, trying to see through the cloud to the canopy above. With a grunt of effort, they took off, Rufus hunched over, covering his head as they crashed through branches.

Suddenly they were up and galloping, the tether tied to the saddle slackening then going taut with each bound. Looking ahead, Rufus could see nothing but the white blanket of fog. Beside him, the grey forms of Tam and Nixus – almost close enough to touch, but indistinct and blurred – kept pace with Lyrinx, bounding over the treetops. Beneath him, the prowlgrin swerved this way and that as she felt her way forward from branch to branch with incredible speed.

With no sun and no horizon visible, it was impossible to tell in what direction they were travelling – but whatever it was, they were travelling fast. With a bit of luck, they would outrun the tree cloud and be able to get their bearings. If not, they risked galloping in circles all day, getting nowhere. Rufus bit his lip, and checked his equipment.

'Good girl,' he whispered, patting Lyrinx's side. 'You'll get us out of here, won't you, girl?'

Two, three, or was it four hours later? Rufus couldn't tell; they were still tree-cresting blindly in the endless cloud. Rufus had tried to keep their spirits up, calling across to Tam, reminding him of the training-cradles back at Scartree where they'd both dreamed, one day, of tree-cresting on their very own prowlgrins . . .

But Tam was clearly in pain. His replies short and terse, he needed to concentrate all his effort in staying in the saddle and balancing as Nixus lurched and swayed, Rufus realized. Finally, as the light began to fade towards the end of that freezing dispiriting day, Rufus knew they had to call a halt. He was about to shout across to Tam when he noticed something. Ahead to their left, there was a curious golden glow, faint but just discernible through the white blankness.

'Do you see that?' called out Rufus.

'Yes,' groaned Tam, with effort. 'We'd better head towards it. At least that way, we'll know we're not going round in circles.'

They tree-crested for another hour, until the glow was unmistakable in the sky ahead of them and the icy white cloud actually seemed to be thinning a bit.

'That's it,' said Tam, hoarsely. Rufus could see him quite clearly now, doubled up in his saddle. '. . . Can't go on. Must . . . rest.'

Rufus and Lyrinx followed Tam and Nixus down into the mid-branches, landing – to the prowlgrins' pleasure – in a spreading darkelm. Rufus dismounted and helped his friend out of the saddle, shocked to see how exhausted and ashen-faced he looked. Tam slumped down on the branch, leaning back against Nixus's soft heaving side.

'I'm going to take a look at that leg,' said Rufus firmly, unstrapping a saddlebag and kneeling next to his friend.

This time, Tam didn't protest, but merely groaned when Rufus eased his boot off. The wound wasn't infected, Rufus was glad to see, but had clearly been rubbed raw against the inside of his boot as Tam rode. He must have been in agony. Rufus shook his head as he applied a thick layer of hyleberry salve and gently bandaged the leg.

'That should do for now,' he said, 'but you'll need to rest. We'll set off again at dawn . . .'

But Tam didn't reply. He was snoring gently beneath the protective bulk of Nixus.

Rufus stood up and turned to Lyrinx, loosening the saddle strap a notch and feeding her a handful of dried thousandfoot grubs from his pack. Looking up he could see the evening sky through the branches of the trees.

'Well done, girl.' He patted the prowlgrin. 'We've outrun the tree cloud. But as to where we are, your guess is as good as mine.'

Although it was now dark, the forest round them was bathed in the golden glow, the source of which, it seemed to Rufus, was just a little way ahead to the east. Curious, he left the prowlgrins gently purring over the sleeping Tam, and climbed down the dark-elm to the forest floor. Stooping at the base of the tree, he drew his knife and cut a wedge before setting off, careful to keep his bearings.

A notch in a green birch and a copperthorn later, Rufus found himself on the edge of a new clearing. Ahead of him, the stumps of recently felled trees stretched away towards a solitary furnace, its lone chimney crooked and twisted like an arthritic finger pointing up at the sky. Around it were huge pieces of rusting metal, the remains of bellows, giant cogs, treadles, truncated metal tubes and unattached pistons. Rufus had seen pieces of metal just like them in the ruins of the evil Foundry Glades. Around the furnace, the crooked chimney belching a thin line of smoke up into the glowing sky, a ghostly army was at work.

Death-cheaters – hundreds of them – fed the massive furnace, passing log after log, one to the other, in a long chain that stretched from the vast heaps of timber piled in the corner of the glade to the roaring mouth of the furnace at its centre. Others operated two giant cauldrons to one side; lowering huge pieces of rusting metal into one, pouring white hot metal into long moulds from the other. Still more of the shuffling half-dead creatures were carefully knocking the cooled metal from the moulds, before stringing up the small globes on long racks that stretched from the furnace to a rough timber cabin on the far side of the glade.

Thousands of metal globes twinkling in the glow, lined up in rows . . .

Rufus shuddered. Just like the rusting metal, he'd seen globes like these before, back in the Foundry Glades, strung from the belt of the black-plumed shryke. It was one of these globes – or rather what it contained – that had killed the three Gyles. Now here he was, crouched behind an ironwood tree, staring at thousands of them in this strange new glade.

This must have been how the old Foundry Glades began, he thought, with one furnace consuming the forest around it like a cancer. One chimney becoming two, then ten, then twenty; all belching out evil-smelling smoke – and weapons of war. And now it was beginning all over again. This new foundry, feed-ing off the scrap metal of the first, dragged here through the forest by . . .

Just then, on the far side of the stockade, there was a disturbance in the trees. A moment later a vast creature emerged, its misshapen head curved into giant tusks on either side of small stalk-like eyes. It was immense, with huge legs supporting a shallow ribcage and stunted-looking arms. Angry welts and weals covered its thick neck and bony back. It was followed a moment later by a second, as big as the first, but with a narrow head fringed by two crests, one above each of its sunken eyes, and a fang-studded mouth that hung exhaustedly open. As Rufus stared, a third came after it, its head embedded between its massive shoulders and a single tusk rising from a carapace-like brow.

The three of them were shackled together by a stiff leather harness that was strapped over their shoulders and round the vast girth of their chests. Taut ropes stretched back into the forest; ropes which, as the creatures lurched forwards – their backs bent and faces straining – revealed themselves to be attached to a huge, flat, and clearly immensely heavy timber cart.

'Nameless ones,' gasped Rufus.

As they came closer, he saw that the creatures were not alone. Hopping from the broad shoulders of one, to the stooped back of another, and onto the horned skull of the third, was the red dwarf. He was clutching a pair of vicious-looking pincer-spikes in one hand, which he wielded with malicious ferocity. He pinched the first creature's ear and stabbed at the

lolling tongue of the second, which screwed its eyes up with pain and redoubled its efforts. The third threw back its shoulders, its tusked head bellowing with exertion, only to be rewarded by a vicious stab in the back from the red dwarf.

Slowly, the heavy timber cart emerged from the shadow of the trees and cast a brilliant glow over the tree-stumps around it. Rufus shielded his eyes against the glare. Strapped securely on the back of the cart was a huge, jagged shard of solidified lightning. Rufus could hardly believe the evidence of his own eyes. The timber cart contained the most precious substance in all the Edgelands.

'Sacred stormphrax,' he breathed.

Rufus had lost count of the times he'd pored over the barkscrolls in the library at Lake Landing, reading of the legendary quests mounted by the knights academic of Old Sanctaphrax. How they'd trained for years. How they'd learned to ride and sail and storm-chase . . . And how they'd set off in their sky ships for the Twilight Woods, chasing those storms that disgorged their lightning into the golden depths – lightning which, the moment it entered the eternal twilight, solidified into a glowing jagged shard.

Hurtling down and striking the forest floor, only the very tip of the lightning bolt would penetrate the ground. But it was enough. Though of normal weight in twilight, in the absolute darkness of the earth, the tip would become heavier than a thousand ironwood pines and begin to sink, ever deeper, below the ground. Slowly at first, but rapidly speeding up as more and more of the lightning bolt entered the darkness, the huge jagged shard would bury itself in the earth. Finally, with a sharp crack, the entire lightning bolt of pure stormphrax would, after a few minutes, disappear below the Twilight Woods, leaving only a thin powder of sepia dust on the forest floor.

A thousand times it must have happened down the centuries. Ten thousand . . . Who could say? The Twilight Woods had swallowed each and every bolt of stormphrax into its dark earth. The questing knight academics' only hope of recovering any of the precious substance had been to be there when the lightning struck, then breaking what shards they could from the jagged bolt before it disappeared. No wonder it was so rare and precious a substance.

But Rufus knew that all this had happened during the First Age of Flight. The ancient knights and their sky ships were no more. Nobody had successfully chased a storm over the Twilight Woods for nearly a hundred years, had they?

The heavy cart, dragged by the poor tormented creatures, came to a creaking halt before the rough log cabin on the far side of the glade. The red dwarf scrambled down from the shoulders of one of the nameless ones and rapped on the thick, copperwood door. In answer, the door was thrown open and the light from what seemed like a dozen lamps flooded out from the cabin's interior.

A tall thin figure, slightly stooped and dressed from head to foot in protective hood, apron, gauntlets and boots, stepped out. He was followed by the black-plumed shryke and at least twelve hulking hammerhead goblins. With their large neck-rings, elaborate tattoos and glittering array of serrated axes, swords and spears, Rufus could tell in an instant that these were savage Deepwoods goblins, raised far from the civilized settlements of the Goblin Nations. The figure in the heavy apron pulled off the tall coni-cal forge-hood he wore, and leered down at the shard of stormphrax, his face illuminated by its glow.

Rufus gasped.

'Getting heavier by the minute,' hooted the red dwarf, complainingly.

The black-feathered shryke reached out and grabbed a group of death-cheaters who were stumbling past in the neverending log-line to feed the furnace.

'Drop those!' she screeched, knocking the logs they were clutching to the ground with her flail. 'And take the lightning inside . . . *Careful!*' she shrieked once more, as the six death-cheaters – two skeletal mob-gnomes and four stooped figures in ragged sky-pirate greatcoats – eased the stormphrax off the cart and stumbled beneath its weight. 'Quickly, before the light goes, or we'll never shift it!'

The shryke cracked her flail over their heads. As they hauled the lightning into the stream of light from the cabin's open door, they straightened up and carried it carefully inside.

Rufus forced himself to look at the face of the figure in the apron. It had been horribly disfigured in some sort of fire or explosion, the features blasted away, leaving a fleshy mass of melted skin and scar-tissue. Only the eyes, piercingly blue, seemed to have escaped, ringed by unburned skin where goggles with eye-pieces of some sort had protected them.

'Do we have a deal?' the figure rasped through the

crooked gash that served as a mouth. 'The contents of the grain stores of the first three villages you raid come to me, plus half of any gold you find.'

'All that! Just for these?' growled the largest of the hammerhead goblins, examining the clutch of metal globes in his powerful fist. 'Sister Blackbeak said your weapons were powerful, but still . . .'

The figure turned his hideously scarred face towards the shryke. 'I paid for my discovery with my face,' he rasped. 'A few trinkets and victuals is a small price by comparison. Show our friend, Gutgurn, here . . .'

'My pleasure, armourer,' replied the shryke, bowing low.

She cracked her flail and set the six death-cheaters

who'd just emerged from the cabin stumbling out across the glade. They tripped clumsily over the tree-stumps as they went.

'Further!' she screeched. 'Further! That's right, keep going . . .'

The shryke took a metal globe from the belt at her shoulder and, closing one eye, took aim. Rufus knew what was coming next, yet couldn't tear his eyes away. The shryke swung her taloned claw in a wide arc round her head and let go. The globe flashed through the air and landed in the midst of the retreating death-cheaters. A moment later there was a flash, a loud *crack*, and all six figures were engulfed in white flames. In moments, the desiccated, half-dead creatures were reduced to ash.

'We have a deal,' said the hammerhead, and motioned to his comrades. They each took four globes and strung them from their belts. 'We'll be back for more,' he growled, 'when we've raided the Goblin Nations.'

The armourer permitted himself what, on his tortured face, passed for a smile.

'Return with the grain and the gold and I'll have some more of my phraxfires waiting for you.'

The goblins set off across the glade at a loping half-run, pausing only to look down at the remains of the death-cheaters before disappearing into the forest. Rufus turned to go. His heart was hammering away in his chest and his mouth was dry. After a day gal-loping through freezing tree cloud, all he wanted to do was curl up beneath Lyrinx in the protective branches of the darkelm tree and forget all about the horror he'd just witnessed.

But he knew he couldn't. Now, more than ever, he knew he had to get back to the Free Glades and raise the alarm.

'*Rufus? Rufus, is that you?*'

Rufus stumbled and almost cried out – but man-aged to stifle his yelp of surprise. It was Cedifice the waif's voice in his head.

Cedifice? Where are you? Rufus reached out to the waif with his thoughts as he followed his tracks back to the darkelm.

'*We're in a bad way, Rufus,*' Cedifice's voice sounded again in his head. '*Ran into a war-party of hammerheads, fifty strong. They got Gaddius, but not before he took ten or so with him. Went down fighting . . .*'

And the others? Rufus reached the notch on the green birch tree and paused.

'*Holt and Hudflux were injured when Dex was killed, and we lost Lance-Corporal Fledder when we rescued them. Sergeant Logglimb has a barbed arrow in his arm, and I've got a few cuts and scrapes – but we'll survive. Left half of the hammerheads dead in return, and shook off the rest. We're holed up in an ironwood pine on the edge of this infernal glade. I've been reading the thoughts of the armourer down there for a day now. They're not good, Rufus. And now he's armed the hammerheads. They've just passed by below . . .'*

Hold on there! Rufus arrived back at the darkelm and began to climb. Tam and I'll come and get you. We got lost in tree cloud. Lucky we did, Cedifice, or you'd be . . .'

'No.' Cedifice's voice was calm but firm. *'You must leave us now. Go back to the Free Glades and return as soon as you can with the rest of the roost. There isn't a moment to lose. The woods round here aren't safe, Rufus. They're patrolled . . .'*

Patrolled?

Rufus reached the branch and shook Tam awake.

'Is that Cedifice?' said Tam blearily. 'Or am I dreaming?'

Rufus was about to reply – but stopped, his mouth open in horror, as he stared past Tam at the treetops just beyond.

. CHAPTER FIVE .

PURSUIT

There, hunched over in their saddles, staring out of the black slits of their rusting visored helmets, twisted pipes and dials encrusting their sepia-stained breast-plates, sat seven ancient knights academic on prowlgrinback. As Rufus gripped Tam's chequerboard collar in a trembling fist and pulled him to his feet, the knights spread out into the trees in a semi-circle around them. Slowly, hardly daring to breathe, Rufus eased himself up into his prowlgrin's saddle. Tam, ashen-faced, did the same.

Lyrinx's nostrils were wide and quivering, and she kept snorting with unease. Both she and Nixus beside her could smell the strange musty odour of decay which was emanating from the half-dead figures in the trees surrounding them.

'What are they waiting for?' whispered Tam, his dark-ringed eyes wide with fear.

As if in answer, the knight in the centre rose in his

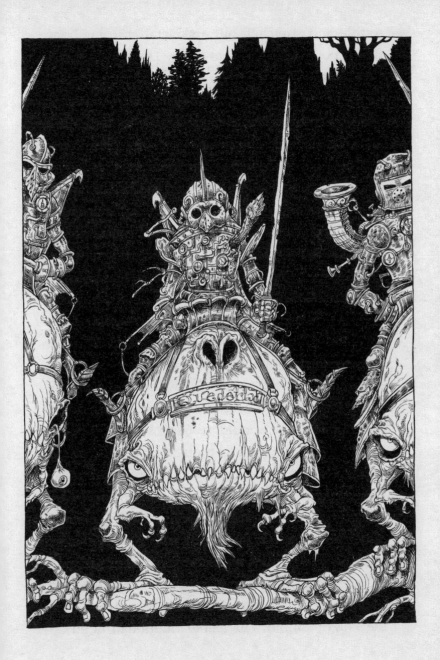

saddle and stretched out a skeletal arm, his bony
finger pointing directly at them. The prowlgrin he
rode was all skin and bone, with wild, swivelling
eyes embedded deep in his bony eye-sockets. Yet
the creature still wore the distinctive bridle, emblazoned with a nameplate, which had been fashioned
centuries before in the armouries of the Knights
Academy.

Quederix, it read, in antique letters.

Quederix's rider was in an equally pitiful state.
He was dressed in armour of a design not seen in the
Edgelands for three centuries – high-crested shoulder guards, a broad 'clamshell' helmet and an
ornately tooled breast-plate covered in a tiny filigree
of pipes and levers, all corroded and pitted.
Everything was encrusted with sepia dust. The
knight was missing an arm below the elbow and the
jagged remains of a splintered tree branch protruded from one shoulder. Whatever his injuries,
they were clearly not fatal though, for like his fellow
death-cheaters, the knight had emerged from the
Twilight Woods' immortalizing light and lived on.

If, Rufus thought bitterly, you could call the
degraded state the once noble knight academic was
now in living at all.

One thing the terrible Twilight Woods had
claimed for ever and could never be restored, was
the knight's mind. His fellow riders had fared no

better. Battered, withered and injured, they all sat slumped forwards on their once magnificent prowl-grins, craning their visored faces towards the two young lancers like a flock of starved vulpoons.

'Behold, fine knights of Sanctaphrax! Robbers! Raiders! Thieves!' The ancient knight's quavery voice rose to a high-pitched scream as he shook his bony finger accusingly at Tam and Rufus. 'They seek to steal the sacred stormphrax we have quested so long to find! Geraldius, sound the alarm! The Most High Academe must be warned!'

The knight on the far left of the semi-circle, his ragged prowlgrin perched in the quivering branches of a sallowdrop tree, raised a curved hammelhorn trumpet of antique design and lifted his visor. A skeletal face, half eaten away, stared back at Rufus as the knight put the trumpet to his shrivelled lips.

A sad and mournful note, deep and sonorous, rose into the night air. In the distance, the piercing shriek of the black-plumed shryke sounded in reply.

'Death to the phrax thieves!' screamed the ancient knight, to the hiss and grind of rusty swords being unsheathed.

'Death! Death! Death!' screamed his six companions, digging their heels into the sides of their emaciated prowlgrins.

'Forest floor!' Tam shouted across to Rufus, and the two of them twitched their reins.

Lyrinx and Nixus didn't need telling twice. They dropped like ironwood pinecones down from the great spreading branch and hit the ground running. Above them, the ancient knights' prowlgrins landed on the branch with a clatter of rusting armour and a cloud of sepia dust. One of their number – a bald prowlgrin with skin like bleached barkscrolls and one eye hanging from an empty socket on a glistening thread – misjudged his leap and came crashing down to earth.

As he hit the ground, his ribcage shattered like the timbers of a storm-wrecked sky ship. His rider, a knight in the piped-armour and heavy dials favoured at the academy during the reign of Linius Pallitax, was thrown high in the air. With a ghostly shriek, the knight jabbed at a lever on his breast-plate and activated his parawings.

Rufus glanced back to see the knight, his black wings spread wide behind him, swooping down through the air. Like a hungry rotsucker, he landed on Tam's shoulders and clung fast. With a loud yelp of alarm, Nixus leaped high in the air, over Rufus's head. As they sped past in a blur of movement, Rufus glimpsed the gauntleted hand of the sinister knight closing round Tam's throat. Urging Lyrinx on, Rufus swerved through the trees after them and took aim with his iron-wood lance at the terrified prowlgrin just in front.

'Go on, girl. That's it,' Rufus muttered encouragingly, as Lyrinx brought her bounding leaps into time with Nixus. 'Just a little bit faster . . .'

A moment later, with a grunt of effort, Rufus lunged forward and felt his lance jolt with the impact. The knight gave a strange gurgling scream as the lance passed through his chest and lifted him from Tam's back. Rufus drew back the lance and the knight – parawings wildly flapping – crashed to the earth and disintegrated in a cloud of bone splinters and rusting metal. Tam was slumped

forward in the saddle, a deep crimson stain spreading across his shoulder telling Rufus that his lance had not only skewered the knight but had also wounded his friend in the process.

'Mid-branch!' Rufus shouted to Tam as he sped past, twitching at Lyrinx's reins.

The prowlgrin leaped into the next tree in their path. And behind him, to his relief, Rufus heard Nixus land on the same branch moments later. He pulled Lyrinx up abruptly and, unstrapping the grappling-hook from his saddle, threw it at the branch above his head. Nixus – with Tam slumped in the saddle – edged along the branch and nuzzled against Lyrinx, while Rufus reached up and tugged on the rope attached to the grappling-hook. The tree branch above them bent down, completely covering them with a thick curtain of leaves.

Rufus secured the rope to his saddle. Then, leaning forwards, he gently laid a hand just above their nostrils to quieten the panting of the two prowlgrins, one after the others. There was nothing to do but wait – and hope they wouldn't be spotted. He peered through the leafy green darkness at his friend. Tam was looking back at him, hunched up and in pain, but clearly aware of their situation. In one fist he clutched his ironwood lance; the other, he pressed against his shoulder. He managed a thin smile, and nodded at Rufus.

Just then, below them, the knights appeared on the forest floor. They were spread out, their prowl-grins trotting through the trees, looking for signs of the two lancers. Stumbling across the desiccated remains of their companion, his parawings still fixed to the empty shell of his armour, they paused and exchanged blank visor-eyed looks.

It was almost, Rufus thought, looking down through the curtain of leaves, as if they envied the ancient knight's death. At last he had been released from the sacred quest for stormphrax to which he, and they, had dedicated their lives centuries earlier.

Rufus shivered. Did their poor twilight-destroyed minds comprehend that the floating city they served was lost; that their quest was at an end and that they were no longer even in the terrible Twilight Woods? He shook his head. What was going through their addled minds, Rufus could only guess at.

The shriek of the black-plumed shryke roused Rufus from his thoughts. Below in the forest, the six ghostly knights turned as the shryke strode into their midst. She raised a glinting taloned claw.

'You sounded the alarm, Centius Thalladix?' the shryke said, addressing the most ancient of the knights.

'Most High Academe of Sanctaphrax,' the old knight replied humbly, bowing his head low. 'Rest assured, the treasury is safe. My knights and I have driven away the thieves. Even as we speak, they'll be drowning in the Mire in their attempts to flee . . .'

In his head, the great knight Centius Thalladix was back in his beloved city, amidst its wonderful floating towers, reporting to the Most High Academe – himself dead for centuries past. The other knights shared his delusion, for all bowed their heads, in turn, to the shryke, though each one of them saw a different, long-dead High Academe standing before them.

'Drowning in the Mire, indeed! You rusting bag of bones!' screeched the shryke, raising her beak in the air and sniffing. 'If that is so, then why can I smell the breath of live prowlgrins above the stench of your decay?'

Rufus swallowed hard as the shryke's piercing yellow eyes turned to the branches of the trees above. They swivelled round until they came to rest on the curtain of leaves shielding Tam and Rufus. Slowly, as Rufus watched in horror, the shryke's taloned claw unhooked a metal globe from the leather strap at her shoulder.

'Tree-crest!' Rufus screamed, releasing the grapp-ling-hook and jerking at Lyrinx's reins.

The two prowlgrins burst through the curtain of leaves that had concealed them, and leaped high into the forest canopy above. Gripping on tight,

Rufus felt the intense heat of the ear-splitting blast as the tree they'd been sitting in burst abruptly into flames. Far below him, the shryke screeched in frustration and hurled another globe.

Lyrinx and Nixus sped over the tops of the trees, leaving the flames and the screeches and the terrible stench of decay far behind. In his saddle, Rufus sat upright, lance in hand, taking in every detail of the surrounding tree-line while Tam slumped forward, holding on grimly as they steered their prowlgrins out across the vast expanse of the Deepwoods. Guided by the light of the full moon, they were riding headlong over the mighty forest in the direction of the Free Glades.

'Tam, how are you?' asked Rufus.

He was standing beside his friend's hammock high up in the top branches of the Scartree.

The pair of them had ridden through the night and most of the next day until – just as Rufus was beginning to fear that Tam could ride no further – they had reached the safety of the Free Glades. Now, an hour later, with the sun low on the horizon, they were on the branch belonging to the Fifth Splinter of the Fourth High-Branch Troop of Scartree Company, Tam's wounds bathed and dressed, and Rufus about to leave.

In the branches all around them, and in the other

405

five trees that made up the Third Roost, there was a frenzy of activity as lancers checked their equipment, readied their weapons and saddled their prowlgrins. The whole of the Third Roost had been ordered to muster and was preparing for battle.

'I'll be all right.' Tam smiled. 'No thanks to you and your clumsy lancework!'

Rufus returned his smile. 'Sorry about that. I'll try a lighter touch next time!' He patted his friend gently on the shoulder. 'I've got to go, Tam. The company marshal has ordered me to report everything I saw to the roost commander himself . . .'

Tam reached out a hand and grasped Rufus's arm.

'Wait,' he said, his face suddenly serious. 'You remember when I told you about my blooding?' Tam's dark-ringed eyes bored into Rufus's. 'I only told you about it because I didn't want you to think that getting blooded was all battle-cries and glory.'

Rufus nodded. 'Yes, Tam,' he said.

'But now you must do your duty. There's a battle coming, Rufus, both you and I know it,' said Tam quietly. 'A great battle. If my blooding was anything to go by, it will be terrible. War *is* terrible – though sometimes it is the only way to protect these Free Glades of ours. It is necessary. Remember that when you ride into battle, Rufus Filatine.'

Rufus nodded again. Tam's grip increased on his arm.

'And promise me one thing, green neck . . .'

'Anything, old campaigner,' said Rufus, staring down at his friend lying there, his shoulder heavily strapped and his leg swathed in bandages.

'That next time I see you,' said Tam with a smile, 'you'll be wearing a *proper* collar!'

The commander of the Third Roost of the Freeglade Lancers stood beneath the huge ironwood pines, their massive trunks rising up behind him like the columns of a great hall. As the branches of the six trees hummed with frenzied preparations, he stared out across the still dark waters of the Great Lake.

The marshal of Scartree Company emerged from the shadows between the mighty ironwoods, accompanied by a young lancer in the green collar of a cadet. Marshal Holdwood, a grizzled mobg-nome, saluted the commander, who remained, back turned, staring out across the lake.

'Freeglader!' he said, touching the crimson ban-derbear badge on his tunic, and motioned for the cadet to step forward. 'Lance-Cadet Rufus Filatine is here to make his report,' said the marshal.

Rufus approached the commander and cleared his throat. Speak simply and clearly, he reminded himself from his training, presenting all relevant facts without embellishment or speculation . . .

'Fifth Splinter, Fourth High-Branch Troop,

Scartree Company set off on deep patrol three days ago . . .' he began.

The roost commander continued to stare out across the lake. 'I'm listening,' he said quietly.

'We tree-crested, then advanced in a mid-branch gallop until we approached the Foundry Glades, which we entered. We found evidence that the nameless ones had been stabled there behind the ruins of the Palace of Furnace Masters, and used to haul dismantled pieces of machinery and forge parts. We were interrupted by a fifty-strong band of death-cheaters led by a black shryke and a red dwarf. The shryke killed three lancers and five prowlgrins of the splinter with a weapon we haven't encountered before – a metal globe that explodes into an intense white fire on contact.'

The commander, still standing motionless, remained silent.

'Sergeant Logglimb and five lancers tracked the death-cheaters, only to be ambushed by a band of hammerheads. Lancer Whytewinter and I were sent back to raise the roost. We got lost in tree cloud and stumbled across a new foundry glade close to the Twilight Woods. An armourer, in league with the shryke and the red dwarf, is producing these weapons – hundreds of them – using stormphrax mined in the Twilight Woods by the enslaved nameless ones. The glade is protected by an army of death-cheaters, and the armourer is selling these weapons to hammerhead goblins and anyone else prepared to pay for them . . .'

'Then this armourer and his accomplices must be stopped,' said the commander, turning round and looking at Rufus for the first time.' He smiled. 'You have done well, Lancer Filatine,' he said. 'Your father is an old friend of mine. Perhaps he's mentioned me?'

Rufus nodded. The commander of the Third Roost had served with the Freeglade Lancers in the War for the Free Glades – but before that he had studied with his father at the Lake Landing Academy. He was a brave, courageous commander, but also private and thoughtful, spending much of his time with the oakelves of Lullabee Island when not on duty.

Rufus noticed the small lufwood disc the commander wore on a leather cord round his neck. On it was a portrait of a young knight academic in armour that reminded Rufus of the ghostly knights he'd encountered back in the forests near the new foundry glade the night before.

'Yes, commander,' he said, looking back at Rook Barkwater. 'My father has often spoken of you.' He looked down, his face flushing. 'It is because of you that I joined the Freeglade Lancers.'

CHAPTER SIX

THE BATTLE OF THE PHRAX GLADE

Commander Rook Barkwater sat straight-backed in the saddle of his magnificent skewbald prowlgrin, Chinquix, and raised a gauntleted hand to the red banderbear badge on his tunic.

'Freeglader!' he intoned in a clear, sonorous voice.

From the six ironwood pines that comprised the Third Roost, four thousand five hundred lancers raised their voices in reply.

'Freeglader! Freeglader! Freeglader!'

The battle-cry of the Freeglade Lancers rang round the Ironwood Stands as the Third Roost began to move out. Old Mighty, Great Acorn, Roughbark, Longspear, Silvercone and finally Scartree; the mighty trees were left empty as their companies formed into troops, five splinters strong, and set off in great rippling waves across the southern pastures towards the distant

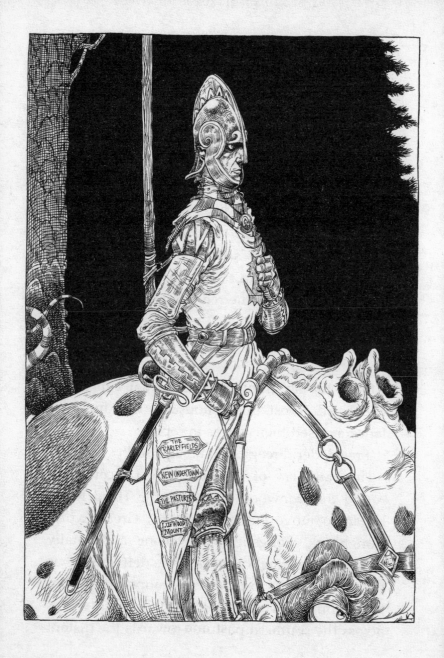

THE
BARLEY FIELDS

NEW UNDERTOWN

THE PASTURES

LUFWOOD
MOUNT

tree-line. All around, flocks of woodsquabs and fieldgrouse flapped into the sky, squawking indignantly, while grazing hammelhorns scurried for cover.

Beside the commander, young Lance-Cadet Rufus Filatine felt his prowlgrin, Lyrinx, tense beneath him and snort with impatience as he gripped the reins. She was eager to join her companions in their bounding gallop towards the forest. Rufus leaned forward and traced a finger round her flaring nostrils.

'Easy girl, easy,' he whispered. 'Not long now, we'll soon be off tree-cresting.'

'Indeed we will,' said Commander Barkwater, turning to Rufus with a smile. 'You'll ride with me at the head of the roost. And I trust you've applied yourself to your tracking studies,' he added. 'I'm counting on you to lead us back to that new foundry.'

'I won't let you down,' said Rufus grimly, remembering his comrades in the Fifth Splinter awaiting his return.

'Then follow me,' said the commander, deftly flicking the reins of his prowlgrin.

Rufus did the same, and together commander and cadet emerged from the deep shadows beneath the towering trunks of the six ironwood pines of the Third Roost and set off at a gallop across the sunlit pastures. By the time they'd reached the tree-line and launched themselves up into the forest canopy, the two of them had overtaken the waves of lancers, and were at the front of the column.

'Tree-crest! Open formation!' Hundreds of waif whispers filled the lancers' heads.

Rufus turned to see wave after wave of galloping prowlgrins burst through the lush foliage and spread out over the swaying treetops like wind through glade barley. The sun, still low in the sky, glinted in the creatures' bright, excited eyes while the trees all round resounded to the noise of twanging and thudding as they leaped from branch to branch.

High up in the sky, a lone caterbird flapped sedately as it soared on rising air currents. Behind him, Rufus could hear the cheers of the lancers as they spotted this omen of good luck – and he felt his stomach give a sudden lurch as he wondered how many of them would survive the coming battle.

Would he be among them? Or was this to be the last time he'd gallop across the mighty Deepwoods on prowlgrinback? Rufus swallowed hard and tightened his grip on the ironwood lance.

Far to his left, a couple of slaughterer hammelhorn-herders from the Silver Pastures, the spider-silk sails of their skycraft billowing out above them, waved and shouted encouragement. Up ahead, a squadron of librarian knights pulled on their loft-sails, realigned their hanging-weights and brought their ornately carved skycraft to a hover. As Rufus flashed past, he glimpsed their swords raised in a salute of respect. Soon they were distant specks on the horizon as the four thousand five hundred lancers of the Third Roost thundered over the treetops.

They tree-crested all through the morning and into the afternoon, heading across the vast forest, with Commander Barkwater and Rufus leading the way. Just as his training had taught him, Rufus had noted the forest formations on that desperate gallop back to the Free Glades with Tam the day before.

He remembered the high black peaks of ironwood pines to the west, and then the undulating expanse of copperwood and crimson larch they had crossed for hour after hour. Before that had come the jagged ridges of smoke-ash and lufwood, and then the low hollows of sedgewillow and blackoak. Now he was passing over them once more, signposts in the endless Deepwoods which pointed back to the horror from which he and Tam had fled.

The lancers travelled on through the night, the sounds of hundreds of waif signallers guiding their splinters mingling with the strange hoots and keening cries of the night creatures that they disturbed in their path. All the while, ahead of them, the golden glow of the Twilight Woods grew on the horizon like a false dawn. Rufus urged the panting Lyrinx on, trying not to think too closely of the terrible glade they were approaching. At last, as the moon sank in a sky now glowing with golden twilight, Rufus raised his arm and signalled for the column to halt. From the tree formations around them, he could tell that they were close to the new Foundry Glade.

Sure enough, Lyrinx's nostrils quivered and her brow furrowed as her sensitive nose picked up the faint, almost imperceptible taint of smoke on the breeze. Commander Barkwater joined Rufus in the top of a darkelm as, behind them, the four thousand five hundred lancers dropped silently down into the shadows below like melting tree cloud.

'You've done well, cadet,' the commander congratulated him, noting the low growls and quivering nostrils of both Chinquix and Lyrinx. 'There is a forest foundry at work close by.'

At that moment, the long sonorous clarion call of a hammelhorn trumpet cut through the air just ahead of them. Rufus looked up.

There, like a recurring nightmare, landing on the branches of a copperwood tree, were six skeletal prowlgrins and their ghostly riders. Rufus noticed the commander's hand go instinctively to the painted lufwood miniature he wore round his neck, the muscles in his jaw clenching as his fingers closed round the portrait of the young knight academic.

'Death to the stormphrax thieves!' the quavery voice of an ancient knight sounded from behind a rusted visor, as he and his companions unsheathed their swords. 'Death . . . !'

The six bony prowlgrins abruptly leaped from the branch in a cloud of sepia dust and flew through the air towards Rufus and the commander. Suddenly, from all about them, the ironwood lances of the five splinters of the Low-Branch Troop of Old Mighty Company thrust their points skyward like the quills of a timber-hog.

Rufus instinctively raised his own lance and felt it buck and jar in his hand as the ancient knights and their prowlgrins landed with a sickening

crunch. The air filled with a thick musty cloud as the knights' paper-thin armour crumpled, dials and pipes disintegrated and their ancient decaying bodies fell apart like broken puppets, the effects of the shrykes' phraxdust finally spent. They rained down, clattering on the helmets and upraised gauntlets of the lancers, before tumbling down through the foliage and landing in a dusty heap at the foot of the darkelm tree far below.

The commander released his grip on the lufwood portrait and brushed the sepia dust from his shoulders.

'Sky rest their poor tortured spirits,' he said quietly. 'The shryke who misused these noble knights shall pay for this.' He raised his head. 'Forest floor, troop formation. Advance!'

As Rufus followed the commander down through the network of branches, the ground below filled with prowlgrins and their lancers, dropping to the ground like ripe fruit.

'*Advance!*'

The waif signallers spread the command, and the Third Roost set off silently through the trees. After a few minutes, the acrid smell of furnace smoke was unmistakable, and the massed ranks of the lancers came to a halt a few strides from a large forest clearing. Ahead, Rufus could hear the awful screeches of the black-plumed shryke and the papery shuffling and clanking of metal of an army of death-cheaters.

'Invaders!' the bird creature screamed. 'I smell them! Hundreds of them! Defend the glade, you mouldering corpses! They must not take the furnace!'

Dismounting, Commander Barkwater called the company marshals of the six trees to him. He drew a circle in the soft soil at his feet with the tip of his sword.

'Old Mighty and Great Acorn on the left. Longspear and Silvercone on the right. Roughbark skirt the glade and attack from the rear.' He issued his orders in a quiet voice, the waifs beside each marshal nodding, their barbels twitching. 'Scartree Company stays with me. We attack in the centre. The whole roost is to converge here . . .' The commander stabbed at the cross in the middle of the circle. 'At the furnace!'

The marshals nodded and disappeared soundlessly into the trees. Commander Barkwater mounted the great skewbald prowlgrin with his clear blue eyes and patted his side.

'Well, Chinquix, lad, here we go again. You and I, riding into battle – Sky protect us . . .' He turned to Rufus, who stared back at him, white-faced and shaking. 'Ready?' he asked.

'Ready,' said Rufus, trying hard not to let

Lyrinx feel his knees trembling.

The commander buckled his helmet and gripped his ironwood lance under one arm. Behind him, tensed in their saddles, the seven hundred and fifty lancers of Scartree Company clustered amongst the trees. From the glade ahead there came the pounding of feet, the clanking of metal and a low chant-like moaning. Commander Barkwater threw back his head, twitched the reins and roared.

'Freeglader!'

Rufus jerked hard on Lyrinx's reins and felt her mighty legs coil, then spring, propelling them both up eighty feet or more into the air. They broke through the branches of the trees on the glade's fringes and sailed out over the glade itself. To his right and to his left were white-tunicked lancers, their ironwood lance points thrust out before them as they reached the high point of their prowlgrins' leap, then hurtled down.

Below him, Rufus saw a sea of ghastly decayed faces with gaping eye-sockets, gap-toothed mouths and grey pock-marked skin stretched over mask-like skulls. With a horrible clanking sound, spears, scythes, jagged spikes and rusting pole-axes were thrust up in the air towards him by a thousand skeletal hands. He bent low in the saddle, braced his lance, shut his eyes and . . .

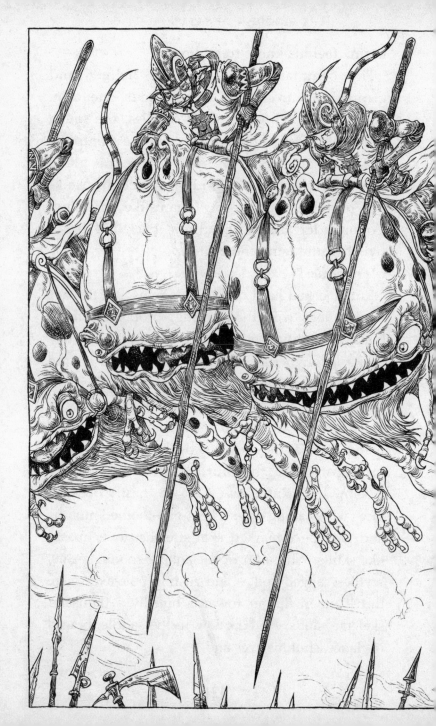

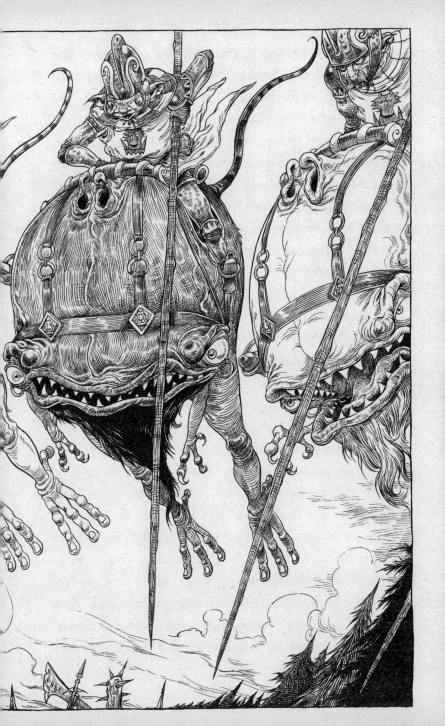

With a sickening crunch and an over-powering smell of decay, Lyrinx landed in the midst of a throng of death-cheaters – before bounding up into the air once more. Rufus pulled his lance back and was shocked to see it encrusted with a severed arm, a breast-plated torso and the gaping head of a with-ered-looking flat-head goblin, its rings rusted and immoveable in paper-thin ears. With a cry of dis-gust, he shook his lance free – just in time, as once more Lyrinx came down heavily amongst the foul-smelling crowd.

All over the glade, great swathes opened up – the ground covered with crushed and skewered bodies – where Scartree Company's prowlgrins had landed and taken off. High-, mid- and low-branch troops spread out like the fingers of a giant hand, the waifs' orders ringing in their heads, before turn-ing in again like the clenching of a fist. All about them, the half-dead death-cheaters scattered like dead leaves before a forest fire.

Twitching Lyrinx's reins, Rufus kept up with Commander Barkwater and the white and brown blur of Chinquix, his mighty prowlgrin. Around him, he saw several lancers buckle, then topple from their saddles, rusting jagged spears embedded in their backs and chests. Glancing down, as Lyrinx leaped high once more, Rufus was horrified to see them disappearing into a wild and frenzied scrum of grasping, flailing claw-like hands as the death-cheaters tore them and their hapless prowl-grin mounts apart.

Down into the throng they came once more. This time, Rufus – jaw set and eyes blazing – thrust his ironwood lance down hard as he landed. Heads, torsos and limbs flew up into the air as a thick cloud of dust billowed all round him. Coughing and choking, hardly able to breathe, Rufus pulled Lyrinx up short and shook his lance clean. As the putrid dust cleared, he saw that the death-cheaters had shrunk back into isolated pockets in the glade around him, like tufts of barley-grass in a trampled pasture. Everywhere else, their hideous remains lay

strewn about in an obscene jumble.

Commander Barkwater landed in front of him. He turned to his lancers.

'Scartree Company, form lines by the splinter!' he commanded.

Suddenly, Rufus found himself in the centre of a row of lancers, their prowlgrins, like his own, coughing and spluttering and snorting with exertion.

In the distance, a cloud of smoke showed where Longspear and Silvercone companies had trampled the phalanx of death-cheaters who were defending the right-hand edge of the glade. To the left, Old Mighty and Great Acorn companies were regrouping, their lances glittering in the early morning light. Everywhere, the army of death-cheaters lay trampled and broken amongst the tree-stumps along the edges of the glade. Their few survivors – injured and limping – stumbled towards the smoking furnace at the centre of the glade.

As Rufus looked, the figure of the armourer emerged from the rough-hewn log cabin at the centre of the glade, his gloved arms full of glittering metal globes. By his side, the black-plumed shryke opened her beak and spat an arc of green bile high in the air.

'It is easy to kill those who are half-dead already!' she screeched scornfully. 'Now, brave lancers, see how you fare against phraxfire!'

She raised a taloned claw, and fifty hammerhead goblins emerged from the sheds behind the glowing furnace, their leather breast-plates festooned with glittering metal globes. They fanned out in a protective arc round the forge and the log cabin. In reply, on three sides, the clatter of lances being levelled at the hammerheads' chests filled the glade.

Commander Barkwater rode forward on Chinquix.

'Those poor wretches that the shryke harvested from the Twilight Woods have found a grateful death on the ends of our lances,' he announced. 'Close the furnace, release the nameless ones you have enslaved, abandon these weapons and your lives will be spared . . .'

The armourer tore off his hood and glared back at the commander, his disfigured face glistening with sweat.

'You Freegladers make me sick! You expect the whole of the Edgelands to live in peace and harmony just as you do.' He sneered. 'Well, I, Lentil Spume have news for you. As long as I live, I will continue my father's glorious work! The Foundry Glades will rise again and Hemuel Spume's death will be avenged! He saw the future, and so have I, even though it cost me my face . . .'

The armourer shook a gloved fist at the commander, the metal globes he held dancing on the ends of their long thin chains.

'*This* is the future! Phraxfire and war! The strong plundering the weak! The rich enslaving the poor. Just as it has always been!'

Behind him, the shryke threw back her black-plumed head and cackled with laughter. 'Do your worst, Freeglade scum!' she screeched.

Commander Barkwater pulled Chinquix back and returned, stony-faced, to his lancers. A waif signaller's voice sounded in their heads.

'*Roughback Company begs to report, commander. We're in battle order in the tree-fringe, but the red dwarf has the nameless ones harnessed to what looks like an old glade-eater. We'll suffer heavy losses in a frontal attack . . .*'

The commander joined Rufus in the front rank of Scartree Company.

'Hold off until we make our charge,' he whispered to the waif signaller with the marshal of Roughbark Company. 'If we can spare those innocent creatures, we shall.'

Rufus tensed in the saddle. This was it. No longer was he to battle against ancient knights who'd lost their minds, or other demented half-dead creatures from the Twilight Woods. Instead, he was about to charge an army of fierce hammerhead goblin warriors armed with a terrifying new weapon whose terrible effects he knew only too well.

For a moment, Rufus wished he was back in his hammock in the Ironwood Stands; safe, comfortable, with a mild case of bark-croup . . .

No! Rufus gripped his ironwood lance fiercely. He was a Freeglade Lancer, and these merchants of death and misery had to be stopped! He waited for the familiar cry, the sound of which would signal his blooding . . .

'Freeglader!'

The prowlgrins of Scartree Company leaped ahead in unison, the riders hunched forward in their saddles with their ironwood lances levelled at the enemy. To the right and to the left, the same battle-cry sounded, as the other four companies did the same.

'Fire!' screeched the black-plumed shryke, and a hail of metal globes shot out from the ranks of the hammerhead goblins.

In his saddle, Rook gasped as the air around him erupted in a flash of blinding light and blast of intense heat. He was torn from Lyrinx's back and thrown through the air.

The ground came racing up to meet him . . .

When he opened his eyes, Rufus's mouth and nostrils were full of the pungent stench of burned hair and roasted flesh. His head rang with a strange roaring, as if a raging wind was blowing directly past his ears, drowning out all other sound. Around him, figures were staggering and stumbling through the acrid white smoke that billowed up from small black craters in the ground like rising banks of tree cloud.

To one side, five hammerhead goblins half stood, half slumped, skewered by a single ironwood lance that had embedded itself in the earth. Just ahead, a prowlgrin lay burned and charred beside the blackened body of its rider. More goblins lay dead around it, beheaded by a lancer's sabre.

Rufus's eyes stung with tears, but he couldn't look away from the horror. Suddenly, right in front of him, a crazed hammerhead loomed up – only to collapse, clawing at its throat as a crossbow bolt embedded itself between its neck rings. Rufus staggered to his feet. He felt light-headed and giddy – but all around him a desperate battle still raged.

The first volley of the phraxfire globes had wreaked terrible havoc on the Freeglade Lancers. Whole splinters had been incinerated in mid-charge, blackened mounds of ash marking the spot where they died. Enough of the lancers had broken through, however, to take their revenge on the fifty hammerheads.

Rufus could now see – something he'd only known before in theory – the unique carnage a well-aimed ironwood lance could inflict. Everywhere, dead goblins lay slumped in heaps. Having thrown the deadly phraxfire globes, their serrated swords and stabbing spears had proved no match for the deadly lances. And, as Rufus watched, the lancers made short work of the few hammerheads who resisted.

Finally, the last survivors turned tail and fled, and the lancers of the Third Roost regrouped around the figure of their commander, standing high in the saddle of his skewbald prowlgrin, sword in one hand, lance in the other. Behind him, the furnace's heavy door had been slammed shut and its valves closed tight. The lancers' grappling-hooks were already clanging against the crooked chimney as they gripped firmly.

Rufus gazed up at the chimney, which tottered then abruptly crashed to earth. Plumes of black soot rose up in a cloud. And at Commander Barkwater's feet lay the bedraggled figure of the shryke; her head separated from her body, her yellow lifeless eyes staring at the noonday sky.

The roaring in his ears cleared and Rufus felt a

gentle shove in the back. Turning, he stared into the eyes of his prowlgrin, Lyrinx, her harness blackened and fur singed, but otherwise unhurt.

'Lyrinx!' Rufus cried, and wrapped his arms round the great neck of the creature. 'Brave girl. Brave, brave girl . . .'

'Open up!' Commander Barkwater's voice sounded from across the glade. He had dismounted and was standing in front of the heavy door to the cabin. 'The battle is lost,' he bellowed. 'Surrender your workshop and what's left of your weapons!'

Suddenly a glint caught Rufus's eye and, looking down, he saw round the neck of the dead hammerhead goblin at his feet a metal globe. Stooping down, he carefully unhooked it and slipped it into the leather pouch on his belt.

All at once, a terrible roar sounded from behind the cabin. Rufus swung round.

'*Stop them!*' sounded the voice of Roughbark Company's waif signaller.

Without a second thought, Rufus grabbed the nearest ironwood lance and leaped into Lyrinx's saddle. He flicked her reins and the two of them sped round the side of the cabin and into the glade behind it. There, trundling full-pelt towards the log cabin, was a great metal plough with a curved spike protruding from its shovel-shaped front, being pushed by the three nameless ones.

Harnessed into place, the creatures were being tormented by the tiny flailing figure of the red dwarf. In its churned-up wake came the battered remains of Roughbark Company who, by the look of their shattered lances and exhausted prowlgrins, had thrown themselves relentlessly against the great contraption.

The muddy path through the glades showed where the red dwarf had forced the nameless ones to propel the plough towards the lancers, while the hideous little creature had devastated their ranks with phraxfire globes. Now, missiles spent, the dwarf was beating a retreat back towards the cabin – though by the speed at which he was forcing the

poor creatures to push the machine, he had no intention of stopping.

Rufus could see, in an instant, that if it wasn't halted, the plough would destroy the armourer's workshop – and take Commander Barkwater and most of the remaining lancers of the Third Roost with it. He urged Lyrinx on and took aim with his ironwood lance. Closer and closer they came to the huge plough and its deadly spike.

'Go on, girl. Go on!' Rufus shouted. 'Now, Lyrinx! Now!'

The prowlgrin leaped high in the air just as the plough's spike was about to run her through. Rufus jabbed down with his lance as they sailed past and landed in the rutted tracks of the contraption.

He raised the lance. On its tip, pierced through his tiny heart, was the red dwarf, his small eyes bulging and his beaked mouth open wide. Behind him, the plough ground to a halt strides from the cabin as the great hunched shoulders of the nameless ones slouched forward and the poor tormented creatures slumped to their knees, panting hoarsely.

Thick tendrils of black smoke began curling up from between the roughly-hewn logs of the cabin and, as Rufus watched, the heavy timbers of the roof burst into crackling white flame. Then, from within the inferno the workshop had suddenly become, the deranged voice of the armourer sounded.

'Nobody shall have my secrets!' he screamed, as the flames that had destroyed his face now claimed the rest of his body. 'Nobody shall learn the secrets of phraxfire!'

Rufus's hand reached for the metal globe in his pocket . . .

Rufus stood before the huge ornately-carved door of the Great Lecture Theatre of the Academy at Lake Landing. He carefully adjusted the fine green and white chequerboard collar he wore before pushing the heavy door open and stepping inside.

'Well, well, if it isn't Corporal Filatine of the Freeglade Lancers,' came his father's gently teasing voice, 'promoted in the field at the Battle of the Phrax Glade by my good friend, Commander Barkwater . . .'

'Yes, yes,' said Rufus, blushing proudly. 'You wanted to see me, Father?'

Xanth Filatine, High Master of the Knights Academy, crossed the wooden floor and clapped a hand on his son's shoulder.

'Indeed I did, corporal. Indeed I did. I have something to show you.'

436

It had been three weeks since Rufus's blooding and promotion, and only now were things getting back to normal in the Ironwood Stands. The strange creatures known as nameless ones had had their wounds treated and had been taken far out into the Deepwoods and released – but not before the librarians had studied them closely and made many notes.

As for the Third Roost, it had suffered badly at the Battle of the Phrax Glade, but already its ranks were being restored by new young recruits attracted by the tales of its heroic exploits. From Fifth Splinter, Fourth High-Branch Troop, Scarface Company, Cedifice the waif, the twins Holt and Hudflux, and Sergeant Logglimb had survived the deep patrol and joined Rufus on the battlefield. Back at the Scartree, they spoke little of their exploits, as was the way with seasoned lancers.

Tam's wounds had mended, and Rufus had found that his own blooding had forged a new and even stronger bond with his friend. So now it was back to the routine of patrols and lance-drill – and the occasional visit to the academy at Lake Landing.

Rufus strode across the vast empty hall with his father, their footsteps echoing round the vaulted ceiling. The pair of them stopped at a small heavy darkwood desk situated in an alcove on the far side of the lecture theatre. Laid out on a tray, and bathed in light, was an array of tiny, intricately tooled metal pieces.

'Remember this?' asked his father, with a smile. 'Tweezel and I have done quite a bit of work on it.'

'Of course,' said Rufus. 'It's the phraxfire globe – but it's in bits . . .'

'Well,' said Xanth Filatine thoughtfully, examining the intricate mechanism of the globe with the tiny crystal of stormphrax at its heart, so dazzlingly bright it was hard to look at, 'sometimes one has to destroy something to reveal the secrets locked inside . . .'

He shook his head and his grip on his son's shoulder tightened for a moment.

'Secrets that you saved and brought back to the Free Glades, Rufus, my boy. Secrets which mean . . .' He turned to his son, his eyes twinkling with excitement. 'Life on the Edge might never be the same again . . .'

THE END

ABOUT THE AUTHORS

PAUL STEWART is a highly regarded author
of books for young readers – everything from
picture books to football stories, fantasy and horror.
Together with Chris Riddell, he is co-creator of the
Far-Flung Adventures series, which includes *Fergus
Crane*, Gold Smarties Prize Winner, *Corby Flood* and
Hugo Pepper, Silver Nestlé Prize Winners, and the
Barnaby Grimes series. They are of course also
co-creators of the bestselling *Edge Chronicles* series,
which has sold over two million books and is
now available in over thirty languages.

CHRIS RIDDELL is an accomplished graphic
artist who has illustrated many acclaimed books
for children, including *Pirate Diary* by Richard Platt,
and *Gulliver*, which both won the Kate Greenaway
Medal. *Something Else* by Kathryn Cave was short-
listed and *Castle Diary* by Richard Platt was Highly
Commended for the Kate Greenaway Medal.

THE
EDGE CHRONICLES
FAN CLUB

Join the FREE Edge Chronicles Fan Club:
read Paul and Chris's diary and find out how they
work together, check out the awesome character
gallery, wonder at the interactive map and download
wallpaper. Plus loads of other stuff to see and do!

www.edgechronicles.co.uk

THE EDGE CHRONICLES

THE QUINT TRILOGY

Follow the adventures of Quint
in the first age of flight!

CURSE OF THE GLOAMGLOZER

Quint and Maris, daughter of the most
High Academe, are plunged into a terrifying
adventure which takes them deep into the rock
upon which Sanctaphrax is built. Here they
unwittingly invoke an ancient curse . . .

THE WINTER KNIGHTS

Quint is a new student at the Knights
Academy, struggling to survive the icy cold
of a never-ending winter, and the ancient
feuds that threaten Sanctaphrax.

CLASH OF THE SKY GALLEONS

Quint finds himself caught up in his father's
fight for revenge against the man who killed
his family. They are drawn into a deadly
pursuit, a pursuit that will ultimately lead
to the clash of the great sky galleons.

'The most amazing books ever'
Ellen, 10

'I hated reading . . .
now I'm a reading machine!'
Quinn, 15

THE EDGE CHRONICLES

THE TWIG TRILOGY

Follow the adventures of Twig
in the first age of flight!

BEYOND THE DEEPWOODS

Abandoned at birth in the perilous Deepwoods,
Twig does what he has always been warned
not to do, and strays from the path . . .

STORMCHASER

Twig, a young crew-member on the
Stormchaser sky ship, risks all to collect valuable
stormphrax from the heart of a Great Storm.

MIDNIGHT OVER SANCTAPHRAX

Far out in Open Sky, a ferocious storm is brewing.
In its path is the city of Sanctaphrax . . .

'Absolutely brilliant'
Lin-May, 13

'Everything about the
Edge Chronicles is amazing'
Cameron, 13

THE EDGE CHRONICLES

THE ROOK TRILOGY

Follow the adventures of Rook
in the second age of flight!

LAST OF THE SKY PIRATES
Rook dreams of becoming a librarian knight,
and sets out on a dangerous journey into the
Deepwoods and beyond. When he meets the last
sky pirate, he is thrust into a bold adventure...

VOX
Rook becomes involved in the evil scheming
of Vox Verlix – can he stop the Edgeworld
falling into total chaos?

FREEGLADER
Undertown is destroyed, and Rook and his
friends travel, with waifs and cloddertrogs,
to a new home in the Free Glades.

'They're the best!!'
Zaffie, 15

'Brilliant illustrations and magical storylines'
Tom, 14

BARNABY GRIMES

CURSE of the NIGHT WOLF

PAUL STEWART & CHRIS RIDDELL

*One moment I was standing there, sword raised,
knees trembling. The next, in a blur of fur and fury,
the hellish creature was flying towards me, its huge front
paws extended and savage claws aiming
straight at my hammering heart . . .*

Barnaby Grimes is a tick-tock lad –
he'll deliver any message anywhere any time.
As fast as possible. Tick-tock -time is money! But
strange things are afoot. One moonlit night, as Barnaby
highstacks above the city, leaping from roof to roof,
gutter to gable, pillar to pediment, a huge beast attacks.
He barely escapes with his life. And now his
friend Old Benjamin has disappeared . . .

A gloriously macabre tale in a
breathtaking new series, packed with
intrigue, horror and fantastic illustrations.

RETURN of
the EMERALD SKULL

PAUL STEWART & CHRIS RIDDELL

*My grip tightened on the cruel stone knife,
the blade glinting, as the blood-red ruby eyes of
the grinning skull bore into mine. Inside my head,
the voice rose to a piercing scream .'Cut out
his beating heart – and give it to me!'*

Barnaby Grimes is a tick-tock lad on a mission –
to collect a parcel from the docks and deliver it to a
famous school. But dark forces have been released and,
as Barnaby returns to Grassington Hall School, he is
about to find out the full extent of the horror.

A spine-tingling tale of a school in the grip
of a terrible curse. Tick-tock, time is running out.
Can Barnaby survive?

COMING SOON!

COMING SOON

THE IMMORTALS

Five hundred years into the the third age
of flight and mighty phraxships steam across
the immensity of the Deepwoods, plying their
lucrative trade between the three great cities.
Nate Quarter, a young lamplighter from the
mines of the eastern woods is propelled on an
epic journey of self-discovery that encompasses
tournaments, battles, revolutions and a final
encounter with the Immortals themselves.

WATCH OUT FOR THE FINAL
EDGE CHRONICLES BOOK
IN FEBRUARY 2009!

Read on for a sneak preview of the
FINAL Edge Chronicles book,

THE IMMORTALS

For the rest of the shift, they worked non-stop on the seam, Nate, Rudd and the other dozen miners who had been assigned to the fifth funnel gallery that morning, cutting slabs of phraxrich rubble, but not finding any more shards. Compared with Rudd, Nate was slow, stopping increasingly often to catch his breath and rub his aching shoulders. The hefty cloddertrog never seemed to tire. By the time the siren went, signalling the end of work, the mine crew had all but filled three of the wagons with rubble.

'Most we've ever done in a single shift,' said Rudd as he gathered up his tools and headed down the ladder. 'And two shards between us! Grint will have to give us a good price.'

Nate followed him close behind. 'I wouldn't count on it,' he muttered.

At the bottom of the shaft, the scuttlers – the lowest and most menial workers in the mine – were already busy sweeping and shovelling away the debris ready for the next shift. As he jumped down to the ground, Nate's ankle went over on a piece of rock, and he stumbled against one of the squat goblins, knocking his broom from his bony hands.

'Sorry, sorry,' said Nate, retrieving the broom and handing it back. 'Oh, it's you, Slip.'

The scuttler – a bandy legged goblin with a look of permanent terror in his eyes – nodded.

'Yes, it's me, Slip,' he said, his voice husky and halting. 'Grey goblin, from the nether reaches, nineteen years of age and in his twelfth year of service . . .'

Nate listened patiently. Scuttlers lived most of their lives down in the mines, always there to keep the oildrums full and the tunnels free of vermin. Although far below the Twilight Woods, the forest's treacherous influence permeated the underground tunnels, seeping through with every droplet of water and breathed in with each particle of phraxdust. The miners, with their shiftwork and distant living quarters, were in little danger in the short term, but for the scuttlers it was simply a matter of time before they ended up completely deranged. That was why, at any opportunity, they would repeat details of their lives, in a vain effort to keep their minds from slipping away forever.

'Bad infestation, Slip uncovered. Piebald rats. Last night,' he said, his husky voice stopping and starting as he concentrated hard. 'Battered nine of them, did Slip. One, two, three, four, five, six . . .' He counted off the number slowly and deliberately. 'Seven, eight, nine. All dead. And Slip laid traps, for the rest . . .'

'Come on, Nate,' Rudd's voice floated back along the tunnel.

Nate smiled at the scuttler. 'I'd best be going,' he said.

'Yes, best be going,' said Slip. 'Best be off. But afore you do,' he said, his voice lowering to an intimate gravelly rasp. 'Afore you leave, there's something Slip wants to tell you.' He reached out and grasped the sleeve of Nate's jacket. 'A warning, Nate, 'coz your father, good he was, to us scuttlers. Gave us time up top . . .'

'A warning,' said Nate softly.

'The mine sergeant,' said Slip, nodding vigorously. 'Grayle Grint. I mean, Grint Grayle. Slip heard him say that flogging he gave you wasn't enough – that next time, he'd fix you for good, Nate Quarter. So, watch out for yourself.'

'Fix me for good? But how?'

'He didn't say,' said Slip. 'Not exactly. But Grint knew your father didn't trust him, Nate. And then he had that accident. Now Grint's suspicious of you. And we don't want no more accidents, do we, Nate? No more accidents.'

'No,' said Nate thoughtfully. 'No, we don't. You see anything suspicious, you come and tell me, Slip."

The grey goblin nodded, his piercing blue eyes wide. 'Slip'll tell you, Nate. Don't you fear. Old Slip'll keep a watch out . . .'

Clapping the scuttler gratefully on the shoulder, Nate set off after Rudd. He found him leaning against the timber lined wall at the bottom of the sloping tunnel of 'the Sanctaphrax Forest'. All round them, like a herd of tilder moving through the trees, the other miners were passing in between the wooden props jutting up at all angles from floor to ceiling as they made their way to the surface.

'What kept you?' said Rudd.

'Slip,' said Nate.

'What, that little scuttler?'

Nate nodded. 'Confirmed my suspicions,' he said, 'that Grint Grayle *does* have it in for me. Slip overheard him . . .'

'Been underground too long, that one,' Rudd interrupted. 'You can't trust the word of a twilight touched scuttler.'

'Yes, but . . .' Nate began.

'I swear, Nate, you're too friendly for your own good,' said Rudd. 'You get the weirdest little creatures latching onto you.'

'Like you, you mean?' said Nate, laughing, and it was Rudd's turn to punch *him* on the arm.

They emerged from the fake twilight of the tunnels into the genuine dusk of the forest, the low orange sun sinking down towards the horizon. Nate and Rudd exchanged greetings with the miners on the night shift, just beginning work. Then they stopped at the tally wagon and gave in their lightboxes, and checked their shift earnings.

'Day shift, ain't yer,' clucked the scrawny shryke in the wagon and checked her list. 'A shard. Good size.' She placed it on the scales and added small ironwood weights until the two trays balanced. 'Will get you . . . fifty gladers. And then your rubble price . . . Three wagons full at five gladers . . . Minus deductions . . .'

'Deductions?' said Nate, staring hard into the shryke's yellow eyes.

'Mine sergeant's upped the stockade tax,' she said. Her eyes narrowed. 'You don't like it, you can sleep out in the woods.'

She cackled as she peeled off promissary notes from a bundle in her taloned fist.

'Thirty-five gladers. Don't spend them all at once!'

Nate bristled, his fists clenched. But Rudd lay a calming hand on his shoulder.

'Take it,' he urged. 'Thirty-five gladers ain't bad for a single shift, Nate, and we don't need the trouble . . .'

Reluctantly, Nate took the notes and placed them in the inside pocket of his tunic. Rudd did the same.

'It's not right,' Nate muttered as they left

the tally wagon and its escort of brawny mine guards behind at the mine entrance.

Falling in with the other miners, the pair of them headed back towards the camps. His hunger and his tiredness seemed to melt away as Nate pounded over the creaking boards, replaced instead by burning resentment at the mine sergeant and his cronies. The other miners, like Rudd, seemed content that their shift was over and they were back at last above ground – and with money in their pockets.

They marched on noisily through the increasingly shadow filled forest. The sun set and darkness swept in across the sky, high above the canopy, pitching the forest below into the impenetrable gloom of night. By the time they came to the fork in the track, the rowdy miners had already relit their helmet lamps, and the yellow beams of light were bouncing from treetrunk to treetrunk.

'You look like you need cheering up, Nate,' said Rudd, glancing round at his friend. He stopped. 'So what's it to be? More slop at the stockade.' He nodded up the left-hand fork, the lamplight shining along the track which led to the camp. He swung round, till the same beam of light danced along the track to their right. 'Or an evening at the Hulks?'

'Hard call,' grinned Nate – and set off after the others along the well trodden path which would take them to the miners' tavern.

'Good choice,' said Rudd, clapping his friend on the shoulders.

The pair of them fell into step with the other returning miners. As they neared their destination, the atmosphere grew rowdier and rowdier.

There were a dozen mining stockades in the area, every one run by a different mine owner and housing anything up to two hundred miners each. Mining was thirsty work and Mother Hinnyplume – an enterprising shryke matron who, some twenty years earlier, had passed that way quite by chance – had immediately spotted a gaping hole in the market. Six months later, the Hulks – two ancient wrecked sky galleons, lodged in a massive lufwood tree, which had been shored up and turned into a tavern for the nearby stockades – was up and running.

At first, the mine owners had tried to shut the place down. They feared that the woodale, winesap and woodgrog on sale in the tavern would lower productivity in the mines. But they were wrong. The miners worked harder than ever, knowing that at the end of their day's work, they were to be rewarded with a night of carousing. What was more, the cut of the shryke matron's profits which the mine owners took, ensured that half the wages they paid out to the miners went straight back into their own pockets.

A cheer went up when the glittering lights of the Hulks came into view at last. Nate smiled as he heard the pounding music, and looked up to see the great timbered sides of the old skyships, peppered with gantries and walkways, and illuminated with strings of lamps. The two mighty vessels had crashed centuries before, and were skewered by the branches of the great tree that now grew around them. Mother Hinnyplume had built on to the original hulks until the former shapes of the great vessels were all but buried beneath cabins, gantries and viewing platforms.

The first of the miners marched up the wooden walkway that wound round the tree, shoved the swing doors open and strode inside. Nate and Rudd were jostled from the sides and behind as the eager crowd funnelled through the narrow opening, laughing and shouting as they spilled into the cavernous hall beyond. Originally the aft hold of the old skyship, it was now open from keel to the captain's cabin, several storeys above. Huge ale vats, embedded in the walls, disgorged a steady stream of frothing woodale into drinking troughs below.

Rudd and Nate drew up a bench and sat down. They weren't the first. The tavern was already half full of workers from the other stockades, loud with deep, hearty voices and gales of laughter.

Rudd leaned across to a passing tavern maid – a young gabtroll with a funnel shaped cap and a filthy apron over her threadbare dress – and took two empty tankards from the upraised tray.

'Stick 'em on the slate, Gelba,' he said. He handed Nate one of tankards and dipped his own in the nearest trough. All round him, the cluster of fellow miners did the same. Rudd raised his tankard high. 'To Gallery Five!' he roared.

'Gallery Five!' The bellowing cry echoed round the hot, dark tavern as the twenty-strong team lifted their glasses and quaffed the woodale to the dregs in one fluid movement.

Two more gabtroll tavern maids brought broad platters of snowbird wings and highly spiced tilder sausages. They laid them in front of the hungry miners, who tucked in with relish.

'It's not so bad, is it?' said Rudd, turning to Nate. 'This life.'

Nate shrugged. His father had hoped for better things of him.

'Food. Place to sleep. Constant work . . . Y'know, I've been hearing all kinds of stuff from Hive. That new pink-eye recruit was saying . . . 'Parently, there's no work to be found. All sorts are living on the streets. Begging.' His face grimaced indignantly. '*Begging!* Can you believe it, Nate, eh?'

Nate shook his head. His friend was beginning to slur his words.

'And, of course,' said Rudd, stumbling to his feet and sweeping his arm round expansively. 'Best of all. We've got all this . . .'

A puzzled frown passed across his face as his arm struck something solid. He glanced round blearily, to find himself staring into the furious gaze of a massive hammerhead goblin. The hammerhead looked down slowly at the woodale dripping down the front of his ornately embroidered top coat, then back into the cloddertrog's reddening face.

'A . . . apologies,' Rudd muttered. He pulled a rag from his back pocket and began dabbing uselessly at the wet patch.

The hammerhead knocked his hand away viciously. Two more hammerheads, even taller and broader than the first, loomed at his shoulders. They had phraxpistols holstered at their sides.

'It . . . it was an accident,' Nate said, climbing to his feet.

The first hammerhead thrust his brutal face into Nate's. 'I know you,' he snarled. 'You're Nate Quarter, the lamplighter I gave a flogging to just last week.'

Nate held his ground. He'd recognized the three of them at once. They belonged to Grint Grayle, the mine sergeant; leading members of the mine guard. They didn't often come to the Hulks – preferring the relative comfort of the mine sergeants' mess – but when they did, it invariably spelled trouble.

'We're not looking for any trouble,' Nate persisted. 'And I'll make good any damage . . .'

The hammerhead in the centre laughed unpleasantly. 'Let's see how you make good this bit of damage,' he said, pulling a heavy ironwood cudgel from inside his topcoat and striking Nate hard across the side of his head.

Nate spun round and tumbled heavily to the floor. For a moment, everything went black. The next moment, there were legs all round him, and arms reaching down towards him. The tavern waif was peering at him through huge black eyes, its ears twitching as it searched his thoughts to find out what he would do next, while Mother Hinnyplume herself, her gawdy red and purple feathered cape flapping, carved a path through the gawping crowd, a flail cracking menacingly in her claws.

'I'll have no fighting in my tavern,' she screeched.

'There'll be no fighting,' came a gruff, slightly nasal voice. '*I'll* see to that.'

Grint Grayle stepped forward from the shadows. He pulled a phraxpistol from his belt and raised it. Nate stared in horror, unable to move. The barrel of the weapon was pointing directly at his chest. Their eyes met. The mine sergeant's jaw clenched, his upper lip curled – and at that instant, Nate Quarter knew with complete certainty that the death of his father had been no accident and that he, too, was about to be disposed of, in what later would be passed off as an unfortunate drunken brawl.

Find out more in
THE IMMORTALS
February 2009